"I'm really not the fainting type,"

Glenna said as Reid cradled her in his arms. "But I guess I'm not as strong as I think I am." Her mouth quivered. "Or as young as I used to be."

Reid saw the look of desolation cross her face, and the bottom dropped out of his stomach. Was she sick?

"What—" He swallowed painfully, and managed to go on with difficulty. "What's wrong, Glenna?"

"Yes, I should just say it." She pushed herself out of the nest of his embrace. It took all of his strength to let her go, and his arms felt as if they'd never be filled again.

She looked at him with so many emotions mingling in her eyes. Then she said, "I'm pregnant," as if delivering tragic news.

* * * *

"Jodi O'Donnell's OF TEXAS LADIES, COWBOYS… AND BABIES has it all—cowboys, babies, a shot-gun wedding, and Texas. The story had me hooked from the very first page. Indulge yourself, and read this book— you'll be glad you did."

—Debbie Macomber
    Award-winning, bestselling author

Dear Reader,

Brides, babies and families...that's just what Special Edition has in store for you this August! All this and more from some of your favorite authors.

Our THAT'S MY BABY! title for this month is *Of Texas Ladies, Cowboys...and Babies,* by popular Silhouette Romance author Jodi O'Donnell. In her first book for Special Edition, Jodi tells of a still young and graceful grandmother-to-be who unexpectedly finds herself in the family way! Fans of Jodi's latest Romance novel, *Daddy Was a Cowboy,* won't want to miss this spin-off title!

This month, GREAT EXPECTATIONS, the wonderful new series of family and homecoming by Andrea Edwards, continues with *A Father's Gift.* And summer just wouldn't be right without a wedding, so we present *A Bride for John,* the second book of Trisha Alexander's newest series, THREE BRIDES AND A BABY. Beginning this month is a new miniseries from veteran author Pat Warren, REUNION. Three siblings must find each other as they search for true love. It all begins with one sister's story in *A Home for Hannah.*

Also joining the Special Edition family this month is reader favorite and Silhouette Romance author Stella Bagwell. Her first title for Special Edition is *Found: One Runaway Bride.* And returning to Special Edition this August is Carolyn Seabaugh with *Just a Family Man,* as the lives of one woman and her son are forever changed when an irresistible man walks into their café in the wild West.

This truly is a month packed with summer fun and romance! I hope you enjoy each and every story to come!

Sincerely,
Tara Gavin, Senior Editor

Please address questions and book requests to:
Silhouette Reader Service
U.S.: 3010 Walden Ave., P.O. Box 1325, Buffalo, NY 14269
Canadian: P.O. Box 609, Fort Erie, Ont. L2A 5X3

Books by Jodi O'Donnell

Silhouette Special Edition

Of Texas Ladies, Cowboys...and Babies #1045

Silhouette Romance

Still Sweet on Him #969
The Farmer Takes a Wife #992
A Man To Remember #1021
*Daddy Was a Cowboy #1080

*Wranglers & Lace

JODI O'DONNELL

grew up one of fourteen children in small-town Iowa. As a result, she loves to explore in her writing how family relationships influence who and why we love as we do.

Jodi is a two-time National Readers' Choice finalist and winner of Romance Writers of America's Golden Heart Award. She's married to the hometown boy she has known since fifth grade and lives near Dallas in a ninety-five-year-old Victorian home with her husband, Darrel, and two dogs, Rio and Leia.

Dear Reader,

All babies are special, but I'd venture to say that certain ones are extra special, by virtue of the particular purpose they fulfill in their parents' lives.

Like my youngest brother, who was special for a couple of reasons. My mother was forty-three when she became pregnant with him. In those days that was a pretty risky age for a woman to be having a child. In fact, my mother had lost a baby, my sister Nora, the year before.

It was a tense, prayerful time in our house, those months before that baby was born. All of us kids knew this would be the last O'Donnell baby, and more than anything we wanted Mama—and Daddy—to go out winners. I say "all" because there were thirteen of us. Obviously, my family already knew how special babies are! Still, this last one, when he arrived hale and hearty, was welcomed with exceptional joy and thanksgiving.

Now, as for my characters, Reid and Glenna...well, they're going to need some convincing on the subject of babies. You see, both of them believe they've entered middle age and that part of their lives—the being young and falling in love and making a family together part—is well over.

I knew it would take nothing less than a baby to show these two just how young and alive and in love they can be.

Of course, right now Reid and Glenna don't know they have this special child—or falling in love—ahead of them. So won't you wish them a little luck now?

Why? you ask. Because being middle-aged and new parents—they're going to need all the luck they can get!

Jodi O'Donnell

Chapter One

Glenna Dunn did not consider herself a woman easily given to tears. However, she believed that once the decision to cry was made, one should make a thorough job of it.

That was why this July afternoon she found herself driving down an isolated ranch road. There were several elements essential to ensuring a truly cleansing cry, solitude being one of them. A person wanted to be able to let it all hang out, shriek or shout as the urge took them, do a little discreet cussing with no one the wiser. Out here in the great wide open was the only place Glenna could think of to find that sort of privacy.

She pulled her pickup onto the gravel shoulder of the road, although there wasn't a living soul in sight who would have been inconvenienced had she parked smack-dab in the middle. But that was the Texas Panhandle for you, its landscape nearly as empty as the vast blue sky above. Just here and there a mesquite tree permanently leaning south-by-southeast due to the constant wind blowing across the plains. Or, if lucky, one might spy an oil pump-jack or windmill. That was about the extent of it, though. As the saying went, there was no other place on earth where you could look so far and see so little.

Right now, such emptiness suited Glenna's state of mind to a T. It would be the perfect backdrop to the sweetest little pity party this stretch of asphalt had ever seen.

Killing the engine, she sat in silence for a few moments, head bent. Then, wrapping her forearms around the steering wheel, fingers hooking the top of it, she rested her forehead on her knuckles. One deep, purifying breath and she was off.

Tears poured from her eyes as great, powerful sobs racked her chest; her nose ran like a leaky spigot. She'd had the foresight to grab a box of tissues, and Glenna groped for one after another, blowing noisily.

As the first storm of weeping passed, anger and resentment and defiance came boiling forth. Now she was getting down to brass tacks. Glenna vented the best she knew how, pounding her fist against the padded steering wheel, her swearing pretty much confined to the oh, hells and damn-it-alls of a churchgoing woman. Which wasn't enough. The tension that had propelled her here still kept her wound tight as a spring, until it seemed she'd never be free of it.

Pitching something would be positively therapeutic, Glenna decided. She lifted her head and, through a glaze of tears, considered the hodgepodge of objects on the dashboard: a pair of leather work gloves, a spiral notebook with a stubby pencil stuck in its spine, a pink baby rattle, small change. Not enough weight in any of them. Then she spied a pair of large needle-nose pliers lying on the floor, and the anger that had begun to level off bubbled upward again. What was Jamey thinking, leaving such a dangerous tool out? Why, little Hettie was getting to that stage where she was into everything and everything went directly into her mouth! With a muttered oath Glenna shook her head. Sometimes her daughter seemed too young to handle one baby, much less two.

Righteously aggrieved, she grabbed the pliers. At least they had the right heft. Perfect for hurling into the scrub, with no one to apologize to and not a moment of chagrin when she'd have to go hunt for them.

Blood now running at a satisfying all-time high, Glenna wrenched open the door of the pickup, ground her boot heel into the gravel as she stepped down—and nearly jumped out of her skin at the sight of Reid Shelton standing not three feet away.

Under the shading brim of a lightweight straw Stetson and furrowed black eyebrows, his hazel gaze was bemused as it moved from her face to her stance to the pliers, business end pointed straight at him.

He took a respectful step backward.

Waving the tool, Glenna opened her mouth to explain. Nothing came out. So she did the only thing she could think of: she got back in the pickup and closed the door.

She debated driving off without a glance but hesitated too long in deciding, for there came a tapping at the window.

She rolled it down. "Afternoon, Reid," she said, curt.

"Afternoon, Glenna," he answered, solemn. He eyed the pliers. "Some kind of trouble with the pickup?"

Feeling her cheeks catch up with her undoubtedly scarlet nose, Glenna shook her head. "No. I was just fixin' to, you know, throw these . . . I mean, haven't you ever needed to—"

She cut herself off. Lord, this had to rank up there as one of the most embarrassing moments of her life. Served her right for staging a world-class hissy fit on a public byway. And then for Reid Shelton to bear witness to her foolishness!

Ever since she'd met this mid-fortyish horse trainer during spring roundup at her son-in-law's ranch, they'd shared what amounted to a game of visual footsie. Those sidelong glances to check the other out, only to have gazes connect like magnets before jerking away. Or at least, hers had. Who knew what he thought of her? Although she had the uneasy feeling she was going to find out very soon, because the way he looked at her right now seemed utterly devoid of attraction.

"You mind telling me how long you've been standin' there?" she asked, entertaining brief hope.

Reid scratched the bridge of his nose. "I believe I came along about the time you were windin' down from whaling the tar out of that steering wheel and had just started, uh, shouting."

"I see." She glanced away and caught sight of herself in the rearview mirror. Lord *above*. Why couldn't she have at least combed her hair before rushing hell-for-bear out the door?

But she knew why, and it seemed no better reason now than it had then. Except she simply couldn't have stayed.

Pushing auburn strands out of her face, Glenna noticed the gray filament among them. By no means was it the first, but to spy one today seemed the crowning insult. Literally.

"I suppose you think I'm plumb crazy." She tried a weak smile that died when her lower lip began to tremble.

Frowning reflectively, Reid propped the butt of one hand on the doorjamb. "I don't guess I know enough about the situation to judge one way or t'other."

"Well, the truth is I'm not prone to exhibitions of high drama, normally. Yellin' and throwin' things and c-crying." Her nose started plugging up all over again, and Glenna dropped her gaze to her lap as she blinked back a fresh crop of tears. Blast it, if she'd been allowed to finish the job properly, she wouldn't be tearing up again! Although the fact that she still felt as volatile as a firecracker factory suggested to her that this problem wouldn't be purged with a temporary wallow in her woes.

"I'm not emotional," she went on, half-aware that she sought to convince herself more than Reid. "Really. Today, though, it's just . . . I don't know."

No, it wasn't merely today's events that had propelled her here, because for weeks now, Glenna had been over-sensitive and uncharacteristically impatient, tense and unhappy. She didn't like being that way, yet she seemed nearly helpless to temper her behavior. And that's what bothered her most of all.

"Everybody needs to let off a little steam now and then, don't they?" Reid commented, bending to lean his forearms on the window jamb. "Used to be when I got that way, I'd rise of a morning, go out to the corral and throw a hoolihan over the neck of the coldest-backed bronc I could find. Then I'd climb on board and warm him up till he got the kink out of his back. Worked wonders for us both."

He chewed on the inside of his cheek. "Of course, nowadays I'd end up goin' ass over teakettle more often than not. Easier just to do somethin' like buy that truck back there."

He gestured behind her, and Glenna hesitated before obligingly twisting in her seat to see a shiny red dual-wheeled pickup parked behind hers.

"Is that new?" she asked—and nearly bumped noses with Reid, which allowed her to observe up close for the first time how dark his hazel eyes were, with their irises shooting out shards of gray and green and gold toward a black rim.

"Yes, ma'am. First brand-new vehicle I ever owned, if you can believe it. Got every feature you could imagine, and some you couldn't. Seven-point-three DI diesel, a back seat with its own doors, air-conditioning, stereo, air bags, dual-speed wipers. I even replaced the ol' CB with one of those cellular phones that lets me talk to practically anybody in the world hands free."

Gazing at his new possession, he tipped his hat back with the edge of an index finger, and Glenna lost herself in the momentary distraction of a thorough perusal of Reid Shelton. He had a wonderfully striking profile with a straight nose, a nice, nice mouth and a firm, strong jawline. She studied the crow's-feet fanning out from the corners of his eyes, the hair at his temple black sprinkled with silver.

She'd never seen him without his hat, and she couldn't help wondering how the rest of his hair had grayed. She had a feeling that, hatless, he would be something else, even if she'd always favored the view of a cowboy in a Stetson and—her gaze drifted lower—a well-fitting Western shirt with a tantalizing sprig of chest hair showing at the collar.

Glenna bit her lip. Maybe that was what made her so jumpy lately: plain old widow-woman sexual frustration. God knew eighteen months of doing without would put even the best of women on edge. After all, she was only forty-one. Forty-*two,* she mentally amended. Still, it was not over the hill, by any means.

Glenna turned away before Reid might catch her gawking at him. If only it *was* as simple as scratching that particular itch, she thought ruefully. But there was no pat answer to the questions in her life, and she really didn't expect to find one. Certainly not in Reid Shelton who, with the courtliness of cowboys, had stopped today only to offer aid if needed—not to get tangled up in her problems, which were no one's but her own.

"That red dually of yours sounds the very lap of luxury, Reid," she remarked lamely.

He faced her again. "Yes, ma'am, my very own Cowboy Cadillac. Better'n Geritol for the middle-age crazies."

She actually laughed, relieved that at last someone had said what she had been so reluctant to even think. "I always thought that some day when James and I could afford a nicer pickup, I'd get him one of those bumper stickers that said Turbocharged Vehicle, Pity About The Driver."

They both laughed at that, except Glenna's mirth faded as she realized she sat in the old, battered pickup her husband had driven for years—and that never would he have a new truck she could tease him about.

Her eyes met Reid's, which revealed a certain sympathy. Then as quickly as it had come, the look was gone from his eyes, almost as if it had never been. And it probably hadn't; she was only projecting her own emotions onto him. Still, she knew some of Reid's history from her son-in-law. Wouldn't it make sense if Reid was experiencing the same feelings of loss she was? After all, they shared quite a bit of common ground, both being of a certain age, both of them widowed with adult children.

Both alone.

She guessed that this, more than any of the other developments in her life she was trying to deal with, had caused her flight today. And was the particular thought that brought back the sting to her eyes.

"Well," Glenna said, staunchly ignoring the quaver in her voice. "I should be going. Thanks, Reid, for bein' neighborly and stoppin'. I'm perfectly fine now, honest."

Even though it was obvious she intended to leave, Reid didn't move away from her truck. "Were you heading into Borger when you pulled over?" he asked.

"Um, yes," Glenna lied, seeing no reason to admit her sole purpose in driving out here was to indulge in a crying jag.

"So was I. I've got some errands to do, make a stop at the feed store." Reid hesitated, the index finger of one hand hooked into the waistband of his jeans as his chin dropped and he looked at her from under the brim of his hat. "We could ride into town together in my pickup, if you were of a mind."

She was touched, unaccountably so, by the simple invitation, especially since she'd had the impression up to now that Reid really *didn't* want to get involved in her problems. Of course, he was only offering a ride to town, not a shoulder to cry on.

Now she paused, considering. Though it solved none of her dilemma, what harm could there be in setting it aside for a few hours, especially when it didn't seem that anything she'd tried yet was helping? A little side trip with no pressure to do anything more than pass the time might be just the diversion she needed to get her over the hump today. As for her fascination with Reid, it probably was nothing more than a product of her repressed sexual urges. And entirely controllable.

This time there was no strain of self-consciousness or tremble of tears in the smile she sent him. "A ride to town sounds fine, but aren't you afraid I'll turn loose the waterworks again and ruin the upholstery of your new truck?" she asked with a drollness that hid the shyness hanging back behind it.

His eyebrows screwed together in consideration as he answered in kind. "That is a poser. Could I get you to hang your head out the window if you feel another one of those squalls comin' on?"

She laughed in spite of herself even as she grew embarrassed, remembering how he'd found her blubbering like a baby. Lord, she must have seemed completely mental!

Glenna smoothed her hand across cheeks sticky with dried tears. "Fine, then. If you'll just give me a moment to jot a note to stick on the windshield in case someone else chances by and wonders if there's a problem. Oh, and to clean up with a little water from the cooler in the back." She pushed her fingers through the tangle atop her head, then gave up with a forward flop of her hands. "There's not much I can do to improve this rat's nest, I'm afraid."

She cut him a wry glance only to find his dark lashes flickering as he took in the whole of her before his gaze came back to hers—and held. It was then she realized: not black, blue. His hazel irises were rimmed in a dark, almost navy, blue.

"Oh," he said quietly, "I think you'll do."

She hadn't been fishing for a compliment, and it wasn't really one anyway, delivered in that understated way of cowboys, and yet a thrill charged through Glenna, producing a gut-deep ache of longing that made her shift in her seat again.

Damn it, she simply *had* to stop acting as if she had nothing better to concern herself with than the color of this man's eyes, the shade of his hair, the breadth of his shoulders—or the kindness in his heart. She was too old for this silliness. A grandmother!

And yet two minutes ago she'd been convincing herself a woman of her years was still entitled to her moments of passion.

What an awkward age! Too old for some things, too young for others. That was why it was called middle age, Glenna told herself, and she must face the fact that she'd reached it.

She knew she had no business getting in that truck with Reid, not if a few softly spoken words could set off such a reaction in her. She would not be one of those foolish, faded women who persisted in staying on the merry-go-round, grabbing for that brass ring, when she should have stepped off long ago and let someone younger have her turn.

But at the thought of telling Reid she'd changed her mind, of turning her pickup around and watching in the rearview mirror as his shiny red truck became smaller and smaller until it was nothing but a pinpoint on that featureless horizon... At the thought of driving home alone...

It's just a ride to town, she reminded herself as she left her truck for the unadulterated comfort of Reid Shelton's.

Chapter Two

Reid paid attention to the road, though he was aware of the woman sitting across the bench seat from him, cold drink in hand. He'd popped open one for himself, and sipped it as Hank Williams, Jr., sang from the radio, the AC keeping the cab of the pickup pleasantly cool. Yes, all the makings of a perfectly normal ride to town. Except Reid didn't feel normal. Not one bit.

That was because of Glenna Dunn.

At first he'd been puzzled at the sight of the pickup parked in the middle of nowhere, then concerned when he spied the figure slumped over the steering wheel, and finally stunned to discover that person was Glenna Dunn, pitching one hell of a caterwaul. Then when she'd turned those miserable gray eyes on him...well, it was to Reid's shame that he'd responded to the rock-bottom desolation in her eyes with a sudden temptation to bring that suffering to heel for her the one way he knew he could.

He hadn't experienced such a reaction in ages, and could only liken it to that of a rodeo cowboy presented with the challenge of riding that bull, taming that bronc—or romancing that woman. He wasn't proud of such a response, but told himself it was natural, even though he wasn't some fly-by-night rodeo buck, hadn't been for coming up on three decades.

Yet he couldn't have turned from Glenna in her misery. She'd looked ready to do something drastic, and he wouldn't have been able to live with himself if he hadn't tried to help her, some way. And he had been surprised—and glad—that he'd been able to find distance by applying one of the horse-training techniques that were second nature to him: When green-breaking a horse, you distracted it with some simple exercise to build up the trust between rider and animal so that it would have a sense of partnership with you when you asked it to tackle the skills that came unnaturally to it, and so tended to be threatening.

Except Glenna Dunn was no skittish filly, and he'd have to be a simpleton to treat her like one.

"Did you have anything in particular you needed to get done in Borger?" he asked, making conversation.

For some reason his simple question seemed to fluster her before she quickly regained her poise. "I was going to do some shopping. Maybe go to the beauty parlor to have my hair done."

"Oh," he said, somewhat disappointed. Her shoulder-length auburn hair was as tousled as a horse's tail, yet it looked natural and unaffected. "Well, I could wait for you while you do your business, or we could set a time for me to pick you up. Either's fine with me."

"Whatever's easiest for you. You've been more than kind already, asking me along."

She sounded anything but upset right now, in direct contrast to how she'd been acting not fifteen minutes ago.

Reid frowned. Somewhere he'd gotten the notion that a storm still brewed in this woman. That was why he'd asked her along; he didn't think she should be left alone just then, although he usually tended to his own business and left it to others to tend theirs.

They drove in silence for several minutes, after which Reid slid her a sidelong glance. Her expression had grown pensive again. So whatever it was *did* still bother her. With effort he turned his attention back to his driving, letting her be. It truly was none of his concern.

Yet when the tires had eaten up another ten miles, he found himself clearing his throat and saying, "You know, Glenna, if you'd like to talk about it..."

She blushed, arrestingly so, which brought a certain tightness to his belly. "It's a bunch of little things, really," she said uncertainly. "I'm afraid in the telling they won't seem like much, at least not enough to nearly go off the deep end."

He wondered why her reticence irritated him, especially when he'd had his own misgivings about opening the subject. "Guess I wouldn't know for sure unless you did tell me."

"Mmm." She slanted him a questioning look before glancing away to frown at her soda can as if it were the root of all her troubles. She lifted one shoulder in a half shrug. "Well, ever since Jamey married Kell Hamilton at the end of May, I've been feeling at loose ends. Till then, I'd been caring for my granddaughter, you know, while Jamey put her life back together. I always knew it was a temporary situation, and I was happy to help her out as long as she needed me."

She wiggled the pop top on her soda can, examining it unduly when it broke off in her hand. "Jamey's been through so much, with that bum of a husband runnin' out on her and her daddy dying, us losing the ranch in

Nevada, and then finding out she was pregnant with Hettie."

"I'd wager you've been through as much, though," Reid noted. "Especially losin' your husband."

"Yes." Hooking her hair behind an ear, she threw him a glance of sympathy. "You'd know how that is, of course. You and Clan. He lost his mother and you your wife, didn't you?"

He squinted against the glare coming off the hood of the truck. "Miranda died of cancer two years ago," he answered—a trifle brusquely, he realized, and so he added on an amending note, "She was forty-three."

"James—my husband? Jamey was named for him— was forty-one when he died," she said in a faraway voice. "Meningitis. Came on real sudden. One day he was there, the next—gone."

It was on the tip of Reid's tongue to tell her she was lucky her husband went so quickly, but he had no appreciation she'd see it that way.

"Jamey seems to have dealt with her daddy's death pretty well," he observed, steering the conversation back to her concerns for her daughter, since that seemed to be what bothered Glenna. "I mean, I've only talked to your daughter a few times, but I know Kell. She's quite a woman in his eyes."

"And she loves him to pieces. Yes, I think she's finally put the past behind her and found happiness. Everyone has. Her little girl will grow up having a real daddy in Kell, and he loves Hettie like she was his own."

She ducked her chin again to focus on the meaningless action of running her thumbnail in a semicircle around the rim of her drink can. "That's the point, though. They're a family now. Jamey and Kell, they're true partners, the two of them. I believe they think there's nothing they can't handle... together. And they should have a chance to work into that relationship without me underfoot."

"I don't know about that." Reid had some knowledge of the setup at the Hamiltons' ranch, since he had an arrangement to use their cattle to train his cutting horses. "Most ranches' survival in the Panhandle depends on the efforts of every available family member. Of course, you're not a native of here—"

But she had been a rancher's wife, and she knew what it was like to be partners with someone, to be in there helping to run the show, as it were.

"Seems they'd still need you, though, don't you think?" he continued. "If Jamey's out tending cattle with Kell, someone needs to watch Hettie."

"Oh, I definitely can help out. And I want to earn my keep, at the very least. But they've got a whole schedule worked out to share responsibilities. That son-in-law of mine is a rare one," she said with a certain pride. "Doesn't mind at all sharin' with the baby's care, even with the cooking and cleaning, so Jamey can have her own time out on the range. Truly, they don't need me. Not at all, although they make every effort to include me in their family. But I want . . . want—"

She bowed her head to rub her temple with four fingers. "Oh, Reid, I feel so selfish. You see, today's my birthday."

"Do tell!" Eyebrows raised in surprise, he almost wished her glad tidings for the day, except Glenna didn't look a mite glad about it. "I understand what it's like not to welcome another year on your age, but why's it make you feel selfish?"

She met his gaze, chin set in defiance. "Because this morning Jamey, her face all glowing and proud and hopeful, told me she had the best birthday present ever."

"Which is?"

"Jamey's pregnant, Reid," she blurted out, as if delivering tragic news. "I know I hurt her—I just ran out without a word. All I could think was that I'm forty-two, and I'm going to be a grandmother twice over before I turn forty-three! I've got decades of my life ahead of me, and already I feel old as the hills. Useless."

Braking gently to avoid a tumbleweed rolling across his path, Reid had to admit it wouldn't excite the pants off him, either, to receive such unexpected news. But he'd concede he might have a different view than most people on the subject, for reasons entirely separate from Glenna's.

"It's a shock, sure, but it's not like it must have been with Hettie—"

"Hettie's different!" she broke in, almost impatiently. "For a while, Hettie was my... I was her..."

There was a moment of silence as Glenna again struggled for composure. Then she said softly into the quiet, "I can see what's happening to me, Reid. For months I've put all sorts of issues in a corner of my mind, and now they're comin' out of the woodwork, all at once. I've got to deal with them, I know I do, but how can I when they're all right there, surrounding me, closing in on me, so that I feel like I've just got to do *something* to relieve the pressure. Something to move forward."

"Like what?"

"I'm thinking maybe I should get a real job, one where I had specific duties. But, yes, the question is, what would I do?" Her eyebrows drew together. "I used to tell myself I didn't have to take any definite steps until I was ready. And I want to stay close to Jamey and Kell. Between us, we all have so little family, and such relationships are precious. I do have an insurance settlement that I can invest and build up for later in my life. Now, though—"

Her fingers whitened as they gripped the soda can. "I wonder, where do I belong right now? Because all I've ever been is a wife and mother. And all I ever wanted to be..."

Glenna's voice trailed off as her expression suddenly grew even more troubled. Quickly she turned her head to gaze out the window, but not before Reid glimpsed a mystification in her eyes he sensed outweighed the anguish that had led her to cry earlier. And it raised in him a vague unease that he should leave well enough alone and discontinue this conversation right now.

Then she straightened her shoulders and went on with spirit, "It's not as if I'm without a few skills. I kept all the books for the family ranch. I'm a fair judge of cows and horseflesh. I just need to put my mind to finding the right position. Or maybe I could get something in Borger. I helped out at the Baptist day-care center there for a while. The minister and his wife would give me a good reference. Of course, the drive from Plum Creek each day would be a long one, but I do prize my thinkin' time. I could see myself enjoyin' a commute."

The words were optimistic, but their tone lacked a little of the same. "It sounds just the thing for you," Reid responded lamely.

"Yes, it does." She continued to study the passing scenery. "Somehow, though, I think I'd still feel so...so..."

So...what? he wondered. There was something going on with Glenna, more than her feelings about becoming a grandparent or having a birthday or wanting a job. Something big enough to have driven her from Plum Creek this morning, but what that concern might be seemed beyond him. Yet a person would have to be made of stone not to want to try to understand, after seeing her tear-streaked face as she'd sat in her pickup.

Then it came to Reid why he'd been drawn to her so strongly today. It was because the bleakness he'd seen in her eyes at that moment had seemed a mirror image of what he'd seen in his own so many times.

He, too, had had his share of tragedy in the past years. He'd watched helplessly as Miranda fought her illness, knowing there was nothing he could do to stem the progress of a cancer that advanced with the terrible purposefulness of a swarm of locusts. He'd had to put everything on hold to nurse her and had lived daily with the apprehension that his business would fail, that he would lose, almost simultaneously, everything that ever meant a damn to him. Indeed, without the help of their son, Clan, the family would surely have lost the ranch.

After she had died, he'd not had time to dwell much on how his life had changed as he concentrated his every effort on fighting for what was left to him. And two years later he was finally back on his feet, at least business-wise. He had clients lining up for him to train their cutting horses. His colleagues had welcomed him back into competition, and he didn't mind saying he was glad to be back. Back on track with his life.

Yet the loss of the past few years had begun to show its effect on him. Why else would he have purchased a pickup half and again more than he actually needed in a vehicle and all decked out like a float in a Fourth of July parade? At the time he'd told himself he deserved it—and he did—and that it would make him feel good. But it didn't.

He looked at Glenna, thought about what she'd told him of Jamey and her family. Oh, yes, he understood what she was going through. He knew, too, that no amount of thinking or crying over the past would make it any easier to bear. And it wasn't any of his affair how she chose to go on with her life.

Still, would it hurt to try to convey his outlook to her?

"Glenna," he said softly. When she remained motionless, he repeated, *"Glenna."*

She turned to him then, her eyes a muted gray in more than just color. He could virtually see the stifling of emotions that were too intense. Too needful. God, he *knew* what it was like.

"I can't speak for you, but I know what helps me," he said flatly. "I stay busy, do what I need to to make a life for myself. And I let my kid live his own, as he's going to, anyway. I mean, what else is there? The frustration of suspectin' life's passed you by will eat away at you, if you let it."

That said, he set his jaw and turned back to the road. It was as far as he was prepared to go for her right now.

Still, Glenna seemed to have gleaned some help from his meager pearls of wisdom, for she gazed at him thoughtfully before saying, "Yes, you're probably right."

They said nothing more until they were entering the Borger city limits. Reid had observed the town's approach for miles, how the terrain changed from flat to a craggy moonscape of white limestone rocks strewn haphazardly amongst the scrub. Great gashes in the earth bled red dirt. The place looked like the leavings of some mining venture gone belly-up. Reid much preferred the scenery around Piney Rise, his ranch.

He cast Glenna a covert glance. No, she wasn't a native of the Panhandle; neither was he. But unlike her, he'd chosen to live here, had craved its untamable nature. Still and all, it had taken some getting used to, this harsh, barren land, this unabated openness. There was nothing, no mountains or valleys, even trees, to break up the space into natural partitions that one could then take in a piece at a time. And so one was relieved the responsibility of even trying to encompass it all.

"Okay if I let you off on Main?" Reid asked.

"Certainly," Glenna answered with subdued politeness, her mind obviously a million miles away. "Anywhere along here."

Reid pulled up to the curb. "This all right?"

"Just fine." She gathered her purse by its strap in one hand and reached for the door handle with the other before hesitating. "So we'll go our separate ways? You run your errands, I run mine? I won't need more than an hour and a half, maybe two, but take your time doing what you need to."

He stretched an arm out across the back of the seat. "I don't mind waiting, like I suggested."

She opened the door and stepped out, the smell from the oil refinery wafting in. "No. I can occupy myself just fine."

They were both trying to accommodate, he realized, both used to doing so with their own needs.

"Besides, this is as good an opportunity as any to pick up a newspaper and look through the want ads," she went on with evident cheerfulness, making Reid wonder if he'd actually found her sobbing her heart out an hour ago. "I'll just find some cozy corner in a café to have a cup of coffee."

"Well, and what more could you want?" he remarked inanely before realizing that no, things weren't at all copacetic, for as Glenna began to close the door he spied in her downcast face a heart-wrenching expression, almost of having been abandoned.

And again he found himself, against his will and definitely against his better judgment, racking his brain for a way to help her. What was it in him that made Glenna Dunn's concerns of such importance to him? Because it wasn't his duty to think of a way to solve her woes and make her happy!

Yet what if he had no place to call his own, a place to be alone, and so he had to drive clear out in the middle of nowhere to find that kind of privacy? How would it feel if he hadn't had his business to throw himself into after Miranda died, if he'd lost forever the definition not of who he'd always been, but who he would always be: a trainer of horses.

And so Reid found himself calling out to her. "Glenna!"

She opened the door and peered back in at him, one palm resting on the back of the seat, inches from his own, as she bent to see his face. "Yes?"

The movement caused a gap in the neckline of her shirt, revealing a curve of breast, and he was instantly captivated by the picture she made. In this light her skin looked perfect, with so few lines around her eyes and mouth it told him he'd been given a rare perspective of Glenna Dunn earlier. How had she managed to remain a woman of soft edges rather than acquiring the hard ones honed of necessity when one fought to make a living off the land? She *was* soft, though. Impressionable as someone much younger and with less life experience might be. And filled with a youthful passion that had reached out to him. Challenged him, so that instead of wanting to talk some sense into her, he wanted to close the inches separating their fingertips and touch her, if only to see whether he could bring some of the fire back to her eyes, answer its heat with a bit of his own.

But she was not, as she'd professed, used to expressing such extreme emotions. No, what he saw now was that she had years of practice dealing with disappointments.

In that, the two of them were as one.

"Uh, good luck," he remarked inadequately. "With your job hunting, that is."

He could tell she wondered if that was all he'd wanted, but she said nothing, purse dangling at her side while she studied him, as if trying to figure out what he hadn't said. Or done.

Which made him uncomfortable—and inexplicably irritated, as he'd been when he sensed her reluctance to talk to him about what bothered her. "Well," he said curtly. "I better get goin'."

He swung back around and reached for the stick shift, glad he wasn't looking at her when she finally said softly, "I'd like to thank you, Reid, for stoppin' today to check on me. And for listening to me, especially after the way I acted. I hope that won't be your lasting impression of me."

Actually, he feared the image of her impassioned intensity would haunt his nights for weeks to come. He shrugged, seeking distance. "Hell, Glenna. It was the least I could've done," he said. The very least.

"Mmm," she said, that noncommittal sound again that could mean anything from yes, no, maybe, to indifferent. Then she went on, "You're right, though. All this is is comin' to terms with middle age."

"You mean your ravin' out in broad daylight like a rabid coyote, or me trying to relive my youth by buying a souped-up truck?" he wisecracked.

As he'd hoped, that brought out her smile—so he could do *that* for her—a warm and grateful one. Then she bantered back, "You know what they say about midlife crises. It's always one of three changes that signals their arrival. Buying a sporty car or switching careers or takin' a lover—"

Glenna cut herself off, blushing again, a glorious rose color that climbed upward from her throat and spread across her cheeks like dawn breaking over the horizon. And made him abruptly, painfully taut.

She recovered quickly, though, giving him a firm nod. "I do believe I'll pick the second option."

With that, she closed the door and walked off, determination in every step.

His gaze traveled upward to caress the sway of her hips, the roundness of her behind in her jeans, and Reid felt himself grow even more aroused. So much for distance, for maintaining control. Or for keeping his mind above his waist. Because now he knew Glenna had at least entertained the same thoughts as he had. But she'd made her choice.

Distracting himself, he concentrated on picking at a nub in the weave of the upholstery, which stirred up what could only be called new car smell. How long, he wondered, until the newness faded, the novelty of owning this truck wore off? Because it would; it was just a matter of time. And then what?

He, however, had made his choice, too.

Reaching up to tug his hat brim level with his brow, Reid yanked the stick into Drive with his other hand and pulled back out into the traffic. So be it. It was no business of his what Glenna Dunn did, especially since chances were she'd find some cowboy who'd play hell trying to meet the wanting in her.

But there was no way he was going to make that mistake again.

Chapter Three

Late that afternoon Glenna entered the mudroom at Plum Creek. She hadn't gotten halfway across the floor before Jamey was at the back door.

"There y'all are!" her daughter said with a brightness that struck Glenna as rather forced.

"Yep, all of us," Glenna replied with her own strained cheerfulness as she hung her purse on a peg before stepping into the kitchen. It hadn't taken her daughter long to pick up that distinct Texanism that could include everybody from one person to the whole world. In this case, though, "y'all" meant two. Glenna turned to find the other recipient of her daughter's welcome standing just inside the doorway.

Yes, Reid Shelton would be joining in her birthday celebration. *Let the festivities begin,* she thought ruefully.

It had all started as they drove back to her truck and, at his encouragement, she'd used his cellular phone to call

Plum Creek and let them know she was on her way home. After she'd conveyed that information to her son-in-law, he'd asked to speak to Reid, and the two had chatted on about the bunch of yearling steers Reid wanted hauled over. As they'd talked, she'd turned her thoughts elsewhere, and that was why Glenna almost missed Kell inviting Reid to follow her home and join the family for her birthday supper.

Reid had hesitated, and she'd been struck by that odd sensation that he wanted not to become involved. She spent an awkward few moments in which she wondered if he presumed she'd somehow engineered the invitation. She hadn't, but, Lord, after her slip of the tongue this afternoon, what *did* he think? And what had been wrong with her to make such a remark?

Then she'd been distracted from such ponderings by Reid saying he'd be pleased to come. And *that* sent another one of those thrills through her. Seeing the red dually in her rearview mirror as she led the way back to Plum Creek had kept her similarly buoyed. Of course, such loop-de-loops in her thinking clued Glenna to the probability that her emotions remained unstable, and that it might be best for all concerned if she cut her losses and called it a day.

Yet that wish was not to be granted.

Resolved to get through this evening one way or another, she now invited, "Come on in and make yourself at home, Reid."

He followed her into the kitchen. Since her daughter was six inches taller than Glenna, she knew Jamey had a bird's-eye view of the top of her head as she passed by.

"Did you do somethin' to your hair?" Jamey asked with her usual bluntness.

"I got some henna highlights put in when I was in Borger today," she answered, newly self-conscious and embarrassed. She'd begun to think the difference to her appearance inappreciable; Reid hadn't said a word.

Did he think she'd done her hair on account of him? Had she?

She was distracted from further stewing about the matter by her nine-month-old granddaughter catching sight of her.

"Ghee!" Hettie squealed from her high chair. Strained peas rimmed her mouth and adorned the front of her bib. Peas were not one of the baby's favorites, a fact evidenced by her disgusted expression when Kell sneaked a spoonful of them into Hettie's open mouth. Lips in a prune, she shook her head as if she had mites in her ears, her copper curls dancing around her face.

Glenna's son-in-law sat on the edge of a chair in front of the little one, his wide shoulders hunkered forward and in his large hand a baby spoon held ready under Hettie's lower lip in case the peas came out again. They did.

"Hettie!" Jamey reproved. "I swear, she's been ornery as a rattlesnake all day."

"Bet you got a tooth coming, don't you, sugar?" Glenna said, bending over Kell's shoulder to make a funny face at her granddaughter. Hettie, in a Jekyll-and-Hyde change of disposition, grinned greenly back. If Glenna knew her granddaughter—which she did—the smile was a blatant attempt to charm her way out of eating any more of those peas.

How she loved this child! Right now it seemed impossible that she did not cherish the opportunity to make her home with her daughter. What could possibly be more life affirming than watching one's children raise children of their own?

Glenna glanced up to find Reid standing just inside the threshold to the kitchen and taking in the scene in the warm, crowded room. *What, indeed?*

She straightened. "Can I get you anything to drink, Reid?"

"Grab yourself a cold one," Kell volunteered, nodding toward the fridge. "We don't stand on ceremony around here."

As Reid stepped over to the refrigerator, Glenna said to her daughter, "I trust Kell told you we're one more for supper."

"Of a fashion," Jamey replied cryptically, concentrating on shredding lettuce for a salad.

"I understand congratulations are in order," Reid said to the younger woman, leaning back against the counter, out of the way, as he twisted the cap off a longneck. "Glenna told me you're expectin'."

Jamey's chin came up, her gaze going not to Reid but Glenna, searchingly. "Thank you, Reid. We're pretty excited about it."

Guilt crept over Glenna, but before she could say anything, Reid went on, "Hope it's no bother, Jamey, me comin' to supper."

Jamey waved away his concerns. "Shoot, no. Fact is I'm lookin' forward to making up for the last time you sat down to the half-burned, half-raw meal I made, right after I'd started at Plum Creek."

"And you came back, Reid?" Kell said with disbelief. "You must be a glutton for punishment, 'cause I can't imagine you got your fill of anything else here."

This effectively broke the strain in the room as everyone laughed, including Jamey, who had indeed prepared some prodigiously awful fare in her first days as Plum Creek's cook-housekeeper.

Yes, it was hard for Glenna to believe that a mere six months ago her daughter had been all thumbs around the kitchen. Yet Jamey had set her mind to doing her best, and she was as good a cook, plus wife and mother, as she'd always been a cowgirl.

So why, Glenna wondered, was she finding it so difficult to adapt and redefine herself the same way?

Kell glanced up at her. "Your hair's pretty, Glenna.
Highlights, did you say? Although to tell the truth, I
don't know that I'd have noticed if no one had said anything."

"That's the point," she told him with a smile, bless-
ing the young man for his diplomacy. Glenna also
thanked God on her daughter's behalf for sending Jamey such a man, especially so soon after her first husband had abandoned her. As a result, Hettie would grow
up knowing only the security of the family Kell and Jamey were building together.

Suddenly the unsettledness that had spurred Glenna
away from here nipped at her heels again. What on earth
would it take to uncork this bottled-up feeling? Or would
she just have to learn to live with it?

She'd *really* end up throwing a wall-eyed fit. Or worse.

Glenna pivoted, with no aim other than to try to relieve the urge to move in some manner, and to her dismay found her daughter's thoughtful and concerned gaze
on her.

Surely, surely Jamey didn't know how unhappy she
was here. But it was time to make amends, as much as
Glenna could.

"Well. I'm sure you're dyin' to wash off the road dust,
Reid," she suggested, trusting he'd take the hint.
"There's a bathroom just down the hall."

She hadn't asked him not to mention her outburst today to the family; she didn't have to. She knew Reid
would keep it to himself. Yet while she'd been glad for his
calming presence up to now, she'd just as soon he wasn't
around when she made her explanations—and apologies—to her family.

He acted unaware of any tension coming from her, and
merely said, "Don't mind if I do."

After he'd left, Glenna stepped over to the sink to wash her own hands, asking, "What can I help with? Kell, why don't I finish feeding Hettie so you and Reid can have a few moments in the living room to talk before supper?"

"Everything's under control, Momma," Jamey answered for her husband. "You're to take it easy. It's your birthday."

"It's not quite exhausting to mash potatoes or stir beans—"

"I know, but we're handling everything."

"Fine, then," Glenna conceded with faint exasperation, and did as she was told, sinking into a chair by the table and trying to regain the lost ground to her composure before going on. Taking a deep breath, she noticed on the table the double-layer cake that held more candles than could be counted in a single glance. However, the Happy 42nd Birthday, Momma written in the icing removed any guesswork.

The kitchen was silent except for Hettie's grunts of satisfaction, since Kell had moved on to her dessert of blueberry buckle. The baby downed each spoonful in one gulp and had her mouth open for the next like a bird for a worm.

"You know, Momma," Jamey said, paying undue attention to the carrots she was chopping, "you could have mentioned when you left this mornin' you had a date to meet Reid."

"We chanced upon each other, actually," Glenna replied, seeing through her daughter's thinly veiled attempt at discretion, and wondered how Jamey would react if there *had* been more to her meeting with Reid Shelton. What might a young woman make of her middle-aged, widowed mother's preoccupation with the first suitable bachelor to come along after her husband's death? Would it seem to Jamey as conspicuously convenient, and therefore foolish, as it did to herself?

"You're right, though, I could have said where I was going today." Rising, Glenna crossed the kitchen to give her daughter a hug around the shoulders. "I'm sorry, Jamey, for runnin' off so quickly and not stayin' to enjoy your wonderful news. Will you forgive me?"

Jamey shrugged unconvincingly. "There's nothin' to forgive. You've got a right to spend your birthday however you want."

"Mmm. It wasn't that I didn't want to stay..."

The sentence went unfinished. She wouldn't lie to her daughter, especially after what the two of them had been through in the past year and a half. "You do know I'm delighted for you, don't you, sugar?" Glenna asked softly.

Jamey gnawed on her lower lip before saying on a relieved rush, "Oh, Momma, I so hoped you'd be!"

"Of course I am." She regarded her daughter's pure profile. "You don't know the good it does me to finally see you truly content," she whispered from the bottom of her heart.

Jamey tipped her chin sideways to touch her cheek to Glenna's temple. "With Hettie, it wasn't the best-timed news. I feel like we both missed a lot of the anticipation of expectin' a new baby with her. I was hopin' this time could be different, to kind of make up for the trouble I was to you. You know?"

Oh, yes, Glenna knew. Jamey *did* still need her mother.

She sent a smile to her son-in-law, who'd finished feeding and cleaning up Hettie and now held the child perched on one hip. In a darling habit, the baby clung to him, clutching a chubby fistful of his shirtfront. "You, too, Kell. You must be looking forward to this little one."

"I never dreamed how much I would be," he answered, one large hand rising to stroke the curls at Hettie's nape as he gave his wife an exclusive, loving glance she returned tenfold.

And sudden desolation, hot and dry as the wind across the plains, swept through Glenna.

Feeling like an intruder, she dropped her arm from Jamey's shoulders and turned away as she sent up a frantic prayer—for herself this time—that she wouldn't start to cry, although no one would think her tears amiss at this moment. Except she had no assurance that she would be able to stop at a few sniffles. The deluge might start all over again.

"Well!" she said brightly, throat tight and eyes stinging. *Please!* she silently begged. "I think I'll just take Hettie into the other room and give her a bottle before supper."

"One of us can do that," Jamey protested. "It's your birthday."

"Which I believe you just mentioned means I can do whatever I want," Glenna observed. "And right now, I want to spend time with my granddaughter, if it's all right with everyone!"

Jamey and Kell stared at her. So did Reid, who she only then noticed stood in the doorway, having returned from washing up, and was witness—again!—to her histrionics.

Crossing to pluck Hettie from Kell's arms before grabbing the baby's bottle, Glenna rushed past Reid, unable to meet his eyes as she left the kitchen.

She sank into the rocker in the living room, situated Hettie in the crook of one arm and stuck the nipple into the baby's mouth. Taking small snorts of inhaled air between swallows, the child stared up at Glenna with anxious eyes.

"Not you, too," she muttered as she willed her own breathing to slow. It wasn't long before Hettie settled, eyelids drooping to half-mast as she lost herself in the familiar routine.

Finding a measure of calm herself from the everyday practice, Glenna leaned her head against the back of the rocker in utter discouragement.

What was *wrong* with her?

But she knew. Had suspected for months, actually. It had simply all come to a head today because of her birthday, which seemed a kind of psychological jumping-off point for the rest of her life—one for which she still had no clear vision. It would help, she supposed, if she knew what she was looking for.

Glenna caught a movement and turned her head to find Reid standing with the longneck dangling at his side between two fingers. The other hand was cocked at the wrist as he hooked a couple of digits in his belt loop in the loose-jointed pose she was learning he struck when thinking on a matter, or looking at her. Studying her, as she guessed he was used to when observing and assessing the horses he trained.

But she was no piece of horseflesh. And she did not enjoy being scrutinized like one.

Glenna pushed off with her toe, rather vigorously, to set the rocker going, as Reid remained where he was. She got that same impression that he did not want to become involved. And no wonder. Still, after a minute he crossed to sit on the sofa opposite the rocking chair, elbows propped on his spread knees, fingers clasping his beer bottle in between.

"Felt a tad out of place in that cozy kitchen, so I thought I'd take my chances in here," he said.

"I promise I won't bite. At least, not so's to leave a permanent mark," she quipped, and he chuckled.

Now that she wasn't in a state of high dudgeon, she realized at least one of her birthday wishes had come true—that of seeing Reid Shelton hatless. And what a sight it was.

He'd evidently wet a comb and used it, for his hair was shiny and springy looking, and lacking the imprint of a sweatband most cowboys perennially wore. Without his Stetson, she could see now that his hair on top was not sprinkled with gray like the sides, but was black through and through, giving him a Clark-Gable-as-Rhett-Butler look—dark, expressive eyebrows, engaging crow's-feet and all. Men were like that, darn them; they became all the more interesting for the marks life left upon them. Yet the shock of black hair spilling over his forehead made him look younger. And made her itch to brush it back.

"Somethin' wrong?" he inquired uneasily. She realized she'd been staring.

"No." Tired of failing at dissembling, she said, "You just look different without your hat on."

He ran a hand over his nape. "I'm not often without it. Makes me feel naked as a peeled egg."

So she wasn't the only one with a few insecurities, to hide under hat or highlighted hair.

The baby's weight on her arm sent pins and needles through it. "I'm sorry, Reid," she said, shifting the child.

"Sorry?"

"About what happened in the kitchen. That's twice today I've put you into the uncomfortable situation of makin' you party to my personal problems." Twice today she'd apologized for her behavior.

Reid lifted his shoulders as if to say these things happen. Which rankled her because they clearly *didn't* happen, not to him. She wished she had his ability to take a step back and put life into perspective. Then she wondered what it would take to shake that equilibrium of his, as hers had been shaken how many times today? It continued to confound her. She simply was not given to the mood swings of an adolescent going through puberty.

Unless, it occurred to her, they were caused by an opposite life change.

The rocker ground to a halt as a cold, hard weight of certitude dropped on Glenna's shoulders, the very realization she'd been trying with all her might to shun for weeks now.

No! she wanted to scream in denial as she had earlier today. *It isn't fair!* The signs were all there, though: the missed periods, the irritability, the hot, tingly flashes that left her either exhausted or restless beyond measure.

Hettie whimpered, and Glenna glanced down to find that she clutched the child to her practically in a death grip. She relaxed her hold, distractedly shushing and clucking reassurance. She didn't need eyeballs in the crown of her head to know that Reid watched her.

Only by concentrating on tucking the child's cotton shirt back into the sides of her homemade romper was Glenna able to suggest matter-of-factly, "I wouldn't hold it against you, Reid, if you decided to leave right now, because I can't guarantee it won't continue to be a bumpy evening, especially after my little flare-up in the kitchen."

She waited, the rocker creaking off the seconds. Then she heard Reid stand in a popping of knee joints, heard the muffled footfall of his boots on the rug. Head still bowed, Glenna hummed a lullaby to Hettie, or tried to, as she had to stop three times to clear her throat. Finally she gave up, and gleaned what peace she could from the suspension of time afforded by this moment with her granddaughter.

"So, is this Jamey's daddy next to her?" Reid's voice came from out of the blue, bringing Glenna's chin up.

He stood in front of the bookcase against the far wall, perusing the framed photographs that sat on the shelves.

"You mean the one with her on horseback?" she answered readily, wondering at his interest but glad for the change of subject. Glad he was still here, for whatever reason. "Yes, that's my favorite of them both. You can see the house and ranch buildings in the background."

"Looks like you had a nice place there," Reid commented.

"Yes, the operation was fine for us. Never would have made anyone rich, but you could make a living."

"Well, and what more could you want?"

Indeed. She and James *had* had a good life together, and for that she would be eternally thankful. But now it was over, and it would serve no good to dwell on it, as Reid had told her today. She must plan her future. She'd done it before, with James. This time, though, she'd do so alone.

"You're right again, Reid." She rocked slowly, thinking. "I saw a couple of interesting ads in the *News-Herald* today," she mused aloud. "One was for an investment opportunity. Maybe that's the way for me to go. The money I got from the insurance settlement isn't a fortune, but it might be enough. I could buy into a business with a couple of other people and help run it. I *could* have a whole new career."

Did her enthusiasm sound as weak to his ears as it did to hers? she wondered. Well, she'd just make herself get excited about the options open to her. What else was she to do?

As if in answer to her mental question, Reid spoke up. "I've got an idea, Glenna." He continued considering the photos. "I've been thinkin' I could use some help with my operation."

"Really?" she asked in surprise. She was *sure* he had wanted not to get involved.

"With my business back in full swing, I'm up to my neck in paperwork that just keeps pilin' higher on my desk. And I need someone to hold down the fort when I'm off to shows.''

"You mean someone who knows a bit about how a ranch is run or kept the books for one? Oh, and has some judgment about horses," she commented perversely, recalling her conveniently cataloging those precise skills earlier today.

He turned and regarded her. "That's right. Problem is I can't pay much, but I could at least provide room if not board.''

She lifted her eyebrows. "You could?''

"Sure. There's this vacant cottage on my property that I put up for Miranda's mother to live in when she came to visit. Gave her some privacy." Pausing, he eyed the level of his beer through the brown glass before taking a quick swig. "It's kind of small but nice, in a pretty spot with a couple of cottonwoods around it and a little creek running by.''

"It...it does sound nice," Glenna admitted, drawn in despite herself. She shifted Hettie to her shoulder, patting the baby's back. "Very nice, in fact.''

"We-ell." He dropped his chin, rubbed it, then looked at her from the tops of his hazel eyes. "To tell the truth, the place hasn't been occupied for five years, and it could use some insulation and a good fumigation." She felt a smile tug at her lips as he went on, "The creek's just a straggle of water and the cottonwoods have got a family of crows roostin' in them that make the most ungodly racket in the morning. And when I say small, I mean the mice get knots on their little foreheads from forgettin' to duck when they come through the door. But other than that, it's a little patch of heaven.''

She actually laughed before bending her head so he wouldn't see how very touched she was by his continued thoughtfulness on her behalf. However, she didn't care for the feeling that he saw her as being so needy, or that he was extending help against his better judgment. Or that if she took his help, it would be for all the wrong reasons.

"Thank you for thinkin' of me, Reid," she forced herself to say, "but it just seems too much. You'd have to fool with gettin' the cottage livable, for one."

Holding up one hand, palm upward, he shrugged. "That'd be the point. See, right now all I've got for spare accommodations is the room off the stall barn, where I put up that young gal who mucked out the stalls and tended the horses in exchange for me helping her train her cutting horse earlier this year. But it's pretty crude living quarters. And I've been thinking I could make the arrangement permanent, take on another loper—a kid to do the stable work in exchange for learning the ropes—and save the cost of a stable hand. Havin' someone come live in that cottage would give me the push to make it habitable again, so that when you were through with it, it'd be all ready for a loper."

"When I was through with it?"

"Sure. It seemed to me today that you really weren't needin' something permanent, maybe just a place where you could get back your bearings, so to speak."

He sounded so logical. And oh, she was so tempted to take him up on his offer, to avoid facing the one circumstance, brought so starkly into focus here on Plum Creek, that she feared she'd never come to terms with.

Hettie gave a resounding burp, allowing Glenna a moment for her own faculties of logic to reassert themselves as she settled the baby and gave her the bottle again.

After a few moments she asked, "What about Clan, Reid? I know he rodeos, but he's the one who should be involved in running Piney Rise with you."

"Well, now, that's kind of one of those situations you have with Jamey."

"How do you mean?"

Turning, Reid squinted against the setting sun blazing through the window. "See, Clan put off his bull-riding career to carry the brunt of trainin' and showin' the horses I managed to keep in the show string so I could stay home with Miranda. So now I reckon he's earned the right to come and go as he pleases, and it wouldn't be fair to continue puttin' the burden of my needs on him," he finished in an odd tone, as if defensive, although whether for himself or Clan, Glenna couldn't tell.

But she understood; it *was* a situation similar to hers. A parent's responsibility was to raise children able to function independently in the world. Implicit in that mandate was one's own self-sufficiency that gave a son or daughter leave to pursue their dreams without the burden, as Reid had said, of their parents' needs. Normally, though, Reid and Glenna would have had their spouses to meet those needs.

On that thought, her gaze floated downward to rest in a study of the precious infant in her lap. "You said I should learn to accept my life as it's become, and if I moved to Piney Rise, I'd be running away from it, wouldn't I?"

"Maybe you would be." His voice was speculative, as if he were searching for an answer he himself had posed. "All I know is, you told me today you felt selfish, Glenna, and that you wanted... a place you belonged. And I couldn't stop thinking, there's no reason under God why this woman should feel badly for wanting that. Wanting something for herself for a change."

Her chin came up, and his eyes captured hers as the spectrum of nature's colors—earth and grass and rain and sky—radiated from them. "At the very least," Reid went on quietly, "you'd have someplace to run to. And it wouldn't be so very far from where you started."

Oh! the longing that sliced through her at his words, that she might again be able to reach out to another as they both went through this trial by fire called life.

That wasn't what Reid was offering, though. Still, Glenna was reminded of how he'd looked as he regarded his new truck. The expression had gone directly to her heart, for she'd seen in his countenance her own turmoil: the regret for moments that could never be reclaimed, possibilities that now lacked a vital element that might have allowed them to be realized.

But they never would be! And she *must* get over it.

Glenna closed her eyes, a bid for strength. "I—I appreciate your offer, Reid, but—" But no, she must make her way, find her peace, by herself. It was how she was going to have to do everything—everything that mattered—for the rest of her life. She might as well get started now.

"I can't," she said simply.

Not waiting for his reply, she opened her eyes to judge the length of the shadows thrown across the floor. "Well. The ranch hands'll be in soon lookin' for their supper. Will you tell Jamey I'll be along in a minute to help her dish up?"

There was his characteristic pause, then he said, "Sure."

So he wasn't going to protest, to try to talk her into it. But then, hadn't he gone far enough just to extend the offer?

With that loose-in-the-hip cowboy gait, he headed for the kitchen. He stopped at the doorway, however, saying, "Oh, Glenna," as if just remembering something.

"Yes?"

"Not that it's my business, but I thought your hair looked natural before you got those highlights or whatever put in."

As it had been when he'd commented on her looks earlier today, his tone was "just fact." And this time she'd take his observation for what it was, without blushing or stammering like a schoolgirl.

"Which is to say I looked my age, forty-two, and like who I am—a grandmother," she said bluntly, which caused a flash of exasperation to leap to his eyes. They darkened with emotion, suddenly making him look a good twenty years younger.

"I'm not talking about the gray, if that's what you mean. I only thought that before you looked—" He gave her one of his perusals, and damn if it didn't set her heart bouncing around in her chest like a BB in a boxcar. "Like *you,* that's all."

With that, he departed, leaving her puzzled. And restless again.

"Well, and what more could I have wanted, right?" She parroted his words with irony to the thoroughly satiated Hettie, who burbled nonsense syllables back.

Half rising from the rocker, Glenna set the baby on her feet just out of range of herself. Hettie swayed unsteadily, arms out for balance and fingers spread wide, as a bird would stretch its wings to gather more air beneath them, before venturing a toddling step forward. Upon reaching Glenna, whose index fingers she grasped in a vise grip, she looked up into her grandmother's eyes and gurgled her delight.

What more could she have wanted? Oh, Glenna knew, with a yearning that scared the wits out of her.

Chapter Four

Reid stayed through supper and birthday cake, begging off from joining Glenna and the Hamiltons for a chat in the living room with the excuse that he had some calls to make before it got too late. In reality, he'd wanted to escape the tension that continued to suffuse the atmosphere, despite everyone putting up a good front, until he himself was feeling a little worked up. Although he suspected that had to do with the conversation he'd had with Glenna—and the resulting tension between them.

She'd warned him, hadn't she?

Despite his claim, Reid didn't head home but pulled off the gravel road leading from Plum Creek onto a rutted cow path, executed a three-corner turn so he faced the way he had come, and turned off his headlights. Clicking the ignition key to the accessories, he listened to vintage Patsy Cline on a slick compact disc—the irony of which privately amused him—while he watched the sky being swept of the last vestiges of daylight.

And wondered what it was about Glenna Dunn that brought out the longing in him in so many ways.

For instance, what had made him want to help her when it was obvious she didn't want him to? Or at least, didn't want what he had to offer. Well, so be it, he told himself as he had earlier. He'd made the effort to be a Good Samaritan twice today, and could count his conscience clear tonight. Or had he been thinking more of his own situation than Glenna's when he'd offered her refuge? As if getting her to see things his way would validate the course he'd chosen to take with his own life—one of acceptance.

Switching off the dome light so he'd remain in the dark, Reid opened the driver's door and set his foot on the running board as he slouched down in the seat, causing the headrest to push his hat up in the back and down in the front, near to covering his eyes. Yes, she'd still been struggling this evening with the same volatile feelings that had made her light a shuck and head for the road today. Yet what of the picture of serenity she'd made with her granddaughter? Whatever Glenna had done to her hair today had made it a little bit darker, the colors in it more complex, and her skin had seemed paler and finer in contrast. Sitting there with Hettie in her lap, she'd looked...young, with the untried faith of youth that made one hold out longer for what one wanted. Longer than, say, someone older and hopefully wiser as a result of living—whether a winner or loser in the game.

Yet, with frustration, he'd seen again this evening that Glenna did hope for or want or need more from life. And still hadn't seen the way in him. Which again had caused that dog of a rodeo cowboy to surge up in him, making him want to do whatever it took to prove he *could* have an effect on her, move her in the one way he knew he could. Not especially proud of that reaction, still he'd managed not to act upon it.

Searching for a logical explanation, Reid supposed he got that impression of expectation and hope in looking at Glenna mainly because it had been a long time since he had observed a woman with a baby. He remembered the first time he'd seen Miranda so, lying in her hospital bed with their newborn son in her arms. But she'd looked not happy so much as almost guilty, in the way someone might who believed they'd undeservedly gotten what they so wished for—which struck him as strange, especially now. Miranda had deserved that happiness of brand-new motherhood, deserved so much more that had never come to pass. He sometimes forgot his part in bringing her that special joy, eclipsed as it was by what he had never been able to give her.

Maybe that was why he was out here tonight, waiting.

Reid sat up straight at the sight of headlights speeding from the direction of Plum Creek Ranch, passing the junction of the cattle trail where he was parked, and heading on out into the country. He gave her a few minutes before starting his pickup and following in Glenna's wake.

Even if he'd suspected she might make another pilgrimage to the Panhandle's particular version of the Wailing Wall, he truly had hoped it might have been averted with his offer of a job and place to live, as today he believed he'd helped her with their talk during the ride to town. Of course, he thought cynically, such measures had merely distracted her from, not cured her of, her ills. So he should leave her to herself, as she wished, and let her get it out of her system, as she chose.

But he continued following her at a distance, noting the flare of taillights as she braked. They blinked out a few seconds later.

Reid coasted to a stop behind Glenna's truck. His boot heels resounded like the strike of a pickax in the deafening silence as he walked to the cab and peered inside. It was empty. He experienced a moment of alarm before he turned and spied Glenna standing a little way off the road, arms wrapped around her middle. She was watching him, calm as you please.

"Evening, Glenna," he said.

"Reid," she said without inflection.

He was glad she didn't ask what he was doing there, because he wasn't sure himself, especially now that he could see she was apparently of a steady mind. He had the sneaking suspicion Kell had been right: he *was* a glutton for punishment.

As he walked closer, she ceased hugging herself and held her hands clasped in front of her, proper-like. He stopped a few feet away from her, stuffing his fingers into his jeans pockets.

"Pretty night for a drive," he remarked.

"Yes."

"I was just enjoyin' it myself."

"Mmm."

She was obviously just fine, and he felt foolish for following her. He kind of wished he'd found her crying and hollering, as he had this afternoon. Maybe then he'd have had a chance of distracting her again. Of helping her, if only for a little while.

Which gave him an idea. Pulling in a deep breath, Reid tipped his head back to look up. "I don't know why, but things this big amaze me," he said after a moment.

Her gaze followed his. "What?"

"The sky. Especially here in the Panhandle, where you've got an unobstructed view from rim to rim. But you can't take it in all at once, just in pieces, since you're only able to look in one direction at a time. I always get this feeling somethin's goin' on in back of me I'd really like to see, like a fallin' star. And you come across one of those so rarely, it's a hard thing to think you're missin' it just because you aren't turned the right way when it happens.''

A coyote yip-yip-yipped in the distance, which started others up in a fracas of noise that went on for several minutes before dying out completely. He continued staring at the great unfathomable dome above him, but he sensed Glenna had turned her attention to him when she asked softly, ''So what do you do?''

He remembered, as they'd driven to Borger, how he hadn't felt he had much to say. Neither did he now, especially talking in parables as he was, but he didn't know what else to offer Glenna. And he got angry with himself all over again—for being here, for wanting to offer her something. For wanting her to want something of him.

''What do you do? Well, you just pick a direction and keep lookin' in it, and you hope that you'll get lucky,'' he answered curtly. ''Or you take the safe way out and focus your energies on the moon. It isn't as excitin' as catchin' a star streaking across the heavens, but you can hang your hat on its reliability, and there's a certain comfort in that, if you know what I mean.''

''I think you mean . . . that I shouldn't wish on stars— wish for a time in my life that can never be again. Don't you?''

Dropping his chin, he concentrated on loosening the roots on a dried-out clump of grass with a boot toe. ''Yes, I do, Glenna,'' he answered, even as he wondered what sort of man James Dunn had been that he could leave such an obviously unfillable hole in this woman's heart.

''Of course,'' she said calmly. ''You told me so today. And I do think you're right, even if it seems like it'll still take me a while to accept the fact.'' She paused, and when he turned to look at her, he found her staring up at him. He saw she wasn't calm at all but fighting to maintain control over herself, so precious to her. So precious to them both. "Now I hope you'll excuse me for bein' blunt, Reid, but I'd like you to leave."

He knew why—she was heading for a big ol' cry, and she didn't want him around.

"Say no more," he told her with a short nod.

Yet as he turned, he saw on her face that terrible fear of being forsaken. She whirled away from him, taking stumbling steps deeper into the night, and he knew she wanted anything rather than to have him see her this way again.

But there was nothing on earth that could have made Reid deny this woman whatever comfort he could give her right then.

Reaching out, he clamped his fingers on one elbow and spun her back around and into his arms. She stiffened, shaking her head violently.

"Reid...no," she cried. "You don't understand!"

"Don't I?" he asked vehemently, one hand under her chin to make her look him in the eye and say it again. *"Don't I?"*

"It's just as you said. It isn't right for me to...to want—" Suddenly, confusion filled her eyes, and she seemed to crumple inward, her face first, then her small shoulders, as she bent over, fists pressed against her abdomen, as if she sought futilely to alleviate a sudden pain there. *"But it's not fair!"*

The fierceness went right out of him as Reid brought her against him once more. Because he did understand. "Hell, no, it's not fair," he murmured into her hair. "Not to you, or me, or to the two that went before us, for that matter."

"That's not...what I meant...exactly...."

Still she struggled; still he held her captive, uncertain who or what either of them was fighting. Then she cleaved to him, arms wrapping around his ribs. She didn't cry, though, just clung to him like a vine, as if she could not get too close, trying, he guessed, to strengthen her connection with the here and now, such as it was, before coming to terms with the way it would be. Yes, he understood what it was like to accept the loss of a future one had always expected to live out. And Reid willingly let her use him for whatever comfort she could, stealing his own peace from helping her face that loss, as he had never felt he'd been able to do for Miranda.

But as the minutes passed, the feelings of comfort changed, and Reid knew it would have taken a better man than him to ignore how soft Glenna's breasts felt against his chest, how her slender frame seemed dwarfed within the circle of his embrace. How her abdomen pressed into his fly.

He closed his eyes and gritted his teeth.

Damn him for the cowboy he still was! Hadn't he sensed this might happen? He truly wanted to give her the emotional support she needed, but just holding her, he was hotter than a two-dollar pistol! What *was* it about her? It wasn't as if he hadn't been with a woman since Miranda died; one of the side benefits of returning to the show circuit was that he never lacked for offers to save on the cost of a hotel room. The circuit had always been a Peyton Place he'd managed to avoid, but recently he'd seen no reason not to avail himself of some enjoyment here and there. Those liaisons, however, had all been aboveboard, understood by both parties for what they meant: a little mutual gratification, and that was all. He didn't think it was that way with Glenna. It would mean more to her, because he knew she wanted more.

Reid relocated his hands to her waist, a covert means of easing the pressure on his groin. She raised her head, and he saw she knew the effect her closeness was having on him. Yet she didn't even begin to try to pull away from him. She just looked at him, that despairing need in her eyes as deep and painful as a jagged wound. It scared the life out of him, because he didn't know if he could fill that need, even for a while.

He shouldn't even try. He knew, better than anyone, how impossible it was. Impossible as roping the moon...

Yet suddenly the moment for decision was gone and he kissed her, her lips trembling and soft under his. She shuddered, making a sound of protest, and he pulled back a millimeter, fighting for sanity, disappointed to his very soul. She didn't want him. But then...dear God...she opened her mouth under his. And, heaven save his sorry soul, Reid couldn't stop himself from trying to help her forget her disappointments, however he could, if only for a while. Maybe forget his own, too.

So he glided his tongue over the ridge of her bottom teeth and met the velvet softness of her own come to find him. He shifted her, one hand spreading between her shoulder blades, the other grasping her waist in an effort to keep himself from smoothing it upward along her rib cage. Yet she surged against him, wresting another groan from his chest. She was so desperate. So passionate, with all those emotions she held inside set loose—and centered on him. And, God, she felt so damned good as her soft body melded to his hard one, which was getting harder by the second.

He felt her fumbling with something and realized she was undoing the buttons on his shirt. Her fingers were cold as they found his skin, and he sucked in a lungful of air even though her touch was heaven.

Too soon! Too much for him to comprehend. To control.

"Glenna," he rasped, lifting his head. If he could just catch his breath, let her catch hers. Glenna gave a small choked cry. He swallowed painfully, feeling for all the world as if he was letting her down.

Looking at her as he still held her in his arms, he was struck again by her achingly youthful radiance that seemed at this moment even greater, if possible, than before. The sight of that glow was a powerful thing. It tugged him toward her as surely as the moon drew the tide to shore. And that was why he said what he did next, almost angrily.

"I don't know why you want to change yourself, Glenna Dunn," he uttered harshly. "'Cause you don't look like no middle-aged lady to me. And you sure don't look like anybody's grandma."

At his words, those great gray eyes of hers turned luminous with the tears she'd been holding back. And Reid realized he *could* give her what she needed at this moment in her life when she searched for definition: a man to show her that, even with all the other changes—the losses she struggled to deal with that aged the spirit more than the body—in this way at least she could feel young and newly hopeful.

God, he *knew*. And understanding as he did, he was as incapable of denying her need as he was his own.

Removing his arms from around her, he lifted shaking hands to the buttons on the front of her blouse, undid them one by one, and spread the material. Her everyday shirts were loose enough that they hid her shape, but somehow he'd known she'd be full breasted, even for her slightness of build. His desire grew apace as his knuckles brushed against the lace trimming between her breasts. One-handedly, Reid slid apart the front clasp of her bra and pushed the cups aside, exposing her to him.

"God, Glenna," he breathed. "You are so damned beautiful."

The sound she made was inarticulate, the message again clear.

He reached out to run a fingertip across the upper slope of her breast before encircling the soft mound, testing its weight in his palm. Her skin was so pale, the moonlight contouring the peaks and valleys of her body; she *was* the moon, with all its mysteries. His hand seemed a shadow passing over her, standing out in stark silhouette as he touched her. Then, watching her face, waiting a moment longer to see if she might have changed her mind, he slid his thumb across her peaked nipple.

Her reaction was electric, as he'd thought it would be. Had hoped it would be. Glenna gasped, and with one arm he pulled her to him, his lips open and hot on hers, so that when the outrush of her breath came, it was into his mouth.

The next several minutes were a blur in Reid's mind as he swept her up and carried her to his pickup. He fumbled for the handle, wrenched one of the rear doors open and laid her back on the bench seat in the cab extension. Clothing was loosened or discarded, and with the sureness of two people with years of experience in giving and receiving sexual pleasure, they stimulated each other with hands and lips and tongues to a fever pitch of arousal. Caresses started out soft and exploring and ended up raking and urgent. Finally he lowered himself on top of her. And into her.

They gasped as one, Glenna making an involuntary sound of satisfaction, and Reid experienced a fleeting moment of believing he could fill the need in her.

And again, he stole his own peace from that knowledge.

Then all thought, all sense of experience or pacing ended as their purpose melded into one. Glenna arched her back, her hands clutching his shoulders to wordlessly urge him on. He aimed to please her, reaching back to tug one thigh higher on his hip and giving him the ability to thrust more deeply into her, again and again, until she cried out, the sound splitting the night.

It was as if he held all the stars in the heavens in his very hands. Then, suddenly, millions of them shot across the path of his vision, a bright white blinding brilliance.

It took a full five minutes for Reid to catch his breath and for the singing in his head to wind down. Only then was he able to press upward from his elbows, easing most of his weight off Glenna. He found he didn't have much leverage, what with his booted toes hanging off the end of the seat. He realized then that the night air was raising goose bumps on his naked rear end.

His head cleared with absoluteness.

Damn him. What was he *doing,* ravishing this woman on the side of the road like some randy rodeo buck! Even if he hadn't known how he could have resisted her silent plea, he should have at least shown her the consideration—shown the control—of driving her home to a respectable bed. But no, he'd taken her on the seat of a pickup truck like a hormone-ridden teenager with no place else to go to get relief. Well, the next time would be different, he made the promise to himself—and to her.

"Glenna, I'm sorry," he said tenderly, raising his head to look at her. Her face was calm, serene, and he thought for a second of how she did remind him of the moon, complete and whole, in and of itself. And for one instant he believed he'd brought her some sense of the completeness she so yearned after.

Then she said, with incongruous sadness, "No, Reid, I'm sorry. I take full responsibility for what just happened."

He stared at her. "What?"

"I had wanted to avoid taking advantage of you, yet now I have. And I am truly, truly sorry for that."

His gut twisted. So what had he expected? Pledges of undying gratitude? Declarations of devotion?

No, but he sure as hell hadn't expected an *apology*.

With a grunt of effort—or self-disgust—he pushed up and found his footing on the ground. He helped her sit up, though he turned his back to let her dress in privacy. He zipped his fly, buckled his belt and buttoned his shirt, stuffing its tails into his jeans, all with the efficiency of a cowboy used to taking his love on the run. So what else was new? It angered him that somehow he managed to take two steps back for every step forward, as if missing some deeper understanding about himself, and about life, that would forever be beyond him.

"I think," Glenna said quietly from behind him, "that it would be best if we put what happened tonight behind us as quickly as possible."

He turned. "Is that right?"

"Yes." Her gaze faltered at the probing of his. "Obviously it was just something we both felt we had to get out of our systems. Rest assured I won't make anything more out of it."

"Me, neither," he said tersely, trying to push down the hurt, wondering if *he* was the one who'd expected more, for once. "But as long as we're makin' apologies, I want you to know I consider it inexcusable that I lost my head tonight, especially when I had no protection on hand. Not that I think you've been with anyone, and I've always been careful, but—"

"Don't worry on that front," Glenna broke in, almost desperately.

Which puzzled him, until it occurred to him what she might mean. He recalled that she and her husband had had only Jamey, and it didn't seem they had planned it that way, just as he and Miranda had only had Clan—which definitely had not been planned.

He hadn't been thinking along those lines, but she was right: there wasn't much of a chance their momentary lapse of reason would have any lasting effects.

Except one. For Reid now knew with certainty he couldn't satisfy the real need in Glenna Dunn.

Chapter Five

Glenna's stomach was queasy. At first she thought it might be so in sympathy for Jamey, who was in the throes of morning sickness—or, rather, late-afternoon sickness. But now, as Glenna drove the pickup with fifteen feet of stock trailer attached beneath the gallus gate to Reid Shelton's ranch, she knew the real cause of her squeamishness. All week the briefest passing thought of her encounter with Reid had turned her tummy over. At the prospect of her seeing him again, it was doing double time, as if trying to keep up with her hammering heart.

But someone had been needed to pick up Kell's horse at Reid's. Gringo had thrown a shoe that morning as Kell helped unload a bunch of steers. Kell had gotten a lift back to Plum Creek, needing to get back to work, and ridden out on a spare.

She came to a stop beside a round corral, fenced in white pipe, as were the other penned areas at Piney Rise.

It gave the place a look and definite air of tidiness and attention to detail that the typical cow-calf operation couldn't quite measure up to. But of course, Reid was in the horse-training business, and his clients needed to feel their tens of thousands of dollars' worth of animals were well cared for, their several thousands more in training and feed well spent.

Piney Rise—1979 read the painted block letters above the stall barn breezeway. She had always meant to ask Reid what possessed him to name his spread thus, on this bald prairie as flat as glass, with the nearest pine tree hundreds of miles away. She'd thought it rather telling of the kind of man he was: a bit of a maverick, not one to fit into any role easily without carving out a few corners to accommodate his particular edges. She knew now he wasn't one to buck the system, and even seemed to think less of some who might try.

Yet for a man who hadn't wanted to get involved with that particular struggle of hers, she'd sure brought him center stage. She still couldn't believe she'd done what she had, made it practically impossible for any man with an ounce of humanity in him—or any kind of a libido—to refuse her in her neediness. However, for one who seemed so in control, Reid had certainly gotten out of control, traded dispassion for passion with amazing swiftness. And extraordinary adeptness. The memory of him giving himself up to her every desire sent heat to her cheeks and another wave of weakness through her belly.

Turning off the engine, Glenna sat for a few moments, getting up her nerve, simultaneously chiding herself for having to. *You're a mature woman, a forty-two-year-old grandmother,* she told herself. Even if the last time she'd seen him she hadn't felt like one. Even if he'd told her virtually the same, and it had been those words that had sent her over the edge.

With a surge of determination Glenna opened the truck door and strode across the yard to the house, a redbrick ranch-style that sprawled out in several directions. Once there, she knocked briskly on the back door, and waited. When there was no answer, she knocked again.

Vaguely disappointed, she'd turned to go when the door opened behind her.

"Glenna!"

She swung back around to find Reid gazing down at her with an expression of surprise—and was it actually pleasure?—on his face that sent her into a paroxysm of pure lust. Oh, but he was some handsome cowboy, with that dark hair and those hazel eyes with their endless facets.

Then one of those damnable hot flashes shimmered over her, bringing her to her senses.

"Sorry to bother you. I've come to pick up Gringo," she explained tersely. "Jamey's not feeling well, and Kell's busy. If you're occupied, I could get your stable hand to help me."

"Bobby Ray's off today." Reid chucked a thumb over his shoulder. "I'm on the phone at the moment, but I'll help you get Gringo squared away when I'm done." He paused in that way of his, as if reluctant to get any more involved. "You're welcome to come in out of the heat while I finish my call."

"Heat doesn't bother me much," she said, wondering if this was how they would be with each other from now on. Curt, polite, defensive. She'd never claim to be an expert on postcoital etiquette in the nineties—or any other decade, for that matter. But it just didn't seem possible she and Reid could be so detached, after sharing their bodies completely.

Well, how had she expected he would act, especially since she'd assured him she wouldn't make anything more out of their moment of madness? What was she still looking for, hoping for?

"Actually, I could probably load him by myself," she said, wishing to escape this place, Reid, and the feelings he roused in her. "I've handled a few cow ponies in my day."

"He looks like he might be starting a quarter crack on the hoof he threw the shoe off of. He's not going to want to walk up that ramp without some persuading."

He had a valid point, yet that didn't temper her irritation when he turned and headed toward the back of the house, as if her waiting for his assistance was decided. She refused to follow, but after a while it became apparent he was taking his sweet time—and it *was* scorching outside, making her stomach squeamish again—so Glenna decided to take his suggestion to step inside where it was cool and hurry him up, as well.

Following the sound of his voice, she found herself in what obviously was Reid's office, with its large partners' desk and file cabinets. She couldn't resist venturing a glimpse around when he nodded and made winding-down noises in his conversation.

The room was cluttered and dusty, the direct opposite of the impression projected by the rest of Reid's operation. The horsehair-covered chair in the corner was piled high with *Cutting Horse Chatter* and *Horse & Rider* magazines. An antique saddle had appropriated the worn brown leather sofa against the wood-paneled wall. On it were built-in shelves holding an assortment of horse-training books and various other items that looked to be nothing but more clutter: a rusty horseshoe, a broken bridle and snaffle bit—well, she'd allow him those—three spurs, none of which matched, leg wraps, and last year's calendar advertising a feed supplement. No less than four coffee mugs, each filled to a different level, sat atop the layer of papers strewn across the entire surface of the desk. Not that it was any of her affair, but she wondered how Reid found anything in such a mess.

Which he was trying to do at that very moment, indicating this was business as usual for him as he sifted through several stacks and talked on the phone at the same time.

"Actually, Bill," he said, "I was thinkin' we'd haul your gelding on over to the Summer Series next month in Kansas rather than the Decatur show. That'll mean the first week in August, if I've got my dates right. Why don't I call you back once I've got my schedule firmed up.... Fine, then. No, I thought you were paid up through the end of the quarter. Hold on, I'll check."

He pulled a piece of paper out from underneath a stack of pamphlets and peered at it before discarding it on top of the heap this time, saying into the receiver, "I tell you what, Bill, I'll look it up later and send a statement of everything I've still got on the books.... Great. Talk to you soon."

He hung up, and Glenna directed her attention elsewhere rather than have him think she'd been watching him—and wondering if his offer of a job helping him with his operation *hadn't* been made out of charity. Yet what did it matter if it wasn't, especially now after she'd turned him down?

Her gaze lit on another set of shelves, covered with plaques and awards, belt buckles and ribbons. Closer inspection revealed they had come from cutting competitions.

"You've got quite a collection here," she observed.

"A lot of them are Clan's," Reid said, coming up behind her.

She wondered how he really felt, aside from still being able to use help with his operation, about his son going off to pursue a bull-riding career. Most people in horse training and showing tended to look down their noses at the rodeo crowd. In their opinion, such cowboys lacked finesse and insight, treating the animals they rode as opponents rather than partners. "A lot of them are yours, too."

"The older ones, sure. From before Miranda passed on."

Glenna turned to find him at her left shoulder, and she was reminded again of his expression as they'd talked of his new truck, what the purchase of it had represented to him, even beyond the coming of middle age.

"I do that, too," she said. "Refer to events in terms of before or after James died."

He reached past her to straighten a plaque. "I guess it'll be a while before either of us stops measurin' time by the passing of the person we spent half our lives with."

"I know. I keep thinking of how James and I would have been married twenty-five years next May."

"May what?"

"Sixteenth. Why do you ask?"

He looked at her strangely. "Miranda and I were married on May seventeenth, exactly two years earlier."

"So. We do have a lot in common." She'd never asked, but had calculated Clan's age to be about twenty-four, a few years older than Jamey. Glenna and James had waited over two years after their marriage for her arrival, as Reid and Miranda must have done for Clan's birth.

It was on the tip of Glenna's tongue to ask if, like she and her husband, Reid and his wife had hoped for more children, only to have that dream go unfulfilled. Except she was afraid such a discussion might lead her to reveal the real sign of middle age she was finding so hard to accept.

Glenna was distracted from her musing by the sight of Reid's own thoughts upon his face. And what she saw there was regret, in the way she was regretful, for the changed circumstances to his existence. Maybe it was that shared emotion, or being with him in the place where he most lived, or merely that appealing shock of hair falling over his forehead, making him look vulnerable, but suddenly a sense of real connection bloomed between them.

This was what she had been looking for today, Glenna realized. Or hoping for. Just some small indication that what had gone on between them hadn't been merely physical, which in turn might give her hope that perhaps that something could be built on, with a little effort.

So did she want to go on—with Reid? For she knew how greatly she wanted to reach out to him and say with an innocent gesture that he was not alone. But to make herself stop there and not brush back that hair and feel it sliding, cool and silky, through her fingers as they curved back over his head to bury in his nape; to have those earth-tones eyes lose their bleakness, grow warm and alive at her touch, as his had done for her...

Glenna pivoted away. No! It was wrong, for herself and for Reid. To try to find answers or solace through him. It was running away again, even if she took not a step in any direction.

"Well," Reid said after a moment. "Let's get Gringo loaded so you can be on your way."

Not daring to look at him, she gave him a nod.

He grabbed his hat as they headed for the stall barn with nary another word between them, back to acting like less than acquaintances. Perhaps it was for the best.

They had nearly reached the stable when down a slight incline Glenna spied a small white house nestled in a stand of cottonwoods. Her steps slowed as she pointed.

"Is that the cottage you told me about?" she said, already knowing it was.

His gaze followed hers. "Yes," he said shortly.

Stopping to get a better look, she saw that it was in pretty sorry shape, with peeling paint and crooked shutters. One side of the small porch listed. Yet the roof appeared whole, if missing a few shingles, and none of the windows, at least on the front of the cottage, were broken.

She was dying to look inside, but could think of no good reason for asking to do so. She'd had her chance at it.

"Well," she said, voice strained. "Let's go get Gringo."

She was barely aware of following him to a stall, where he haltered Gringo before leading him outside to the stock trailer. She snapped back to attention, though, when he loaded the buckskin, then turned him around so the horse faced the back.

"What're you doing?" she asked, surprised more than anything.

He paused in securing the cross ties. "Trailering Gringo."

"But you put him in backward."

Reid continued unperturbably tying the gelding in. "I've been trailering my horses this way for some time, and I've found over the long haul, so to speak, that it's less wear and tear on their legs as well as their nerves. I know it doesn't seem like it'd be so, but it is."

"I don't think Gringo's used to bein' hauled that way, though," she protested, even as she watched him settle into the stall as calmly as if he'd never been loaded any other way. "Or that stock was meant to be carried backwards in this trailer."

"Most trailers, I'd say you're right. But some stock trailers you can go either way. There're tie-downs on this end, so that's probably the case with this particular one. And Gringo doesn't seem to be shying." Reid rested his palm on the side of the horse's neck, just laid it there as he waited. Any nervousness the gelding might have exhibited melted away. "The proof'll be in the ride. Let me know if he thrashes any. But most horses find they have more balance this way, and they tend to be calmer."

He looked down at her as she stood on the ground next to the ramp, and apparently saw the doubt lingering on her face. He frowned but said, as impassive as ever, "Of course, it doesn't really matter—backwards or forwards—for as far as you're goin'. We can turn him back around, if that's what you'd be more comfortable with."

"Don't be silly." She was actually the one being silly, questioning Reid's judgment when it came to horses. She helped him bring up the ramp and latch the back. That done, he saw her into the pickup, even closing the door after she'd climbed in.

So she was leaving, with the two of them still treating each other like polite strangers. And *that* situation didn't seem any more right to her than their forced intimacy.

"Maybe we're like Gringo," Glenna said spontaneously, then amended, "Well, maybe *I* am, at least."

Reid's eyes widened in surprise. It *was* a strange statement, especially coming out of the blue as it had.

"I mean, maybe the reason it's been so difficult for me to contemplate the future is because of the direction I've been facing, straight ahead, thinkin' that's the way I had to do it. Except, what if I faced the other way? Maybe I'd find some of the answers I'm seekin', not in what's ahead of me but what's behind me."

She glanced up expectantly, and found Reid looking at her in that way of his, as if he wanted nothing more than to remain uninvolved, which was a sure way to get her dander up. Then he did answer, albeit stubbornly. "But you can't, Glenna. Like I said the other night, you've got to pick a course to follow and just hope it's the best one—"

"Without even tryin' a different way?" she interrupted with faint exasperation.

Her heart surged with hope when Reid's eyes burned hot at her contentiousness, so that he looked ready to come through that open window and . . . and do what? Shake some sense into them both? Or sweep them away again to that place where she might confirm what had happened between them had been for a reason. It just wasn't like her to act as she had. She'd bet cash money it hadn't been like him, either.

Was *that* what she'd wanted to confirm today?

Then he said calmly, "I guess we just have opposite ways of lookin' at things."

"I guess so," she said, disappointed in him when she knew she had no call to be. Maybe he was right and she was reaching for the impossible, but Glenna had to continue to try, with or without Reid's concurrence. That decided, she still couldn't help pondering what it would take to move this man, to spur him from his stoic acceptance. For she knew she'd seen the same need in him, as in herself, to be at peace. And she didn't think such peace attainable until a person understood the whole of their life—past, present and future—in a way that still eluded her and Reid, and perhaps forever would.

"Well." She reached for the ignition key and started the pickup. "Thanks for your help today, Reid. I'll be sure to show Kell how you loaded Gringo."

He nodded. "You might want to take the ride a little more gently this time, till he gets used to the change."

So. They were back to being polite strangers, perhaps now for good. Which settled one question in her mind— their indiscretion *had* been a one-time slip, because Glenna knew herself this much: she was not the kind of

woman to give herself time and again to a man with
whom she was not of one accord. Of one heart.

She expertly backed the pickup and trailer away from
the corral, turned around and headed out to the main
road without a backward glance.

Chapter Six

August hit the Panhandle like a hot anvil dropped from the sky. The heat was oppressive, depressive. Even the wind did nothing to alleviate the stifling pressure as it came out of the south in furnacelike blasts.

Not that Glenna wasn't used to hot weather. She'd been born and raised in Nevada, and dealt with extremes on both ends of the climate spectrum as a matter of course. But this heat wave made her feel wrung out and dog tired from sunup to sundown. Which at first didn't concern her greatly since it certainly kept her from dwelling too much on other matters—such as the fact that she'd been able to do little to either come to terms with or enact a change in her life. She felt too worn down even to sustain the head of defiance she'd worked up against Reid and his stolid acceptance of the way things were. But maybe, it occurred to her, that was because she'd finally come to a place in her thinking Reid had reached long ago.

So it wasn't until the morning she was out in the barn, one moment pitching straw into the stall she'd just cleaned, the next coming to from a dead faint in a pile of that straw, that Glenna got her first inkling something *had* changed. Perhaps her tiredness and the squeamishness she'd been so willing to attribute to nerves weren't born of some recent resignation to her circumstances.

Barely stopping by the house to change her clothes, wash up and tell Jamey that she was leaving, Glenna hopped into the pickup and took off for Borger. As she drove, she forced herself to put her mind on hold. Don't jump to conclusions, she told herself without alarm. There'd be time enough for thinking—and worrying— once her suspicions had been verified.

Luckily, her doctor could work in a moment to see her, after which she did spend a few fingernail-chewing minutes waiting for the results of her test. Even suspecting the outcome did not prepare her for his calling her into his office with the news that she was pregnant.

"But, Dr. Kirby—" Glenna tried to collect her thoughts enough to ask the million and one questions she knew she'd think of later. "I haven't had a period in months. And besides, I thought ... I thought I was going through the change."

"Certainly that was a possibility." Elbows propped on the armrests of his high-backed leather chair, he steepled his hands. "But remember I told you it could just as likely be the stress of losing your husband and the other upheavals to your life that was causing your amenorrhea."

"Of course I remember, but—" But she hadn't believed it. Or perhaps had until the telling signs of menopause had led her to that conclusion. "I figured there was some other reason I couldn't have children, besides being too old to. I mean, my husband and I tried for years after our daughter was born."

"It's normal for women to become less fertile as they draw closer to the end of their childbearing years, but the possibility of conception still very much exists. As for being too old to be pregnant, you're in a higher-risk age group, that's true, but you're in good health and with proper care I see no reason you shouldn't have a perfectly normal pregnancy."

Dr. Kirby turned away from her as he reached into his credenza, and she got the impression he was reluctant to look at her when he asked, "Am I correct in assuming you aren't married to the child's father and that this pregnancy will be as much of a surprise to him as it obviously is to you?"

There was no point beating around the bush. "Dr. Kirby, I'm not even in a relationship with this man. We only had...had sex once."

The doctor swung around. "Well," he said on a gush of air, "it seems you've beaten some very high odds, indeed."

He made no judgments, his eyes kind and understanding as he said, "You have certain options, as you are probably well aware. My advice is to talk to the child's father as soon as possible to discuss whether to go through with—"

"I would never...never have a..." Glenna couldn't even say what the doctor was inferring. "It's not an option, no matter what he wants."

Dr. Kirby nodded. "Fine. I'd like to see you as soon as possible for a complete physical and pelvic exam. I'll be able to tell you your due date then. In the meantime, here are a few pamphlets for you to read." He paused. "And my advice still is to let this man know of his obligations to you and the baby." He smiled reassuringly. "You're not in the same position as a young girl who has become pregnant, Glenna. You *do* have choices."

"I'll try to remember that," she answered as she rose on wooden legs to leave his office.

Once outside, she didn't know what else to do except head back home. But she stopped on the same ribbon of road she had before—the day Reid had found her crying. The evening he'd found her trying not to cry, but needing to do *something*.

She didn't cry now, however, just sat staring dully out the window at the bleak, sunburned landscape that surrounded her. Oh, she knew it surrounded her on all sides; she didn't need to turn in a full circle to comprehend how alone she was right now.

Alone—and pregnant. At forty-two, with her second grandchild on the way.

The sheer outrageousness of the situation devastated her.

Glenna dropped her forehead to the top of the steering wheel. Once! She'd had sex with Reid only once, and she'd gotten "caught." The doctor had been wrong; she was *exactly* like some naive teenager, with a woman's body and an adolescent's judgment.

Then it really hit her. *She was pregnant.*

With an inarticulate sound Glenna tore open the door of the pickup and threw back the lid of her son-in-law's toolbox that was sitting in the bed. She snatched up a wrench, and in one fluid motion, spun around and hurled it into the scrub. But it didn't help, even when she turned and caught up another tool, a hammer this time, and flung it out over the flat land. No, the childish action only raked up anger in its wake—at herself, mainly, for being so damnably reckless, but also at fate, for causing this to happen. *Why* had it happened? And why now, when she would have given anything for this to have occurred twenty, ten, even five years ago, with her lawful husband?

Scalding shame made beads of perspiration pop out on her forehead. Glenna wiped it away with shaking fingers as she slumped against the side of the truck, fading in the heat after her exertion. Yes, she was faded—and foolish, for doing what she'd so *not* wanted to do by staying on the merry-go-round to try for that brass ring. Her time had passed for such experiences, whether she accepted it or not. Yet now there could be no looking back to try to come to terms with what might have been, as she'd suggested to Reid.

Reid. She was angry with him, too, incredibly angry. By God, he should have been more responsible! But she should have been, too. Oh, so should she.

A thousand times in the past several weeks she had wished to have back that point in time when she gave in to impulse or instinct or whatever it was, and had sex with Reid. Yet a thousand times more she'd relived its every minute, every second, as if trying to spot the one element that had previously escaped her. *Something* that would ease her disappointment with herself since, given the chance to repeat that moment, she knew she'd act in the same wanton manner. And it hit her, fully, the extent to which she had taken advantage of Reid.

So came guilt to complete the gauntlet of emotions she'd run through today as Glenna realized she would never be able to hide from the fact that she had wanted to do anything rather than face the end of her reproductive years.

How could she tell him? she wondered. There was no question of whether she would; she wouldn't cover up the mistake with another. Her cowardice went only so far— as did her courage. What would he think of her? Would he...would he hate her for the complication she brought to the steady existence he'd fought so hard to regain?

Lord, she wanted to run, as far as she could! She couldn't, though, not this time.

What *would* she do? The thought of continuing to live at Plum Creek with Jamey and Kell practically made her stomach curdle. Now, more than ever, she did not feel part of their family, would always be an awkward addition to it, like a strange-looking upper story tacked onto an obviously one-level house.

She might have no other choice. Moving to some city and getting a job didn't seem feasible. Who would hire an unmarried pregnant woman only to have her take weeks, maybe months, off in less than a year? And during that time Glenna knew she'd be paying all her own living expenses, then afterward paying for infant day care once she was able to go back to work.

Suddenly the money she'd gotten from James's insurance settlement seemed to dwindle to nothing before her eyes.

She had thought herself alone before. She hadn't known the meaning of the word.

Too dazed to think of what should come next, Glenna made herself step off the road and into the brush to find Kell's tools, at the very least. She spied the wrench first, dropped to one knee to pick it up, found the effort needed to rise overwhelming, and sank down in the bristly grass, drained of emotion or motivation to do anything but remain in this spot forever. She needed to move, though, get out of the sun, return to the pickup. It was past noon, too, and she hadn't had lunch. Though the thought of food brought a surge of nausea to the back of her throat, she knew she should eat something. However much she might be avoiding contemplating the future, she needed to think of her baby.

Her baby. She tried to visualize it. A little redhead, as Jamey had been. No, she realized, this baby would probably be black haired, as Reid was. But she couldn't imagine the look of a child of this man, himself still so new to her.

Desperately she laid one palm on her still-flat belly. Warmth, the living kind, seeped reassuringly through the layers of cotton and denim. It was only her own body warmth she felt, she told herself, but then it wasn't, either. It—this baby—*wasn't* just a concept, a memory or a wish. It was real.

That's when the tears came, tears of relief, for Glenna was consoled, soul deeply, that this part of her life wasn't over—that she had not been, as she'd so feared, forsaken. And she was thankful for this chance, however it had come to her. Oh, she *cried,* because she realized what she'd been terrified of facing for months was not that her future lay down any number of unfamiliar roads she must decide which to pursue. No, what she'd feared was that the rest of her life had already been mapped out and stretched before her all too clearly across the years.

And that it was as barren as the Panhandle landscape.

But it wouldn't be, not now! she thought, fervently pressing her other palm over the one that lay against her abdomen. She wasn't alone, even if she still felt empty inside. For how was she to reconcile her conscience to having created a new life with a man she didn't love, and who didn't love her?

Glenna squeezed her eyes shut to hold back a fresh onslaught of tears. She wouldn't think about it now. It couldn't be helped; what happened had happened, and she had to put it behind her, pull herself together, and go on as best she could. Which, she realized ruefully, was really a variation on Reid's outlook. She only hoped he'd see this situation that way.

Yes, she'd wondered what it would take to jolt him out of his complacency. Glenna had a feeling she was about to find out.

Reid had been feeling cooped up, a sort of penned-in sensation that had only seemed to grow stronger over the past few weeks, which puzzled him. Not that he hadn't felt this way before, because he had, but he'd always been able to correlate the onslaught of such edginess with some event.

But life was going along much the same as it had always done, especially in the past few weeks. Yet still he was itchy as a rodeo cowboy with his eyes ever on that next ride down the road.

So this afternoon, right in the stinking hottest part of the day, he saddled a big bay gelding named Rogue and rode north, the only direction where lay some distractive scenery. Not much of it, he'd be the first to admit, but at least he had a destination, because he didn't like the impression he got that he was pulling a Glenna Dunn: not going anywhere in particular, just anywhere but here.

From a mile away Reid spotted the hackberry tree that marked the edge of the Canadian Breaks, which were just that—deep, wide breaks in the earth's crust cut out a millennium or so ago by the Canadian River. Looking out across the flat terrain, a person might not believe such a crevice existed. From a certain vantage, there appeared to be nothing but more acres of scrub and mesquite stretching as far as the eye could see. Yet one sensed the change rather than saw it, even if it was hard to miss the signs of the vegetation growing more abundant and less stunted, along with the slow but steady incline of the land.

Then in the next instant he was upon it, the ground shearing off in front of him, plunging nearly straight down two hundred feet to the sandy brush lining the untroubled riverbed where the Canadian, no more than a stream, meandered its way eastward. It was like a roller-coaster ride, both visually and audibly, that screaming, stomach-churning descent before the hushed leveling off at the bottom.

Pulling up under the hackberry, he dismounted and looped the reins over the saddle horn as Rogue started to forage in the meager scrub, Reid checking to make sure no locoweed or bitterweed grew underfoot. He stepped up to the brink of the precipice, boot toes practically hanging over the edge, and looked out across the Breaks, wondering, as always, at the gravity-defying lean of the junipers growing out of the nearly vertical face.

He had lived in the Panhandle more than a decade, and the novelty of the Breaks never ceased to enchant him. Never ceased to bring him a measure of calm and control.

He discovered such peace was to be short-lived, however, when he heard a noise behind him in the distance and turned to see a pickup bumping toward him. It ground to a halt thirty feet away. Out climbed Glenna Dunn.

And he realized then what he'd wanted to get away from today were thoughts of this woman. Yet that apparently wasn't to be, because here she was, as if conjured from those thoughts. He couldn't imagine why she'd come looking for him, for she obviously had. One didn't just go off-roading around here without a specific destination in mind.

He cursed himself for feeling something more than curiosity as she approached.

She wore her usual jeans and sleeveless cotton shirt that nevertheless made him go rigid as a fence post. Especially when she came walking toward him, her hips swaying with each step as she picked her way between the prickly pear and yucca.

She stopped in front of him, her face looking particularly pale under the flat brim of a light gray gaucho hat that suited her in both color and style. Those silvery eyes of hers reminded him of placid pools of water.

"Hello, Reid," she said with the same calm reminiscent of that disastrous evening he'd tried to ease her burdens by making love to her.

He removed his straw Stetson to swipe a shirtsleeve across his perspiring forehead, and dangled the hat from one hand as he reached up and hung his wrist on a low branch of the hackberry. "Afternoon, Glenna."

Her gaze slid past him and widened in mild surprise. "I didn't know you were so close to the Breaks." Her head swiveled slowly from side to side as she took in the broad expanse. "This sure is different from the Breaks near Borger," she commented. "Starker. Striking, in its own way."

"Well, it isn't much compared to the Palo Duro Canyon area over by Amarillo. But I'm kind of partial to this section of the Breaks, I guess 'cause they're practically in my backyard."

For lack of anything better to do, he squatted to scoop up a tiny hackberry, hard and red, and sidearmed it into the crevasse. He didn't know what impulse made him add, "Spring's really the prettiest out here, with the wildflowers blooming. Prairie zinnia and the purple dayflowers called—"

Reid cut himself off, realizing the more common name for the flower here in west Texas was widow's-tears. He thought again about how Glenna was not a native of the Panhandle, of how she had been pretty much plunked down in a place not of her choosing, to live out the rest of her life. To feel thusly trapped would bring out the rebelliousness in him, too.

"It certainly sounds pretty." Her smile came and went with the breeze. She shaded her eyes. "Is that a pine tree growing up on the very edge of that ridge?" she asked wonderingly.

"Yep." He didn't have to look to know what she referred to.

"So this is the pine of Piney Rise. Did you plant it?"

"Nope."

"No? How did it spring up here, of all places?"

Was there some reason for this conversation? he thought, even as he answered. "I figure there was a fire here sometime in the past, and it sprouted up after that, a seed brought by some bird. Purely accidental, as are most happenings in nature." He wondered at the way her skin got even paler at his remark.

Craning her neck forward, Glenna took a few tentative steps closer to the edge before backing up quickly. "Hoo," she said on a rush of air. "Doesn't it make you dizzy, bein' that close?"

He shrugged. "You get used to it."

Glenna said nothing in reply, and minutes went by. He wished she'd say what she'd come here to and end this suspense, because he didn't like the expectant feeling he was getting the longer she stayed. She must have something powerful on her mind to cause her to hunt him down.

But she remained staring silently out across the Breaks, only she'd taken to her old habit of wrapping her arms around her middle, as if she was trying to hold something inside. Or maybe holding everything else out. He wondered what would happen if he reached out one hand and wrapped it around her calf in a familiar caress, if it would unleash the passion in her as he'd seen his touch do before. Because he had brought her that release and relief; if no other, he *had* met the physical need in her.

At least the day she'd come for Gringo he'd resisted giving her false hope for getting much more from him. So what did she want today from him?

Damn him if he'd ask.

He didn't have to, for a second later Glenna blurted out, "I've had an idea, Reid." Then she pressed her lips together, again as if she barely contained some emotion inside her.

Curiosity got the better of him. "Which is?"

"I was thinking what if...what if I did move into your cottage, finished fixing it up for you, in exchange for the job as your bookkeeper or secretary or whatever you want to call it?"

You could have knocked him over with a feather. Slowly Reid rose and faced her.

"Why now, and not before?" he asked, not bothering to keep the suspicion from his voice.

"I had a chance to see your setup," she answered forthrightly enough, though he sensed that wasn't the whole story. "And it's just as you said. N-not that I thought you'd lied. I mean, you've got a definite need for someone to answer phones and open mail and organize the books, order supplies, maybe even keep your schedule. I could do that for you, so you could devote yourself to training and showing horses."

She looked up at him, gray eyes luminous. "You've worked so hard to get back to doing what you want with your life. I'd like to help you continue reachin' for that aim."

There was no doubting the sincerity in her voice, and a tiny sprig of hope sprang up in him. Could it be he hadn't damaged himself in her eyes, either by not understanding her needs, or by thinking he could satisfy those needs any more than temporarily by recklessly making love to her? For she obviously understood him, understood what he wanted and who he wanted to be: a horse trainer and not the cowboy whose impulses and inclinations he was afraid would always rule his judgment.

Was this understanding what he wanted from *her?*

"So, what's in it for you?" he asked, still skeptical.

"A place to belong, of a fashion."

"But I thought you said you'd feel like you were runnin' away if you left Plum Creek." He had to know. "Are you still? Or would you be runnin' to...somethin'?"

"Is it possible to do both?" she said, her own hope obvious.

His eyes roamed over her upturned features, and he astounded himself by asking, "Would it be worth it to try?"

Her gaze faltered under his seeking one. "Reid, I need to tell you somethin'. I should have done it right away, but..."

She took a deep breath, or tried to, as she pressed her hand against her stomach just as she had on the eve of her birthday, as if in pain. She went pale, alarmingly so, and said quickly, "Could I sit down for a moment?"

Without waiting for his permission—as if she needed it—Glenna bent at the knees, then buckled. Reid closed the space between them, catching her by the waist. She slumped against him, eyelashes fluttering, voice reed thin as she protested, "I'm all right. I just got a little woozy for a second."

"You're almost fainting, even now," Reid disagreed, his concern making him abrupt. In one easy motion he slung her into his arms and gently set her against the trunk of the tree, where there was the most shade. Quickly he sidestepped over to Rogue for his canteen, then back to kneel beside Glenna. For lack of a better option, he pulled from his hip pocket a fairly clean bandanna, doused it with water and smoothed it over Glenna's forehead and throat. Dissatisfied with such an incomplete effort, he removed his shirt, stuffing it under the back of her neck for a makeshift pillow as she rested her head back against the tree trunk. He offered her the canteen, from which she drank gratefully before struggling to sit forward.

"Reid, I—"

"Hush. Just lie back and rest."

Glenna quieted, eyes closed, her breath shallow but evening out. She looked so defenseless, so vulnerable, so alone. And she wanted so little, really—to belong somewhere, to find fulfillment in some purpose. It wasn't that much to expect of life, as he'd told her, and for one instant Reid let himself get caught up in the fantasy of being the keeper of those dreams.

It didn't take more than a few minutes for her to get a bit of her color back, especially when he fanned her with her hat, sending the damp tendrils around her face afloat in the cooling breeze. Slowly her lashes drifted open. Her gaze found him, slid down over his naked chest and back to his face as hers gained even more color. Then a look he barely had time to place crossed her gaze—as Miranda had looked holding Clan in her arms those many years ago—before Glenna's eyes filled with tears. She turned her head away from him as if in shame, pressing the back of her hand against her lips to stifle a sob.

Reid didn't understand what was wrong, but he couldn't help himself; he had to give her comfort. He slid a forearm behind her shoulders and nestled them in the crook of his elbow as he cradled her against his chest. "Shush, now," he murmured. "It's the heat that's got to you. I'm fairly wiltin' with it myself. Here, drink some more water and you'll feel better."

He held the canteen to her lips again. Half-choking on her tears, she managed to get a few swallows down before closing her eyes once more, resting her cheek against his biceps as the tears continued to slide from beneath her lids.

"I'm not the fainting type any more than I'm the cryin' type," she said tiredly. "But I—I guess I'm not as strong as I think I am." Her mouth quivered. "Or as young as I used to be."

Though her eyes remained closed, he saw in her expression that same look of desolation he'd seen before. And again he was reminded of his late wife, this time in the midst of that deadly cancer. It was the moment after all that could be done for her medically had been done, when she'd come to grips with the fact that what was to follow must be faced utterly alone.

The bottom dropped out of Reid's stomach, dropped out of his world. Was Glenna sick, too? *No! It isn't fair!* he thought. He realized the denial was *her* cry, made that night of her birthday. Had she known something then?

Reid resisted the urge to crush her soft body to him and never let go, never venture one second into the future where he might have confirmed what he feared in his heart.

This couldn't be happening, not again.

Was this why she'd come to him today? For help through some devastating ordeal that she was trying to face, having no one else to go to, no one else who could understand as he might? Fantastic as it might seem, was he being given the chance to rewrite part of his past, to come to terms with it, as Glenna had wondered whether he had the need to do?

For Glenna's sake, he hoped not. God, he hoped not.

But he had to know. "What—" He swallowed painfully, managed to go on with difficulty. "What's wrong, Glenna?"

She opened her eyes. "What's wrong, Reid?" she echoed weakly. "Or what's almost...strangely...right?"

She sounded so fatalistic. She couldn't give up hope!

"Just tell me!"

"Yes, I should just say it." She pushed herself out of the nest of his embrace. It took all of his strength to let her go, and his arms felt as if they'd never be filled again.

She sat with her forearms on her knees, her head bent. Reid again couldn't prevent himself from sending a hand out to smooth back her hair and tuck it behind one ear, then slipping a finger beneath her jaw to tug her chin up with infinite tenderness.

And Glenna looked at him, so many emotions mingling in her eyes—though he thought maybe a little less of the desolation he'd seen there before.

Then she said, "I'm pregnant," the same way she'd blurted her daughter's announcement, as if delivering tragic news.

Poleaxed, Reid dropped his hand and rocked back on his heels. Of all the truly tragic possibilities he'd expected, this wasn't one of them. And the thought that came to mind first was: this could not be happening to him, not again.

"Say somethin'," Glenna whispered.

Chapter Seven

Hell, what could he say?

"You're...you're sure?" Reid asked through lips that had gone, along with the rest of him, completely numb.

"Yes." The word was soft but definite.

Somehow he found his legs and stood, took a few steps in one direction, stopped automatically to pick up his hat, and took a few more steps, toward the edge of those wide, deep breaks.

Not sick—pregnant.

Reid sent a brief prayer of thanks sailing upward that Glenna was not suffering from something terminal—though why he might have been so devastated by that fear didn't bear examination at this time—before he wondered if *he* was suffering from something terminal. Like stupidity.

Damn him! Had he learned nothing in the past three decades? Apparently not; maybe he never would. He'd always perceived life proceeding along in a linear fashion, with events coming one after another, those once past forever gone. But now Reid got a sense of it being more cyclical, like the seasons. Or like a spiral, spinning ever downward, dooming him to repeat his mistakes, over and over again, because of a flaw in his nature that could not be corrected, no matter how hard he tried.

He had gotten a woman he barely knew pregnant.

Reid peered down into the split in the earth as if he would find there a different solution to this problem than the obvious one. For the first time, he got not one shred of solace from this view, which had always made him feel that at least here, if no other spot in the world, he had a measure of control. He wondered if he'd ever feel that way again.

Well, he'd better speak his piece now or lose his nerve.

"I'll marry you, of course," he said firmly.

"Reid, no," Glenna said in a stricken tone. "I don't expect you to do that—"

"Then what do you expect?" He turned and gave her a hard look. "That I won't live up to my obligations? What kind of man do you think I am?" Abruptly, he recalled her earlier suggestion of her moving to Piney Rise to live in his cottage and work for him. "And what was all that stuff about before? Your wantin' to help me do what I love." And he'd lapped it up like a dog!

"I meant it, every word!" She gave a huff of exasperation. "Look, I know I said I'd never bring up what happened between us that night by the road—and believe me, after today I won't—but I don't want you to think I ever thought that you and I would...that there would ever be, you know, repeats of that episode."

He went cold, as if he stood in a deep freeze instead of one-hundred-plus-degree heat. It was one thing to think that the most they had shared was the scratching of a mutual itch—as long as that itch was scratched, which Reid had believed it had been. It was another matter to have it spelled out to him that he had so failed to satisfy her in a moment of clear physical need that she might never want that connection again with him, as he so did with her.

Yet here she was, wanting something from him again, though not sexually, not "expecting" too much lest she be disappointed yet another time. Somehow that idea cut a little deeper, especially since he realized he'd been foolishly hoping there had been more behind her suggestion to come live and work on Piney Rise. That was right, *he* had wanted more, in this woman's way of wanting more that had apparently rubbed off on him.

Suddenly feeling conspicuously naked, Reid strode over and scooped up his shirt to put it on. However, he was distracted from buttoning it and tucking it in by what he wanted to say.

"You were probably right to refuse to take me up on my offer when the subject first came up, thinking you'd avoid dealin' with certain issues if you left Plum Creek," he said icily. "Because I won't have a woman using Piney Rise to hide in shame from the world." *Not again.*

"But I wanted to run and I didn't!" Glenna held up a hand in appeal. "Don't you understand, Reid?"

"Pardon me, but I don't," he retorted without an ounce of sympathy for either of them.

The hurt that shone from her eyes was a tangible thing. Well, damn it, she'd hurt him, too.

"Fine, then! I've done my duty by tellin' you about this baby. I won't bother you again." She shoved off the ground and surged to her feet. It was too quickly. She swayed, would have fallen had Reid not grabbed her by her upper arms to steady her.

Her hands came up, pushing against his chest in ineffective resistance. "Let me go!"

"What, and watch you topple over the edge of that embankment?"

"I'm not even near it!"

"Close enough, and you're so disoriented right now I could see you headin' for it without even knowin' you did. And don't forget, I've seen you with your blood up. You're like a spooked horse."

Bolts of lightning shot from those stormy eyes. "Don't you dare compare me to some skittish mare who changes directions with the wind!"

"Then don't you dismiss me as a shiftless cowboy without the decency to look after his get!" he shouted back.

Glenna stared at him, and he at her, unbelieving of the way they were acting, completely out of character. Reid saw all the anger go out of her as surely as he felt it leave his own body. They were both running, running scared. Running for—or was it from?—their very lives.

For one instant longer Glenna continued to resist him before her head fell forward in absolute frustration.

He knew the feeling. Her auburn hair brushed his collarbone, her fingers dug into his pectorals, and with all his might Reid resisted the urge to curl his fingers around her nape, settle his other hand against the curve of her back and pull her flush against him. Resisted the urge to act on his first instinct, which was to show her he did understand her woman's body even if he might never understand her woman's heart.

But she didn't want that from him.

Still, it must have taken a lot for her to approach him, to risk having him come back with a denial of his own, given how he had behaved the day she came for Gringo. As if he didn't care.

"All right, explain it to me, Glenna," he said, still gripping her arms, giving her a single shake. "Make me understand."

"Oh, God, Reid, how can I when I barely do myself?" she whispered bleakly. "Maybe you're right. Maybe I'm still avoiding the real heart of the matter. Why and how all this happened in the first place."

Head still bent, she said, "You know, I thought I was doin' real well by makin' up my mind on the way over here to accept this . . . this development and look ahead. Like you would. I guess I hoped I'd prove somethin' to you, as well as to myself, by having a plan all ready that would allow me—and you, I mean, if you wanted—to take care of the baby. But I see now I was bein' selfish again, because I was thinkin' of me first. Of what you would think of me."

"Why would you feel you've got to prove something to me?" he asked, thoroughly bewildered.

"Because you're doin' what I want to do, even if I'm not able to find the way yet that'll work for me. You're makin' the journey back to a normal life all by yourself. After the way I challenged that effort the day I came for Gringo, I guess I didn't care to dwell on the possibility that you might see me as someone who hadn't the same ability to adjust. And accept."

Within his hands, her shoulders slumped, almost in defeat. "Now, though, I've got to think of this child first, what's best for it. However she came about, she deserves the best future that can be had." Her voice wobbled. "I'm not completely naive, Reid. I know how hard it was for Jamey to find work with an infant in tow. And she even had me to mind Hettie. It'd be very difficult for me to survive on my own with this baby."

He still didn't get it. "So why do it? Why not stay on Plum Creek?" *Especially if living with me would be such a hardship.*

She raised her head, shaking it definitely. "I've thought it over, and I just can't. Part of the reason's the same as before—they're a family and I don't fit in. I won't put that burden of trying on them. Or you. That's why I offered to work for you, take care of your books and manage your office. Make your life less complicated, sort of to balance out the real complication I'd be bringing into it. It's fair that you do provide your support to me and this child. And I to you, as much as I can. I've even got my insurance money I could contribute to your operation.''

That sounded more to Reid like a partner than an employee. More like a...a wife. A rancher's wife. But she'd said she didn't want that from him. And he *still* didn't understand.

''Why not just inform me of my obligation to support you and move somewhere you'd never have to deal with me at all?''

At his question, Glenna's gaze dropped, and she apparently realized only then that she touched him, her fingers spread on his chest. She jerked them away, two bright spots staining her pale cheeks. It occurred to Reid that he touched her, too, held her by the shoulders, and he abruptly released her.

In that way of wrapping her arms about herself, she slid her hands up to cover the places where his own had been.

''Why?'' she echoed faintly, avoiding his eyes. ''It wouldn't be fair...to you. I know neither of us asked for this baby, but now that she's on her way, you have an equal right to input on how she's raised. An equal right to her love. And she has a right to two parents who love her, even if they aren't—''

Glenna broke off, tears welling up in her eyes. She blinked them back as she said almost inaudibly, ''I just want it to be fair, for all of us.''

But it isn't fair! That same cry of denial she'd made filled his head. Yet she was trying to be—with him. She wasn't running, just as she'd said. He couldn't help admiring her courage as she quested for the truth in herself. He found himself moved by her consideration of what he might want out of all this, and not just what he was obligated to provide.

So what did he want? He thought of Glenna as she'd lain there close to a faint while looking for all the world as if she merely slept, even dreamed. He thought of his own brief dreams in which he'd indulged. And which he must now set aside, perhaps forever this time, and face the cold, hard realities of his nature.

Thus resolved, Reid said matter-of-factly, "You were right to come to me, Glenna. Right in suggestin' you move to Piney Rise. It's where you belong now."

Her chin trembled perilously as she murmured softly, "Thank you, Reid."

Thanks for what? he thought cynically but didn't say. Yet, strangely, her gratefulness made him feel a whole lot better about this scrape he was in...no, that they were both in.

"So we'll move you over as soon as we can." He planned aloud. "I wouldn't expect you to work." Even as her mouth opened in protest, he added, "Except I know how it is to have somethin' productive to do to get you through rough times. But—"

He hesitated, clearing his throat, scratching his chin. Uncomfortable as hell and stalling. He had to say it, though. "The only way this'll work, Glenna, is for us to be married."

Her eyes widened in dismay, which he stalwartly ignored. "Reid, I told you, I don't expect that. I won't ask it of you."

"I know you won't, but it's what *I* can bring to the table—my name and my protection of you and—"

Our baby. Why couldn't he say it? Glenna seemed to have no problem doing so. But it wasn't real to him yet. He didn't know when it would be. All he knew was that he had to get this point settled and taken care of now, before they went any further.

Setting his stance against her refusal, Reid said, "The matter isn't negotiable."

"I won't cover up my mistake," Glenna returned just as decisively, though her chin wobbled again. "I'm willing to own up to it, even if I don't want to wake up every mornin' and face walking into Jamey's kitchen and havin' everyone uncomfortable with my growing waistline or avoidin' talking about Jamey and Kell's baby because of me and my baby."

Yes, she could call it hers, and for some reason he couldn't.

"But it's not yours, it's mine." He gestured impatiently. "My mistake, I mean. Because I should've known better."

There. It was out, and he waited for her to ask how it could be more his transgression. He wanted her to ask so that he could make his own explanations as to his reaction to this development, for he didn't have the courage himself to come right out with it.

But Glenna didn't ask, only looked at him sadly as she said, "Oh, Reid, we both should have known—what was in our minds and in our hearts. What...happened between us," she went on haltingly, "wasn't just sex, I know that now. It was both of us trying to find something—release from problems, or avoidance of them— through sex, but it didn't make it any more right."

Her features were drawn, the expression in her eyes so regretful. "You were correct in saying I was running from Plum Creek out of shame. I *am* ashamed, for making a travesty of what should be an expression of love."

And she was correct, for Reid knew with perfect clarity what she meant, and he confronted his own culpability. He'd known Glenna felt this way even as he had encouraged them both to be swept away by their passion. He'd known she wanted more, had known the odds against him being able to give it to her.

Would their child have to take the hit, though, for them both not knowing better?

"Look, Glenna, I'm not trying to cover anything up, but I ask you—what choice have we except to marry?"

"And I'm asking you how we can compound our error by getting married. Don't you see? It'd be wrong for us to live truly as man and wife." She sounded desperate. "We hardly know each other, Reid. I meant what I said. I won't share your bed."

Oh, but that hurt! Even knowing that was how she felt, he was cut to the quick at hearing it said out loud. And, God help him, Reid struck back in his pain.

"Fine, I won't look for you in it," he snapped. "You can have that damned cottage all to yourself. But I'm tellin' you now, I will not have it ... *our child* go through life a bastard. Is that what you want?"

"No!" she cried, again so very desperate.

"Then don't make him pay for our folly," he said, wondering that he sounded just as desperate. "I won't do that."

Her eyes searched his for a long moment before a look of profound relief filled them, bringing his own relief. And hard as it had been for them both, Reid knew he'd done the right thing. It had actually been what he'd had to do—in his heart. What he could do for them all, if nothing else.

But God, he felt hollow inside!

"So we'll get married," he said curtly.

Arms wrapped tighter than a straitjacket around her middle, Glenna nodded her acceptance.

"I'll leave the whole thing to you, then, however you want to arrange it," Reid continued. "I know you attend one of the Baptist churches in Borger, so you'll probably want to have the minister there do it. Although if you just wanted to go to the courthouse, I'd be all right with that, too. And the sooner the better, I'd say.''

It sure wouldn't be him who'd bring up considering waiting a while to see if the pregnancy carried; damn him if he'd have it look as if he wanted out of the situation.

''That'll be fine.'' Her voice was subdued, resigned. Accepting, as he'd once wished she would be, and now bereft of all that incredible, passionate defiance that had drawn him to her from the first. He recalled how it had unearthed in him that cowboy need to meet the challenge of that passion. Well, now it looked as if he had, and he couldn't feel anything but sorry for his damnable shortsightedness.

''I'd even be willin' to foot the bill for a ceremony or reception,'' he added, wanting to make amends in any way he could.

That brought the stubborn light back to her eyes. ''It's the bride's—my place—to pay for those kinds of costs.''

''This isn't exactly a conventional wedding—''

''I can afford it.''

They were both trying to accommodate, both used to doing so. Not wanting to ask too much or give too little in the equation.

''All right.'' He acquiesced. ''But that brings up another matter. You mentioned investing your money in Piney Rise. I won't take your savings, Glenna.''

''I want you to have it, though. I want *us* to have it.'' She gazed at him beseechingly. ''Please, Reid. If this arrangement is to work, it's what I need.''

Yes, they were both used to accommodating, dealing with disappointment within themselves, by themselves. Yet they had certain wants—no, needs—that would not be compromised.

''We'll talk about it,'' was all he'd promise. As time went by, she might not want to be bound to him so definitely....

He simply couldn't think of such a possibility right now.

"You probably shouldn't drive," he said gruffly, buttoning his damp, wrinkled shirt and stuffing its tails into his jeans in a replay of the evening this whole mess got started. "You still look a little peaked."

She seemed about to protest again, then merely said, "You're right. What about your horse?"

"Rogue? He knows the way home."

To prove his point, Reid whistled the bay over, gave it a slap on the rump and a "Git, now," to send him trotting obediently off through the scrub in the direction of Piney Rise.

Glenna watched him go, an intrigued frown on her face. "He'll really go home?"

"Yep."

She turned to look at him. "You're really a very talented horse trainer, Reid."

Embarrassed, he scoffed, "Shoot, Glenna, I probably learn as much from each horse I train as they do from me."

"Mmm," was her only comment. She retrieved her hat but didn't put it on, just let it dangle between her shoulder blades by the stampede strings as her gaze took in the stark beauty of the Breaks one more time, allowing Reid to take in the whole of her. One more time.

God, this marriage was going to be a living hell. How could it not be, having her close and yet so far away.

He cleared his throat. "Well. Let's get you home. To Plum Creek, that is." They started off in the direction of the pickup, and he took her elbow, thinking that he at least had that right. He would protect her, to the best of his ability. "Would you like me to be there when you tell Jamey and Kell?"

"That we're gettin' married?"

"And why."

"I'm not sure I'll tell them that part."

The shock rocked through him. "But I thought you said you weren't going to cover up anything. Even if you were... ashamed. And they'll figure it out eventually."

"I see what you mean. I just can't imagine right now how one goes about telling a grown child, with a child of her own, that her parent has to get married."

He definitely could see what she meant.

"What about Clan?" Glenna asked. "How will he feel about our gettin' married and the reason behind it?"

Reid's stomach clenched. Yes, how would his son feel—that is, if the boy deigned to show any reaction at all? Clan—so uncompromising of weakness in himself. And in others. Briefly, Reid debated, not for the first time, whether it was how Clan was like him or how the boy was different that bothered him most about his son.

He had to remember Clan didn't know the whole story.

"I reckon Clan'll deal with it," Reid finally said as they reached the pickup.

He circumvented further discussion by opening the passenger door and helping Glenna inside before going around the front and slipping in behind the wheel. He was reaching for the ignition key when she stopped him with a hand on his arm.

He glanced up.

"I promise, Reid, I'll be a good mother to this child," she said, again with that edge of desperation. "And a good... a good partner."

She hesitated for an instant, then nodded, as if convincing herself more than him. "Yes, I must look at it that way. We're partners with the aim of making a life for this child."

He noted her omission of promising to be a good wife. But then, neither would he be a good husband, as long as they were married in name only. And even if they did share a bed, it would hardly guarantee their happiness.

Partners. It was probably better this way, he thought as he drove them away from the Breaks, to start out from the first not pretending they felt more for each other. Not trying for more. And failing.

Suddenly ten thousand lonely tomorrows stretched out before Reid, making him want to run for the hills, escape the fate he'd wrought upon himself—and Glenna.

He couldn't think of that now, or he'd never make it through another day.

Chapter Eight

As weddings went, Glenna mused as she dressed in her bedroom at Plum Creek, this one was bound to be as peculiar as a snowstorm in summer. Which had never happened, so far as she knew, even in the oddity called west Texas weather.

First, Jamey wouldn't hear of there not being a full-fledged wedding. Why not? she'd asked when Glenna had told her daughter of her decision to marry Reid. She saw right away that Jamey obviously failed to grasp the circumstances behind what Glenna perceived as a hastily announced engagement, followed by a hastily planned ceremony. Of course, who would even dream that two people of Reid's and her ages would "have" to get married?

Regardless, Glenna just couldn't make herself come out with the full story, even if the reason, as Reid had said, would be more than apparent within months. Sometime before then, she would tell Jamey, Glenna decided. Yet, as she'd asked Reid, how did one introduce such a subject? And who would believe it had happened the way it had, anyway? Glenna was having trouble grasping it herself, and she'd been there.

And so she found herself being swept along in Jamey's plans to have the ceremony take place at Plum Creek, as Jamey's had been a mere three months earlier. Her daughter wanted to do all the cooking and, even if she wasn't the seamstress her mother was, she wanted to help Glenna shop for a dress. Glenna hadn't planned on buying anything new—and definitely nothing in white. Lord *above*. But some part of her womanly pride exerted itself, and she settled on a slim Western-style skirt with a matching short-sleeved blouse in a cool green-and-blue print that she could use as a church dress. Or at least would after the baby came, because already the waistband seemed a little constricting. Heaven knew she hadn't needed to get a skirt with a waistband, could have done nicely with an elastic waist, but again some bit of pride had goaded her into buying a style that was form-fitting, perhaps in some sort of symbolic denial. Who did she think she was fooling, though?

Glenna's stomach lurched at the thought. *Don't you dare do me this way,* she mentally warned it, and took a fortifying bite of the soda cracker she'd sneaked from the kitchen. Yet her insides continued to churn and her forehead broke out in a cold sweat. How had she let Jamey talk her into this charade?

Stocking footed, Glenna padded into the bathroom to wet a washcloth, and she applied it to the back of her neck, hoping it would cool her off. In the mirror she surveyed her hairstyle, which had sprung from the same aim. She had pulled her hair up on top of her head in a soft knot, with wispy tendrils floating down. Actually, she had secretly hoped wearing it this way would make her look more bridelike. Younger.

"Glenna Dunn, *you're* the fool here, no mistake," she muttered to her reflection, and reached up to remove the pins. She decided then and there that the secret to feeling young was not having too damned many mirrors around.

"Momma, what're you doin' with your hair?"

Glenna turned to see Jamey enter the room. "I'm takin' it down before it falls around my ears," she explained, coming back into the bedroom, collecting pins in her palm as she went.

"But it's so pretty that way. I've even got some baby's breath to put in it."

"Heavens, no!" She would look foolish with flowers in her hair, as if trying to appear a blushing virgin. *More like an aging Mother Nature.*

Glenna caught sight of her daughter's downcast expression and relented. "All right, I'll keep it up, but no flowers."

"Here, let me help you." Jamey hastened over to take the hairpins from her. She positioned Glenna in front of the mirror and, lower lip caught between her teeth, tried to restore the topknot to its former state.

Jamey looked very pretty today, Glenna observed, watching her daughter in the mirror. Her long, dark red hair swung loose around her face, lending even more purity to her features. Despite the bad spell after her father had died and her marriage to Henry McSween had failed, Jamey seemed untouched by that strife. Such was the resilience of the young. Yet Glenna couldn't remember Jamey being any different than she'd always been, one to meet life head-on, even to bend it to her will, which was different from Glenna's own way of doing things.

That is, until recently.

"Good God, what have I done?" Glenna said suddenly.

Jamey shot her a brief glance in the mirror. "Somethin' wrong, Momma?"

"Jamey." She took a deep breath and looked her daughter straight in the eye. "The only reason Reid and I are getting married is because I'm going to have a baby."

There, it was out—or at least as much as she had the courage to own up to at the moment.

Jamey said nothing for a few minutes, her hands stilled on Glenna's hair. Finally she mumbled through the pins in her mouth, "Are you sure?"

Glenna's jaw dropped. "That's all anyone's got to say? *Are you sure?*" No how or when or why?

Her daughter took the hairpins from her mouth. "Of course I know you're sure about the baby comin'," she said patiently. "But what I meant was are you sure the baby is the only reason you're gettin' married? Because there must be somethin' between you two for you to get pregnant."

To her utter mortification, Glenna blushed. Her daughter was far too used to discussing the breeding habits of cows and horses as a matter of course. "Well, there isn't," she said bluntly. *Not anymore, if there ever had been.*

"I see." Jamey gnawed on her lip. "That sure doesn't sound like you, Momma."

"That's where you're right," Glenna answered. "But there's no denyin' it was me who got into this mess. So I've got to do what's right for the baby—if for no one else. But how can I...oh—" she blinked rapidly, fanning her hands in front of her face "—I should have known better than to bring this up now. I simply can't walk into the living room and have Reid see me with red-rimmed eyes. I won't do that to him."

"I've got some eye drops, so don't worry on that score," Jamey volunteered. "Let's talk about this." She stooped to peer into Glenna's face. "Now, I realize this is a little more than the usual cold feet, but can you honestly say you don't have some tender feelings for Reid?"

Carnal, yes, Glenna thought ruefully. But tender? In an instant she was transported back to the afternoon by the Breaks when she'd looked up to find Reid, bare chested, bending over her, concern written in every line of his face, strength and dependability carved into every muscle of his hard torso. And then when she'd touched that chest, actually experienced that strength living, happening, beneath her hands...

Yes, she had to admit what she felt for Reid was more than an indebtedness to him for doing so many things, foremost among them insisting upon this marriage. She hadn't realized how she'd feared facing the stigma of illegitimacy that would follow this child until he'd confronted her with the prospect. And since then she had thanked him in her heart a million times for being such an upstanding man.

"Maybe I do have tender feelings for Reid," she said, adding as she dropped her gaze to her hands, twisting around themselves, "but tenderness, even respect, do not constitute love."

"They're a fine foundation for it, though. Don't you think you could learn to love each other?"

Could they? Perhaps once, she and Reid might have had a chance to get to know and come to love each other. She'd sensed as much the day he'd come to her rescue by the side of the road, that even with their difference in views, they might have come to some understanding, with a little effort and time. But now, how could they, after what had happened and the reason she feared in her heart that it had?

She met her daughter's eyes in the mirror as Jamey stood behind and off to one side of her.

"Do I think Reid and I could learn to love each other?" she repeated. "I think I'd be foolish to hold out for that end."

"Would you, Momma?"

Glenna shook her head, which caused a section of hair to slip, and Jamey fastened it up again as Glenna said resolutely, "Look, I am fully aware of the reasons Reid and I decided to get married. They're not the best for why two people should make their lives together, but that can't be helped. I just had to let you know, sugar," she went on in a milder tone, "that I'm not trying to cover up a mistake, truly I'm not. I'm trying to make the best of the situation. But let's call it what it is and not pretend it's something more."

She reached up to stay her daughter's actions. "That's why I've been so resistant to havin' a wedding. It hasn't seemed fitting that this union be celebrated so specially."

Jamey appeared to digest this speech. Then she moved around to Glenna's other side, tucking here and pulling out another tendril there as she went. "It's a rare moment when I feel I have more experience than you, Momma, but I know I never felt truly married the first time, and part of that was because I never had a real wedding. Not that I think the marriage would have lasted any longer than it did if we had, but this marriage to Reid, you do mean it to last, however it might have come about in the first place."

She turned Glenna to face her. "I know you, Momma. And you seem to know Reid, at least to the degree that you're willin' to make a try at this marriage. So I would hate for you to regret not marking this moment when it all begins, because you won't be able to snatch it back once it's gone. We've both had enough regrets to last us a lifetime, so why let yourself in for one more when you have the chance right now to avoid it?''

Glenna stared at her daughter. She hadn't thought of it that way before, but was she trying to avoid making another mistake by agreeing to this wedding? Was it a chance to make something right in this whole situation?

"How did you get so wise?" she asked, mouth quivering.

"I take after my mother," Jamey quipped.

The younger woman stooped to bestow a kiss on her cheek, which Glenna returned, and they ended up hugging, desperately so, and even crying a little, for weddings of every kind were special affairs, by their very nature of marking both beginnings and endings in one's life.

"Now," Jamey said as they continued to hug, "am I allowed to say congratulations about the baby and tell you how happy I am, not just for you but for myself, as well, because now we really have some anticipatin' to do."

"Do you mind?" Glenna asked, on tenterhooks for Jamey's answer. "That I'm sort of stealin' your moment in the sun?"

"Momma." Her husky voice was tenderly admonishing. "There's enough sun to go around. And even if there isn't, it's your time to shine. You deserve it."

Did she? Glenna wondered, for she hadn't told her daughter the real secret she kept locked in her heart of hearts: that she had used Reid Shelton, that fine and honest man, to give her the renewal of life she'd despaired of ever having again. But such a confession seemed impossible, mainly because she realized Jamey's purity came from her being in the first blush of love. And Glenna, with her flawed motives, had no right to cast a darkening shadow on *that* divine season in the sun.

"Enough!" Jamey straightened, daubing with a tissue at her tears, then Glenna's, so their mascara wouldn't smear. They took turns using the eye drops, then the lip gloss, like two girls primping in the rest room at the school dance. "Okay, I left the baby's breath out of your hair, but you will carry the beautiful bouquet of pink roses I ordered special, won't you?"

"Yes," Glenna acceded readily. Even if she wasn't showing yet, she wanted to walk into the living room with something to hide her abdomen, more for security than anything else.

They met Kell in the kitchen, since he was to give Glenna away. With a parting smile of encouragement, Jamey preceded Glenna into the living room, in which the furniture had been moved against the walls to accommodate the small assemblage. The Reverend Mr. Morris stood at the far end of the room in front of the bay window. Glenna had gone ahead and decided to have the Baptist minister say the vows. It was a demonstration of faith on more than one level, for she wanted to show Reid that she believed in this marriage as much as she could.

The hired hands, Charley and Purdy, both with hair slicked back and mustaches waxed, sang "I Cross my Heart," a George Strait ballad popular at country weddings, to the strum of a guitar. Advancing into the room, Glenna barely distinguished the other people there, such as the minister's wife, who held Hettie. Her attention did light on Clan, standing next to his father. Black haired and sharp featured, the young man seemed an image of Reid as he might have looked twenty years ago, and more than just in looks. His expression was as impassive as she'd often seen Reid's. She still didn't know what Clan thought of this marriage or even what Reid had told his son. Did the young man resent her taking his mother's place? Not that Glenna was, or could, in several capacities. But how to tell Clan that? Had Reid tried?

Finally Glenna could avoid it no longer; she looked at Reid, and found him so handsome she got palpitations. He stood straight and tall in black slacks and a Western-cut suit coat in a muted black-and-white weave. He wore a pair of spit-shined lizard skin boots, and at the throat of his stark white shirt was a silver-and-onyx bolo tie. The shock of ebony hair that perennially fell over his forehead had been combed back, making him look unusually somber. Was he thinking back to his first wedding, how he had been filled with hopes and dreams for a life together with Miranda—and was he comparing that day to this one?

Remorse, disappointment and longing hit her in one dose. *Was* she holding out for more from this marriage?

She saw Reid's lashes flicker as he completed just as thorough a perusal of her before coming back to her face. Their gazes met, locked, and something about the light made his eyes glint like shards of color coming through a kaleidoscope. Then Glenna actually saw the heat of emotion in those changeable eyes flare momentarily before going out, as if snuffed forever.

Her knees nearly buckled with the shock of it. Oh, God, this marriage was a charade. A travesty, without love.

Glenna was on the verge of turning and running or, at the very least, stopping the ceremony, when Kell let go of her elbow, and Reid took it. He threaded her arm through his own, settled her palm on his hard biceps and pressed his hand over hers. Involuntarily, Glenna spread her fingers, and his wove between them, curling and squeezing, hard, as if to bring her back to her senses, remind her she wasn't alone, that they needed each other now more than ever. They were in this together.

Again, tears started to her eyes, and she gulped them back urgently. She couldn't cry now! She had to be strong, if for no other reason than not embarrassing

Reid. She mustn't make him sorry for marrying her, not when she'd promised he wouldn't be.

At the thought, a measure of calm settled over Glenna. Because she found she could be strong—for Reid's sake.

Keeping that thought at the forefront of her mind helped her get through the short ceremony, up to the repeating of vows, when she faltered slightly. She and Reid faced each other, holding hands, and promised to take the other as lawfully wedded husband and wife, for richer or poorer, in sickness and in health, till death did them part.

"I do," said Reid, gaze never wavering.

"I do," said Glenna, wondering if every bit of her heart showed in her eyes.

The moment they were pronounced man and wife, she suffered an onslaught of panic—or anticipation—as the minister invited Reid to kiss his bride. Those dark lashes flickered again, concealing his expression, as he leaned forward. Reflexively, she closed her eyes, waiting, yearning.

She felt a perfunctory peck on the lips.

Glenna hid her disappointment as best she could, chiding herself for wanting more.

The reception went smoothly enough, until Glenna returned momentarily to her room across the breezeway to powder the shine off her forehead, and heard voices through the open window. She peeked through the blinds and saw Clan, now in shirt sleeves, collar open and tie who knew where, standing at the open door of his pickup truck. Reid stood in front of the truck, the tails of his suit coat pushed back and hands in his pants pockets.

"Sure you won't stay?" he asked. "Jamey must've made enough food to eat through next Tuesday."

Fidgeting, Clan looked off into the distance. "Naw, I need to get on the road to Arizona."

"Oh. Well." He shifted on his feet. "I appreciate your takin' time out of your schedule and bein' here, son. It . . . it meant a lot to me."

"Sure." Clan dropped his gaze and toed a pattern in the dirt beneath his boot. "You know, I've got a meetin' in Tucson to talk to a potential sponsor."

"Do tell!"

"Yeah. Now that it looks like I've actually got a shot at makin' the Finals this year, they're willin' to invest some money in me."

"That's great, son."

Clan shrugged, concentrating on opening and closing his right hand, which Glenna remembered he'd injured directly before roundup time in May. "It'll help to have a sponsor, that's for sure, but it doesn't make up lost time for when I was out with a gimped-up hand."

"Well, it won't be for lack of persistence if you don't make the Finals."

Neither man said anything for several moments, and Glenna got the impression that this conversation, such as it was, signified more communication between father and son than either had had with the other in some time.

She knew she shouldn't eavesdrop, but she couldn't make herself back away from that window.

Reid cleared his throat. "Before you go, Clan, I want you to know my marrying Glenna doesn't change anything at Piney Rise."

"Dad, really." For the first time, Clan looked at his father, and though his tone was just short of patronizing, Glenna sensed the hurt hiding behind it. "I think we both know this changes a lot of things."

"No, it doesn't—"

"Come on, Dad. I'm a big kid now, I can handle the truth."

"But I'm tellin' you the truth. I mean it, Clan. Even though you're on the road, you should still consider Piney Rise your home."

Clan stared at Reid, disbelief written clearly in his features. "Is that right? So were you even going to bother to tell me?"

"*Tell* you?" Even from as far away as she stood, Glenna could see Reid's ears turn red, though whether it was from anger or embarrassment, she didn't know. "Tell you what, by God?"

"I mean, I know I'm not around for it to make much of a difference anyway, but why the hell are you fixin' up Grandma's cottage if not for me to clear my stuff out of the house and put it there!"

Now Reid stared at his son, the seconds ticking off. For a moment Glenna had been confused, but now it seemed clear that Reid hadn't owned up to their mistake—and was apparently debating whether or not to at this moment. It wasn't that she didn't understand, but his reluctance hurt. With him unaware she watched, it seemed particularly telling of his feelings about the circumstances wrought upon him.

Then he answered his son tersely, "It's for Glenna, all right? I've been fixin' it up for Glenna to live there."

In that moment she knew the real shame Reid faced. It probably would have been easier telling his son he'd gotten a woman pregnant at his age. Because what this said was that, whatever the reason he had married her, it was without love.

Her heart contracted in her chest, for Reid's burden was her burden.

Clan just stood there looking at his father. "If you needed help that bad with the business, Dad, money or manpower, all you had to do was ask."

Reid said nothing.

Shaking his head almost in disdain, Clan muttered a dismissing "Look, I'm outta here," and climbed into his pickup. Within seconds he'd backed up and pulled away, tires spitting gravel and dust flying everywhere.

Reid watched him go. Then, with one hand, he ran his fingers through his hair, dislodging the front clump of hair to resume its usual place on his forehead. That world-weary gesture, more than any guilt she might have experienced for eavesdropping, made Glenna whirl away from the window. If she watched one second longer she'd find herself rushing to his side. And she couldn't do that. Because she wanted to offer him more than support and understanding, one parent to another. Wanted to make it up to him for the trouble she'd caused—as a true wife would. But she didn't have that right. And it struck her fully what Reid had given up for her, for she knew instinctively that this man of honor would never seek physical comfort from another woman as long as he was married, even if it was in name only.

There was no way she could ever make that up to him, not by taking care of his business, his house or his child.

Wrapping her arms about her torso, as if warding off a sudden chill, Glenna glanced around, her gaze falling on her bouquet, and she lifted it to her lips, the scent of already fading roses filling her head. She would preserve them, she decided, for Jamey had been right; she should make the most of each chance she had to avoid creating more regrets in her life. What other direction was open to her?

"Welcome to your future, Glenna Shelton," she whispered.

The sun had already set on their wedding day when Reid turned the dually into the driveway at Piney Rise, Glenna sitting across the bench seat from him. A Dwight Yoakam CD had filled the silence on the ride from Plum

Creek. He didn't take offense at the lack of conversation; they were both tired after the long afternoon.

He pulled up next to the house. His house, that is. Out of the corner of his eye he saw Glenna regard it, her expression composed, though her hands twisted in her lap. She was nervous, too, about making it through this awkward moment.

"Let's get you situated," he said gruffly, adjusting his hat, this one a fine 15X beaver in black that was really too hot to wear past March and certainly not before November. But it was his dress hat, one he always wore for special occasions.

He fetched her bags, shoving one under an armpit and carrying the other on the same side so that he could take her elbow to help her across the uneven ground to the little white cottage under the cottonwoods.

"I hope you won't be disappointed," he said. "The place isn't more than twenty feet square, with no dividing walls, so there really weren't many options for where to put your things I moved over earlier this week. Of course, you can change the furniture around however you like. I mean, I can. You shouldn't move stuff yourself."

She gave a soft smile. "I'm sure everything'll be fine."

It was a short walk, a pleasant one, in fact, especially at this hour. The sky glowed a rich sapphire at its height, with just the hint of rosy-violet seeping down its western rim, indigo blue creeping upward in the east. A full moon became more distinct by the second, ushering in what would have been their wedding night if they'd been a normal couple.

He went ahead of her to open the door, setting the bags down just inside, against the wall. "Well, here it is," he announced unnecessarily, switching on the overhead light as he doffed his hat and held it nervously in front of him.

Glenna hesitated, and for a second he got a wild impression that she waited for him to sweep her up in his arms and carry her across the threshold. Then she stepped across it herself, glancing around.

"Now, to your left is the kitchen area," he hastened to explain. "There's no stove or oven—I forgot to ask if that'd be a problem—but there is a hot plate and a mini-microwave I picked up for a song. I hoped... thought you might want to take your evening meals at the house, but whatever you'd like to do..."

He laid a hand on top of the microwave. "It seemed handiest to set it on the half fridge here next to the counter, but you can arrange it however works best for you. Your table and chairs need to sit up against the wall when not in use, otherwise you won't have room to get into the closet over there."

He knew he was rambling but felt the need to fill the vacuum created by Glenna's silence. She opened one of the cupboards and tentatively peeked inside.

"I'll hang some shelves if you need extra storage," he suggested.

"Mmm."

Trying not to be disappointed at her reaction, or lack thereof, Reid pointed as he moved across the room. "And this spot right here seemed perfect to me for a little sitting area. Your rocker, end table and a lamp beside it."

"Mmm," was again all she had to say.

"This, of course, is the bedroom area. I went ahead and put on a set of sheets I had at the house, just so you wouldn't have to make the bed the first night you spent here." He gestured aimlessly with his hat. "Don't trouble yourself to wash these when you're through with them. Oh, that reminds me. You'll have to do your laundry up at the main house. Sorry about that."

Reid finally wound down as Glenna continued to say nothing, just walked slowly around the interior of the cottage, gray eyes contemplative as she looked it over. He tried to see it as she might, and failed. Too much of himself was in this house.

In the past week he had put hours and hours of work into the place, patching walls and repairing the roof. He'd weather-stripped the doors and blown a few hundred dollars' worth of insulation in between the walls and in the crawl space above the ceiling. In short, he had done the best he knew how to make the place as homey for Glenna as possible, but in the end it was still just a prefab bungalow.

He felt it fell far short of making up for anything.

Reid jammed his fists into his trouser pockets. "I did warn you it was small."

No comment from Glenna, her lips thinned to a straight line as she held them between her teeth. She returned to the center of the room and made a slow circle, ending up facing away from him, and he couldn't help but make an extended inspection himself—of her.

She'd looked more than beautiful today, slim as a slip of a girl, yet no one would mistake her for a teenager. No, she'd been every inch a lady, composed and calm, throughout the entire ceremony and reception. His heart had nearly burst with pride. With some other emotion, too, deeply visceral, as a pounding hunger would be.

She was his wife now.

She still wore her wedding outfit, still had her hair pulled up as she'd worn it today, and it ringed her head in an auburn halo, exposing the nape of her neck to him. He wondered what would happen if he came up behind her and touched that vulnerable expanse of skin. But would he be able to stop there, hold himself back from wrapping his arm around her waist and lowering his head to taste the delicate curve beneath his fingertips?

Could he stop himself from wanting more?

He waited, and when after several minutes neither of them moved, Reid did approach Glenna. He stopped just behind her, his hands gripping his hat in front of him.

"Look, Glenna," he said in a low voice, "you don't have to move in here if this cottage isn't everything you expected. Or wanted. I'll make some kind of arrangements for you here on Piney Rise. I don't know what, but I'll think of something."

She spun to face him, shaking her head and blinking rapidly. "But it *is* everything I expected. More, in fact. Much more."

Why did he doubt her, just a little bit?

Now it was she who rambled. "I—I guess I just lost myself for a minute, wondering which window would provide the best light for me to do my sewing, imagining what kind of curtains I'd put up, and if I might hang wallpaper."

Was it merely him, or did her enthusiasm lack something?

Her forehead wrinkled. "Of course, if you'd rather I didn't do any decorating to the place—"

"Shoot, you can paint the walls polka-dotted for all I care. I just want you to be comfortable."

I want you to be happy, Reid thought but didn't say. They stood very close, the warmth of the day seeming to linger still on their clothes, the tension of it in their bodies. Yes, he wanted her to be happy, but whether he would ever be able to make her so remained a vast uncertainty.

Then he realized why she'd been turned from him, for her eyes were shimmery with tears. "Reid, I—" She swallowed, dropping her chin. "Even a blind man could see the hard work you've put into this place. I don't...I don't deserve it."

"*Glenna.*" Unable to stop himself, he slid the edge of an index finger beneath her chin and forced it up. "What do you mean, you don't deserve it? Don't deserve what? This cottage?''

She hesitated, lower lip caught between her teeth, before nodding. "This—and your consideration.''

"You aren't entitled to every bit of care I can provide?'' He wasn't angry with her, just frustrated that she might doubt she merited certain rights that seemed so basic to him. "I mean, what kind of a man would I be if I didn't see to my wife's wish of having a place to call home?''

She shook her head. "I don't know. I can't imagine it.'' She smiled then, tremulously. "What else can I say, except thank you, Reid.''

With his thumb he brushed away one tear that had fallen to her cheek. "I wish I could do more,'' he said simply. *Much more.*

His fingers still cradled her cheek, and it seemed as automatic as a reflex for him to lean toward her, ever so slightly. Her pupils flared, another involuntary response, as she lifted her chin. And looking down into the reflective pools of her gray eyes, Reid knew that she'd lied, or that he'd misunderstood her, or something. Because she wanted him—he knew it with every instinct ever born in him—and she wouldn't want him now if he hadn't been able to satisfy her before.

That still gave him no call to take advantage of her. Again. Because he *wasn't* some shiftless cowboy.

He dropped his hand and stepped back, breaking the spell.

"Well.'' He cleared his throat. "I should be going. Good night, Glenna.''

"G'night, Reid,'' she said softly.

He got out of there before he could let himself respond to the look that came to her eyes, that of having been forsaken.

Reid let himself in the back door of the main house and into the darkened kitchen. Long familiar with the layout, he didn't bother to turn on a light as he made his way to his bedroom. He undressed in the silence, made a trip to the bathroom and was in bed in less than five minutes.

Linking his hands behind his head, he stared at the ceiling and ticked off all the things he needed to do to Glenna's house: get a new air conditioner, first. Replace the flooring in the bathroom. In addition to no washer or dryer, the cottage was without a telephone. He would talk to the phone company about splitting the line and running a wire out to the cottage. In addition to a phone, though, he should see about rigging up some kind of intercom system between the cottage and the house, so Glenna could buzz him when she needed help of any kind. Such a device would be doubly handy when she became heavily pregnant. And after she gave birth.

He blinked. Surely Glenna didn't intend to raise the kid in that little place, did she? The cottage was barely big enough for one person, much less two. He wondered if she had thought that far down the road. Perhaps not. The situation had only occurred to him just now, along with another: how was it going to look, his wife and child living in a one-room cottage while he rattled around this big house by himself?

Mighty peculiar, came the answer, just like the rest of this arrangement.

But where would Glenna live, if not in the cottage? The ranch house had only two bedrooms. He'd be damned to hell and back before he'd ask Clan to take the cottage. Of course, after today maybe Clan was so fed up with his old man's foolhardiness he'd move away from Piney Rise of his own accord.

The boy didn't even know the half of it.

On that thought, back came the indignation, in spades, that he had felt this afternoon in response to the look his son had hit him with. It was none of Clan's business what Reid did with his life. Yet that indignation was again tempered by his suspicion that Clan's disdain had only been a front for the real emotion the boy was experiencing. Was his son afraid that by marrying Glenna, Reid might completely disregard his old life?

Would he?

And then there was their child. He knew he'd only been putting off the inevitable by not telling Clan that Glenna was pregnant; again, it was essentially none of the boy's business if she was. But he'd feared, in a way he wasn't yet sure he understood, that such news might cause him to lose his son before he had really gotten a chance to try to win him back.

Reid sighed tiredly, bringing his thoughts back to the matter at hand. The fact remained that Glenna couldn't continue to live in the cottage past her pregnancy. He didn't know why he'd agreed to the arrangement in the first place, and blamed himself for once again being shortsighted. If he'd made the effort to think more into the future, rather than just going with the quick fix he and Glenna had settled upon, he would have seen the impracticalities of their plans, on several different levels. Did either of them really believe that they'd forgo for the rest of their natural lives the physical pleasure two people could share with each other?

Yes, he'd jumped the gun there, too, promising never to darken her bedroom door because his ego had been wounded. But that was before he'd seen the look in her eyes this evening. He knew, with the intuition that he'd built through the years from watching and studying horses, that she wanted him, and whereas once he'd been discouraged that she might want him only physically, now Reid was glad. She had married him, however, with the understanding that they'd live as a married couple in name only. It was what she wanted, for whatever reasons.

What about *his* needs, what he wanted? Or was this whole thought process just a way to come up with an excuse to get her into his house and consequently into his bed?

He shifted to his side and, lying there in the dark, Reid felt that old discontent creep up on him, creep into him, making him want with a powerful, pounding yearning to take off for somewhere else. It didn't matter where. The next state. The next rodeo. Just anywhere but here.

Except he had a wife now. Again.

Chapter Nine

Glenna heard the back door open and close, announcing Reid's arrival at the end of the day, and her stomach did its usual nervous flip, as if she were a misbehaving child caught red-handed. Even after two weeks of working in his office—and finally completing a much-needed overhaul of the contents of his desk—she still felt like an interloper to his domain. Normally she'd finished up for the afternoon and was long gone by the time he returned to the house, but today she had remained, needing to go over a few matters with him.

Judging from the sounds coming from other parts of the house, however, he was probably unaware she waited for him. She was reluctant to go in search of him, had yet to explore much more of the house past his office. Part of that was pique. She had mentioned to Reid she'd be glad to clean as part of her duties, and he had told her rather brusquely that he had a woman come out once a week to take care of all that. It had been on the tip of

Glenna's tongue to retort that she'd only offered because, from the looks of the place, it wasn't getting cleaned too well by anyone. But she was determined to respect his privacy, especially since she'd been literally tearing up his retreat.

"Reid?" Glenna called softly, going to the office door and listening as she absently rubbed her back, which had begun aching toward the end of each day. She heard running water and guessed he'd gone straight to the bathroom to wash up.

She waited a few minutes more and called again, "Reid?"

The water was shut off, and even though Glenna knew he was on his way up the hall, she jumped when all of a sudden he came around the corner, still wiping his hands on a towel.

"I thought I heard your voice," he said, giving his face a quick scrub with the towel. "Is everything all right?"

His hazel eyes were alert, his expression openly concerned in a way she hadn't seen once past their wedding day. Past their wedding evening, actually. That hank of black hair jutted out over his forehead, sexily so, and Glenna managed a croaky, "Everything's fine. I had a few questions for you, is all."

He extended his arms, palms upward. "I'm at your disposal." *Oh, would that he were.* Of course, taking him up on a like offer was what got her into this predicament in the first place.

Shaking off such thoughts, Glenna turned and marched back to his office.

"I'm sorry to trouble you," she apologized, sitting in Reid's large leather chair and scooching it closer to the desk as she picked up the clipped stack on top of the neat pile of papers. "I wanted to go over the travel plans I've made for you for the show in Terrell this weekend."

Reid had followed her into the office, and now he took the copies she unceremoniously thrust at him as she continued, "I got you a pretty good rate, even at this late date, at a motel a few miles from the show arena. The gal with the Terrell Chamber of Commerce said it was nothin' fancy but clean. And I was able to get the schedule from the show secretary. The first Open go-rounds start Friday mornin'. You're showin' Sonny Wescott's gelding in the morning's second set and Bill Roanoke's mare in the afternoon's third set. Finals are Saturday night. On Saturday day, you've got the Classics first go-round, with the Wilkersons' stallion midafternoon sometime. I called those clients who said they were attending the show and let them know when their horses were on, in case they didn't know already. Sonny wanted to make sure you knew to save time for dinner with him Friday night."

"Will do."

"Oh, and Bobby Ray knows to lay fresh straw in the trailer and load provisions for the horses on Thursday morning before you take off."

"Good."

Glenna hesitated, wondering if she should tell Reid she had reservations about the job the twenty-year-old stable hand was doing. Except she didn't know if she'd stop there or go on to ask why, if Clan considered Piney Rise his home, he couldn't pitch in to help his father with the operation when the young man wasn't on the road. But then, Clan hadn't been home once since she'd moved here. She was reluctant to ask Reid if that was normal and risk stirring up the issues he'd obviously struggled with in his conversation with Clan on their wedding day. "I figured you'd want to get your tack and show clothes together yourself. Let me know if you need any help."

"Fine."

His replies were so terse she glanced up inquiringly, only to find Reid half sitting next to her on the edge of the desk, ankles crossed, boot toes cocked upward. His shirt sleeves were rolled up on his forearms, and he'd propped his elbow against the back of the arm resting against his middle as he read the papers in his hand. Or seemed to read them.

On the verge of offering him the reading glasses she'd spied the first day in the pencil drawer of the desk, Glenna forgot all about any kind of glasses as she lost herself in studying the dusting of black hair on his forearms and on the backs of his tanned hands. The memory of them moving duskily over her body sprang unbidden to her mind, making a flush start from her chest and move upward to her cheeks.

At least she knew now that her hot flashes weren't caused by menopause, Glenna thought dourly, hardly reassured. This feeling of being in heat all the time wasn't much better. It occurred to her, as it had the day he'd come upon her crying, that she looked far from her best these days. Her face was puffy and her eyes ringed with circles from lying awake at night while she wrestled with her conscience. She'd discovered that having made her bed, she was finding it very hard, literally, to lie in it.

Her gaze climbed upward and found his penetrating one upon her, which made her stomach do another of those flips. This one was a little more portentous, though, and Glenna recalled she'd forgotten to eat the midafternoon snack that tended to keep nausea at bay, at least until she had made it to the privacy of her cottage.

"Are you sure you're feelin' all right, Glenna?" Reid asked.

"Yes," she answered on a jerky nod, turning her attention to the next stack of papers. "Now. I've finally come up with as complete a reckoning as I can of each client's account. The only one I haven't got a firm grasp on is the Villers'. From what I can tell, you were workin' with their two-year-old mare, Lots O'Lass, which they sold, and Little San Donner, another two-year-old—this one a gelding—that you apparently agreed to continue trainin', but for a higher fee. And then Lots O'Lass—'' Glenna shuffled the papers ''—came back under the Wilkersons' ownership. After that there's some kind of funny-money arrangement goin' on that completely lost me.'' She sat back with a huff of frustration.

"You couldn't figure that out, huh?" Reid said thoughtfully. "You see, the mare's a fine horse with a lot of potential, but of the two, Donner showed more promise. Initially I agreed to work with them both to see which the Villers should put their money into, because they couldn't afford for me to train up two Futurity contenders. I recommended they go with Donner and sell Lots O'Lass. I even found a buyer for her in the Wilkersons, who'd been looking around for a mare they could build up a show reputation with and in a few years breed to Sally's Doc Time, their champion stallion.

"So," Reid went on, squinting one eye in concentration and pointing from left to right as he talked, "the Villers agreed to take compensation for Lots O'Lass in the form of the Wilkersons payin' part of Donner's training fees. Both the gelding and the mare had already been started off at a lower rate—because I was just gettin' a feel at that point to see which horse showed more promise—but when we decided to go ahead with a full program for Donner, I upped the rate to the Villers. I kept it the same, though, for Lots O'Lass because the Wilkersons have two horses with me now, and those clients get a break on my fees."

He looked at Glenna innocently. "Does that clear things up?"

She could only shake her head in wonder as she made a note for her records. "'Pay no attention to the man behind the curtain,'" she quoted the sonorous Wizard of Oz, adding the aside, "who's runnin' this show by the seat of his pants."

Reid laughed, and the charm his smile brought to his face nearly took her breath away. She wondered if Reid, of a nature, was really more carefree than he'd been with her—or perhaps than he'd been since the drastic change losing Miranda had brought to his life.

She didn't think she'd ever know for sure, as long as neither of them let the other too close.

"I did warn you I wasn't much for keepin' up my accounting," he said, then added seriously, "You've done a great job here, Glenna, and I want you to know how much I appreciate it."

"I'm glad to be of any help I can," she told him, meaning every word. Encouraged by the easiness of the moment, she asked shyly, "What would you say to getting a computer? They have some tracking and accounting programs now designed specifically for horse-training and breeding operations that'd make all this record keeping easy as pie."

"Tryin' to drag me along as you rush breakneck into the twentieth century, are you?" he quipped.

"I'd think you would be all for progress, especially when it comes to your business. And besides—" she cocked her head to one side, indicating the small table in the corner, "—that dusty typewriter of yours should have been retired years ago. It's skipping *o*'s. Watch."

She removed the cover from the typewriter and turned it on before rolling a piece of paper into the platen and typing the standard "The quick red f x jumps ver the lazy br wn d g."

"This is a delicate piece of machinery," Reid protested. "You just don't have the right touch."

"And I can't set tabs," she went on, ignoring his excuse.

"Maybe you're not doing it right. Wait, I think the manual's around here some place."

She continued tapping out *o*-less words while Reid rummaged through the shelves she'd yet to organize. With a sound of triumph he held the manual aloft.

"And you thought I'd never find it," he said, perching one hip on the edge of the desk as he flipped through the manual.

"I didn't say a word," Glenna returned virtuously, feeling suddenly happier than she had in a long time. "So what are the instructions for setting tabs?"

Out of the corner of her eye she saw him reach for the pencil drawer of his desk before seeming to stop himself. He held the booklet out to her. "Here. Look it up and see."

She knew then what the situation was with those glasses. And she couldn't resist trying to prolong this moment of lighthearted closeness between them.

"Oh, go ahead," she urged. "I'm tryin' to get the right touch for this delicate piece of equipment."

She busied herself at the typewriter so that he had no choice but to thumb through the index himself. He turned slightly away from her, and she bit back a smile as he held the manual in front of him first with arms bent, then lengthening the distance between it and his eyes until he had tucked his chin against his neck and stretched his arm to its full reach.

She pivoted, catching him. "Well? What's it say?"

He had on his face the most adorable expression of chagrin. Lifting an eyebrow at her, Reid opened the drawer and took out a pair of glasses, the kind with rims only around the bottom of two half lenses.

With aplomb he set the glasses on the bridge of his nose. "It *says—*"

Glenna collapsed with laughter before he could go on. Again with exaggerated dignity, Reid crossed his wrists on the thigh propped on the edge of the desk and regarded her reprovingly but with acknowledged humor. She got a sudden sense this was how he would deal with a cheeky child.

Their child.

She hadn't really dwelt on what kind of a father he'd be, wondered if he had thought about it. Tenderness for how he had changed his life thus far for her—and how he would have to change it in the future—welled up inside her, and Glenna again couldn't help herself. She stood in front of him, adjusting the glasses, and said consolingly, "Look at it this way. Your eyes aren't goin' bad, your arms are simply too short."

Reid raised his hands, fingers circling her wrists. "Glenna." The word was a warning. The humor abruptly vanished.

Their faces were inches apart, and her gaze met his. In it she saw embarrassment, sure, but also self-consciousness. And why wouldn't he be? She knew how sensitive she'd been about certain signs of aging, at the feeling she was playing at being young, when she should have accepted her fate. Why would she think Reid would be different?

Glenna became immediately contrite. "You know what I think, Reid?" she asked softly. "I think your glasses are darlin'."

He was darling, with his expression of flustered discomfiture at her words. That look went straight to her heart. Straight to her core.

He was darned sexy, is what he was. And they weren't bantering, they were flirting. Dangerously so. As if they weren't married and expecting a baby. As if they were two youngsters falling in love.

Glenna pulled her hands out of his grasp.

"I shouldn't have teased you, Reid," she said formally, trying for some distance. "I guess I never thought you'd be sensitive about needing glasses when you're so...accepting of everything."

"I fight battles with myself just like you," he said quietly, removing the glasses and folding the earpieces against his palm.

She reddened. "Of course. I didn't mean to imply..."

What did she mean, then? She felt that old restlessness come upon her again. "But shouldn't it start getting easier? Isn't gainin' experience and some sort of sense you're comin' into your own what we have to look forward to?"

"That depends on what you mean by comin' into your own."

His gaze held hers, eyes sparking green and gold and silver within the circle of that midnight blue. Drawing her in, pulling her toward him with the soul-deep understanding within them. How she'd missed that connection with this man, as brief as had been the moment she'd experienced it; as much as she feared she never would again.

The heat rose up in her like a firestorm.

With effort, Glenna took one step back, a feeble effort to stop them both from making any more of a mistake.

But the mistake had already been made. Hadn't it? Then, simultaneously, he stood, she reclaimed the step she'd taken, and she was in his arms, their lips finding the other's with unerring accuracy. His mouth slid over hers in a moist, leisurely touch that did not press but pulled, and Glenna found it was not enough as she parted her lips, seeking a more intimate contact between them.

Still Reid wouldn't give in to her silent demands. Rather, his tongue grazed across the tip of hers with velvet strokes that took the strength from her legs, making her knees nearly buckle.

He was there for her, as always, catching her against him with one strong arm across her back, the index finger of his other hand snaring her to him by the belt loop of her jeans.

Finally he held back no more. His mouth covered hers, hot and urgent.

God, she'd missed this. Wanted it with an appetite honed sharp by just the taste of ecstasy they'd shared. Glenna pressed closer, twining her fingers not altogether gently into the hair at the nape of his neck, as she found, at least temporarily, an outlet for her restlessness.

Yes, she was restless. And needy and all the other cravings she'd been denying for much too long. The yearning grasped at whatever morsel of satisfaction it could. And Reid gave every bit of himself over to it.

His ability to do so did—and didn't—surprise her. She'd guessed he was a man who found his fulfillment in seeing to others' needs. Not that he could only find happiness through them, but he was simply a person who cared, quite naturally, about the happiness of others.

How selfish of her always to take and take and take from this man, and give so little in return.

"No." Glenna shook her head, effectively breaking the kiss. "No, it's not...fair!"

Her voice was almost frantic, and he dropped his arms immediately, even as his gaze again held hers, the message clear—this they could do for each other, was what truly bound them together. They were prospective parents, yes. Man and wife, if only in name. But first there had been this between them.

Yet even if it wasn't just sexual attraction, Glenna thought desperately, it still wasn't everything it should be between them, either.

It took every bit of her strength to wrench her gaze from his. She simply couldn't meet his eyes. If he continued to look at her burningly, she knew she would shame herself again by finding whatever comfort she could in his embrace, and damn the consequences.

Looking for something, anything, to do, she switched off the typewriter, put its cover back on with trembling fingers.

"So. The accounts are reconciled," she prattled. "Honestly, I don't know how you managed on your own for so long. Of course, you probably relied on your wife to take care of you before—"

She could have cheerfully torn her tongue out and left it for carrion. Nothing like reminding Reid that *she* was his wife now, had "taken care" of things for them both for the rest of their lives.

Glenna was staring at the papers in front of her, sick at heart, when a large hand covered hers as it lay on the desktop.

"You *are* feeling poorly, aren't you?" Reid asked. "Your hands are like ice. Damn, Glenna, why do you work so hard?"

"It's my job," she protested lamely. "You yourself said that you needed someone to hold down the fort for you."

"That was if you were only an employee. But now you're my...my partner."

"Am I? We've never spoken again about my putting money into the business."

"Then let's do it," he said with a lift of his hand, as if he'd never been the one to object. "Let's draw up the paperwork and get goin' on the deal."

So at least she knew what she was to him—certainly more his partner than she could ever be his wife, but even that role Glenna doubted her rights to. And she knew the other reason she'd remained here tonight.

She dropped into the desk chair, thinking back to the conversation she'd listened in on between father and son. "What about Clan, Reid?" She made herself ask the question that had haunted her ever since that day.

"What about him?"

"I know you said once that he'd earned the right to come and go as he pleased, what with putting off his bull-riding career to help keep your horse-training operation going. But what about now?" She raised her eyes to his. "Are you sure he wouldn't like a little more responsibility in runnin' Piney Rise? To be your partner instead of me?"

"Why would he when he's at his busiest since he took up ridin' the bulls?" Reid asked with a little of the defensiveness she'd heard from him before when speaking of Clan.

"Maybe Clan's waiting for you to say something. Waitin' for you to offer some of what you've been so willin' to give me."

"If you feel you've got too much on your plate, all you've got to do is say the word, Glenna," he said. "I don't expect you to work as hard as you have been."

"I didn't say that!" So they were back to arguing. In her mind, it was better than the distance they'd kept from each other, even if this backlash of emotion was likely a result of the kiss they'd shared. But did she want to push Reid right now?

Glenna took a deep breath, which helped to calm her on more than one front, for her stomach had gone from churning to roiling—ominously so. "I just thought my being here might be causin' a rift between you and Clan.

And that it might be helped if you took the first step toward reconciling.''

The warmth left his expression completely as Reid slid his hip off the desk to turn away, taking a few steps toward the door before stopping. She got the feeling he would have liked to terminate all conversation by leaving. But he didn't. Very quietly he said, ''I appreciate your concern, Glenna, but I'm dealin' with Clan just fine. I don't tell you how to deal with Jamey, do I?''

''You have, though. And why not help each other with our grown children?'' Glenna chewed on the inside of her mouth, fighting back nausea and trying to concentrate. ''Look, Reid, I think you're right, to a certain extent, that we should let young people work out their problems for themselves, even if it's hard for us parents to let them. But I'm wonderin', if we *have* garnered some wisdom as a result of living, why not help your children avoid making some of the mistakes you made?''

''Glenna.'' Again the word held a mild note of warning, and she knew that for Reid to have issued this one, she had stepped over the line with him. But it was their old argument with each other, that basic division in outlook: he preferred never to look back, and she never to look forward. But that had changed now! And now it was different between them. They couldn't agree to disagree, because they shared common ground that neither of them could walk away from. She wanted so badly to talk to Reid about not the children already born and raised, but the little one on the way. That was the connection they shared that must be strengthened, for the sake of their child.

''Don't you wish *someone* would benefit from all the heartache you've gone through?'' she asked in complete exasperation.

At her question, he wheeled around, making her jump. ''Don't interfere, Glenna,'' he said fiercely. ''How I handle my son is between me and him. It's got nothin' to do with you, so just leave it."

She pushed out of the desk chair and faced him squarely. "All right. I won't point out that obviously there is a rift between you and Clan. But I will tell you, Reid Shelton, that when it comes to *our* child, I won't sit back and just let life happen to her. I'm through with living my own life that way, because I *do* try to learn from my mistakes!"

Suddenly her stomach revolted with a vengeance. Glenna shot out of the office in a panic, racing for the bathroom down the hall. She barely made it in time.

Dimly, she registered that Reid must have followed on her heels, for he held her head for her as she proceeded to empty the contents of her stomach into the toilet. When she'd finished throwing up, Glenna slumped against the bathroom wall, eyes closed in humiliation.

She heard the toilet flush and the lid turned down before she was unceremoniously hoisted up by her armpits and plunked on the commode. Reid filled a glass with water and pressed it into her hand.

"Go ahead and give your mouth a rinse," he commanded softly.

She obeyed, her embarrassment growing as she spit into the sink with a shudder and a mumbled "Ugh" afterward. She didn't have the will to look at Reid and so continued to sit, eyes closed and chin upon her chest. She did work up the gumption to apologize. "I'm sorry, Reid. I was never this bad with Jamey."

"Are you sick that often?" he asked gently.

She nodded. "Every morning and afternoon. But then, I'm discovering there're a lot of things about this pregnancy that're different from the first. I'm already retaining water like a camel. And my back aches." And the raging hormones that put her into an instant state of arousal when he was close. "Of course, what can I expect?" she asked ruefully. "I'm no spring chicken."

"Neither of us is, Glenna."

"Yes, and I bet two months ago you were thinkin' that now that Clan had gotten to a certain age, you were done with parenting. And here you are—" She wasn't about to tell him what she'd heard pass between him and his son. "Here you are havin' to deal with the prospect of at least a whole twenty years more of it. It can't be that much of a thrill."

The water ran again, then her chin was tugged upward as Reid, crouching in front of her, soothed a cool washcloth over her cheeks and forehead, his lashes lifting and lowering as his eyes followed the cloth's path.

"Isn't there something a doctor can give women these days to help the nausea?" he muttered, not addressing her remark. Which led her to believe he *had* rued that very situation. And for the life of her, she couldn't make herself press him any further than she already had. Not about their child.

It'll work out somehow, some time, she told herself. Don't force it.

"I think so, yes," she answered wearily.

"Then what's the reason you're puttin' yourself through this misery?"

To try to be of as little inconvenience to your life as possible, to make up for the complication I've brought it. And here she'd gone and started an argument. Why couldn't she let well enough alone?

"I—I suppose I could call my doctor and see what he recommends," she allowed. "Maybe when you go into Borger sometime next week, you could pick up a prescription."

"Why not drive yourself in tomorrow?"

"I don't have a way into town. Jamey and Kell are so busy right now, I hate to ask if they could bring the pickup over—"

The hand holding the washcloth dropped to her knee. "And I don't have a perfectly fine working vehicle sitting idle in the barn?" he asked with sudden impatience.

She stared at him in amazement. "That's your new pickup, Reid."

"It's a piece of machinery, Glenna!" Once again, his fierceness startled her.

"But you're so proud of it. It's your—" *Your baby.* She could see on his face he knew what she'd been about to say. He'd bought that truck as a way to ease into middle age, and here she was giving him a real baby to shoot that expectation all to hell.

Yes, the mistake had already been made.

"Look," Reid said firmly, "tomorrow mornin' we're goin' to Borger and get you something for this morning sickness. You'll drive, though, so you can get familiar with the truck and ask me any questions you need to about it. And, Glenna, you're never to consider that pickup my possession alone. Never to consider this pregnancy your burden to bear by yourself. Good God, I can't believe I didn't know how poorly you were feeling," he finished with disgust.

Continuing to frown pensively, he set his palms on his thighs and rose. He folded the washcloth and hung it on the rod. "Maybe you're right. Why shouldn't someone learn from our experience . . . our mistakes?"

"What do you mean?"

"I mean this arrangement is dangerous, at best." Eyebrows drawn together, he stared almost unseeingly at his hand resting on the towel rod. "What if you have an emergency when I'm on the road? You'd be here alone, with no way into town. I don't know why I didn't think of it sooner. I'm not going to have you bein' on this place by yourself. Or livin' out in that cottage alone.''

"What's the cottage got to do with anything?"

He finally looked at her. "Have you thought of how you'll manage out there when you're seven, eight, nine months along? Or afterward?"

He had a point, she thought as she protectively laid her palm on her abdomen. Was she, despite her resolve, putting her own concerns before this child's well-being? For she'd known the minute she'd stepped into that cottage two weeks ago she'd never be happy there. Not when she wanted more than anything to be with Reid in his house, in his bed, as it should be with a married couple. But intimacy of that sort, between two people who didn't love each other...not only was it wrong, it wouldn't make either of them any happier.

Would it?

"So what's the solution?" she asked.

That shock of black hair sprang out over his forehead as he ran his fingers through it. "I'll arrange for Bobby Ray to stay over on the weekends I'm away to shows—he can sleep in that room off the stable—and I'll move you into the house next week when I get back."

Glenna shook her head, steadying herself on the sink as she stood. "Reid, I already told you I don't expect to share your bed," she protested, surprised to hear her tone was almost panicked.

"And I heard you just fine." His hazel eyes glinted discerningly. "I'll take Clan's room. He's rarely home, but when he is, I'll sleep on a cot in the office."

"It would hardly be fair for me to make you roust yourself from place to place, like a wanderin' cowboy. Not in your own home."

"Damn it, Glenna, it's your home now, too! Just like it's our truck, our business, our bab—"

His fingers closed on the towel rod, knuckles turning white, and again she had the impression he would have given anything to leave. "I ask you, what kind of a man would I be if I didn't do everything within my power to take care of you?"

The pain in his voice went straight to her core. She raised her eyes to study his strong profile. He'd asked her that before, and she was freshly touched by what he was willing to endure for her sake, racked anew by the conviction that she did not deserve such consideration. But she wouldn't tell him that again, since this fine, upstanding man would continue to deny she had any reason not to expect that from him.

"I don't know, Reid. I just know I won't have you see me as someone who takes and takes, and gives little in return," she said softly but definitely. "At the very least, it isn't fair."

She realized the resemblance the tone of this conversation bore to the one they'd had by the Canadian Breaks the day their worlds had been torn asunder—and such fragile worlds they'd been, Glenna realized now. They had come apart as easily as tissue paper, only to be hastily patched back together just as flimsily as they worked out how to deal with this pregnancy.

Yes, she wanted to give more to Reid, a repayment of sorts for what he'd given her in this child. Give him at the very least her support, her comfort...

In the form of that sweet release they'd found in each other's arms?

But it had happened for all the wrong reasons! Glenna reminded herself vehemently. Sure, he'd made her feel as she never thought she would again—so young and alive— but she had no right to seek him out that way, not after she'd played him falsely once before because she hadn't truly known her own mind.

Yet if it had been some involuntary urge that had driven her before, why did she continue to want him even more intensely? Like now, with her stomach still feeling turned inside out, she had to physically restrain herself from reaching out and brushing his hair back, pulling his dark head down to her breast, taking him in her arms, into herself.

Wouldn't *that* be the very least they could do for each other?

"All right, Reid." Glenna finally relented. "I won't have you worrying about me, so I'll sleep here in the house. But I'll take the cot. It'll be more comfortable for me than you, even though I'll feel like I'm completely runnin' you out of your last refuge." And bringing her one step closer to intimacy with this man. "Maybe in a few months we can put the single bed from the cottage in the office. But for now I'd like to keep my things—my furniture and some of my clothes—at the other place."

Wrapping her arms about her middle, she met Reid's gaze and held it, and tried to believe, make him believe, she wasn't running again. But even if she convinced him, she would never be able to fool herself that she wasn't evading something. Someone. And this time it was him.

He marked her declaration with a nod of his head as he finally let go of the towel rod and turned to leave. Yet he paused at the door, hand on the knob.

"Glenna, I . . . I'm sorry for the way I spoke to you. About Clan," he said, his voice low. "After that, I know I don't have the right to ask what I'm about to, but I will. And that is . . . don't shut me out. Whatever you do."

He left without hearing her response, which Glenna whispered to herself. "I don't want to, Reid, truly I don't."

But how could she let him even an inch into her heart without him discovering how she had selfishly upended his future in order to secure her own?

Chapter Ten

Glenna awoke with a start, disoriented until she peered around the darkened room and remembered where she was. She lay on the cot in Reid's office, was still unused to being here, even though September loomed just around the corner. They'd been married a month. She was eight weeks into her pregnancy. And it had been too many nights to count since she'd slept straight through till morning.

Then she heard the back door open and close, quietly, and realized that a very real intrusion had woken her.

Someone was in the house.

Not truly alarmed, Glenna pushed back the covers, flicked on the lamp next to the cot and set her bare feet on the rug as she began considering who it could be. Bobby Ray would have knocked, even if some emergency had arisen. Reid had gone to a show and wasn't expected back till tomorrow night. Clan? The young man hadn't returned to the ranch in the entire time Glenna had lived here, and she doubted he'd make an appearance in the middle of the night. But if either of the men had had a reason to cut their competition short and come home, it wouldn't be a good one.

She rose and padded to the closed door, listening, palm automatically covering her abdomen. Sure enough, she heard footsteps head for the back of the house where lay both bedrooms.

Glenna opened the door and saw the light coming from the hallway around the corner. She took a few steps toward it.

"Reid?" she called softly. "Clan? Is everything okay?"

"It's me, Glenna," she heard Reid say. He came into view at the end of the hall. "Sorry to wake you. I was trying to be quiet."

"Th-that's all right." The light was dim, but she could see he'd already started getting ready for bed, for his shirt was untucked and unbuttoned, and hung open to reveal his chest, shadowed with dark hair.

"You weren't supposed to be back until tomorrow afternoon," she continued a trifle worriedly. The finals for some of the classes could go late into the evening, and so he usually booked a room for that night and drove back the next day.

"I know. I...finished early."

"You mean one of the horses didn't make it past the prelims?" she asked, rather surprised. She'd learned Reid rarely failed to reach the finals. Then her concern deepened even more when she saw his reaction to her question. She'd never seen him look so haggard.

She took a step toward him. "What's happened, Reid?"

He sighed. "Nothing earth-shattering. Go back to bed, Glenna. I'll tell you in the morning."

She took a few more steps closer. "No, tell me now or I'll get even less sleep than I already am."

"I told you that if the cot was uncomfortable to sleep in my bed," he countered pointedly.

"Don't change the subject." Now she sighed. "Reid, I don't want to argue with you." She leaned her forearm against the wall and studied the hand spread on its surface. "Doesn't it work both ways?" she asked softly.

"What works both ways?"

"You asking me not to shut you out."

Out of the corner of her eye she saw him drop his chin, push back the tail of his shirt to hook his index finger in his belt loop, as he was wont to do when thinking. Even peripherally, she could see he'd gotten further undressed than she'd previously noted, for he'd removed his belt. The top button on his jeans lay undone and open, revealing a firmly muscled stomach.

Resting her forehead against the back of her hand, Glenna closed her eyes. She wanted to provide Reid with emotional comfort, not physical, she admonished herself.

"It's Doc," he finally said.

She looked up. "The Wilkersons' stallion?"

"Yes. I had to withdraw him from competition."

"Why?"

He hesitated, and Glenna knew she might never again see him look so shaken. "He...he foundered. Acute laminitis."

Her hand covered her mouth as she gasped involuntarily. "Oh, no, Reid."

"'Fraid so." He rubbed his forehead, as if massaging away a headache. "I noticed it first thing when I got to his stall at the arena on Friday morning, and had the show veterinarian treat him. I think we were able to avert any permanent damage to Doc's feet. I stayed with him through yesterday to this afternoon, when the vet said he might be able to travel. I've already called our regular vet to come out first thing tomorrow and check him over."

He sighed, and Glenna knew he must feel the weight of the world on his shoulders right now. "I'm glad the haul home was relatively short," he continued, almost to himself, "even if I made sure the floor of the trailer was padded to within an inch of its life. I wouldn't have risked it, but Doc seemed to know what was goin' on, and somehow I knew he wanted to be here rather than with strangers."

His voice dropped to a whisper. "He's a champ, that one."

"Will he show again?"

"The show vet said probably so. But it was close. So damned close."

"How do you think it happened, Reid?" she asked. There were many ways a horse could contract laminitis, and the particular circumstances of each instance—how and when and how much—greatly influenced the animal's recovery.

"It was water founder. The day before I left, I'd worked Doc, since he hauls easier and performs better if he's gotten some of the P and V out of him beforehand. When I brought him into the stable I was in a hurry and told Bobby Ray to water the stallion and rub him down. Bobby Ray must have let him drink all he wanted rather than walking him out first to cool down."

He stood deathly still for a moment, then in a blur of motion his fist shot out and struck the wall, making Glenna jump back a foot.

"Damn it!" he said from between clenched teeth. "How could I have been so careless?"

"But it was Bobby Ray's fault—"

"No, it was my fault! Those horses are my responsibility! It's my job to see to their needs and take care of them."

His vehemence, once again, surprised her, but she understood his distress. Having a horse founder was not the kind of thing that would destroy a trainer's reputation, though it certainly did it no good. More than that, though, was dealing with the fear of a fine animal's productive years being cut short; that one might have had a hand in such misfortune through neglect of some sort would consume a man such as Reid. She knew the pride he took in his work, the attention and care he gave to each one of the horses entrusted to him. And his clients were right to consign their prized possessions to his custody.

How could she help him recognize that right now?

"Come into the office and sit down," Glenna instructed briskly. When Reid made no move to cooperate, she closed the space between them and took his arm, pulling him along as she returned to the office. She pushed him gently into the desk chair as she went to the cupboard in the far wall and retrieved the bottle of whiskey she'd found there once she got around to organizing that corner of the room. She wasn't a drinker herself, but she knew the value of a medicinal shot of liquor now and then, especially on an isolated ranch where proper medical attention was over fifty miles away.

Taking her water glass, she poured him a healthy shot, which he threw back handily then stared at the resulting emptiness.

"Have you told the Wilkersons?" Glenna asked, knowing the horse's owners hadn't attended the show.

"I called them right away. They said that they trusted me to do whatever I thought best."

"And so you have and will. *We* will." She knelt in front of him, wanting so badly to reach out to him right now. "It won't happen again, Reid. I promise you. You're a *good* horse trainer, totally competent and dependable," she told him emphatically. "Don't ever doubt it. And now that you've got me to help so you can concentrate solely on seeing to the horses' needs, you'll be even better. We're in this together, remember?''

''No, Glenna. Not this.'' He wouldn't meet her eyes. ''I've no one to blame but myself for this development.''

''What nonsense. Are we truly partners or not?''

He paused before asking, ever so quietly, ''Are we?''

''Yes,'' she vowed without hesitation. ''It's the way it has to be if Piney Rise is to survive. If *we're* to survive.''

Yes, it had to start with them, or neither of their futures would ever be realized.

And so Glenna did what she had been wanting to do, needing to do, dying to do, for ages: she reached up, fingers spread, and dragged them backward through that thick, black shock of hair. The cool silkiness of it sent a purely sexual charge to the center of her abdomen as she buried her fingers in his nape. Reid's lashes lifted, and he looked down at her, hazel eyes kindling with fire, just as she had imagined they would do. Just as she had dreamed.

His gaze slid over her, and it was only then that she realized she wore only a thin cotton nightgown that hid very little of her body.

He swallowed but didn't look away.

''*Glenna,*'' he said hoarsely. The word held that mild note of warning she'd heard before. It told her she'd stepped over a line with him. Perhaps she had, one across which she could never look back, only forward, as he had always wanted her to do. But even though they still maintained those separate views, it was different between them. They shared common ground that neither of them could walk away from.

She'd always known they had too much in common to turn away without regret for what might have been.

Wordlessly she tugged at the back of his neck as she raised her chin, and he needed no further encouragement as he covered her open mouth with his. His hands, hot as brands through the thin material, encircled her waist and brought her between his legs as he slid forward in the chair. Brought her flush against the cradle of his desire. Of both their desires.

He kissed her as a man desperate for breath. The air left her lungs, given to him readily, for she didn't need it as much as she needed this feverish, urgent melding of lips and tongues. Her free hand slid under his shirt, found the warm, heated skin of his chest, and she was instantly aroused, liquid with her passion for this man. And she could feel every contour of his hunger for her against her swollen abdomen. Swollen because of him. Because of her.

They both pulled back, ever so slightly, breath mingling, hearts thundering, eyes wide and wondering as two adolescents sharing their first kiss. Then he muttered an oath that was lost when he took her lips again, roughly, in a way that was age-old with experience, ripe and fully developed as the whiskey she tasted on his tongue.

"Please," she whispered against his mouth. "Oh, please, Reid."

His fingers clenched in her hair as he held her away from him and peered into her face. "Are you sure?" he asked, just as he had when she told him she carried his child. But she knew what he meant this time. It wouldn't be just for tonight. If she came to his bed, she'd stay there. Permanently. And she would be his wife, truly. "What do you want from me, Glenna?"

He waited, gaze keen on hers as if watching for the slightest, even involuntary, reaction to reinforce or belie any words she might say. And Glenna knew she must say the words. Nothing must be implied tonight.

"Take me, Reid," she whispered. She was still unable to say, *Make love to me.* Frightened to death to ask that of him if that wasn't what *he* wanted. Or having given it, what he might expect in return. No, it wouldn't be just sex, even if it still wasn't quite everything this act of intimacy should be between two people.

But it just might be enough.

And it was, apparently, for at her words Reid rose, swept her up as if she weighed no more than a child. He paused, though, looking down at her in the pale light, eyes glittering. "Your bed," he asked huskily, "or ours?"

"Ours," Glenna murmured.

He kissed her again, hard, then strode past the cot where she would have slept that night. Or not slept but lain in restlessness to know he was so close, and yet so far away. But he wasn't far away. He was with her now. And now, not yesterday or tomorrow, was what mattered.

In his room Reid laid her gently on the bed, then sat to tug his boots off. "The rest is easy," he told her.

And mesmerizing. She watched as he peeled out of his shirt, his jeans, his briefs, and then he took her hands to pull her to her feet for her turn. He laid his palms flat against the outsides of her thighs as he kissed her behind her ear, a nuzzling downward to her throat as he inched her gown upward, past her hips, her torso. Over her breasts, her arms, her head to sweep it completely off, leaving them standing face-to-face, chest-to-chest, naked as the day they were born.

Though she was dying to peruse all of him, she was glad for his closeness and the dark that prevented him from taking stock of her own body. Her pregnancy had already changed it, even in a few months, bringing a fullness to her hips and abdomen she knew only hinted at what would come. How would she look, she wondered, forty two and heavily pregnant? Would it age her, wear down this older body of hers that wasn't used to having such physical stresses placed upon it, didn't have the resilience to bounce back once she was through bearing this child? Would Reid want her then?

Lord, she wanted to hide.

Instinctively, she crossed her arms in front of her, but Reid had already turned away. He went to the window to lower the shade, and she got her wish as he was silhouetted against the faint glow streaming in from the yard light. Her insecurity forgotten, Glenna drew in a quick breath, sinking back on the bed, for he was splendid. Lean of hip and thigh, firm of belly, and broad of shoulder and chest, as perfectly formed as a sculpture. No one would ever think without knowing as fact that Reid Shelton was forty-six years old. He looked in his prime—which he was, she realized.

He must have been able to see something of her, or at least of her expression, for Reid suddenly crossed to her. Surprising herself, Glenna leaned back on her elbows, no longer uneasy but inviting. His gaze swept down, then upward, and for the first time she was glad of the fire that rose up in her, for she knew it would be met and driven higher.

He set one knee on the bed next to her hip and placed his hands, arms locked, on the mattress on either side of her. "I want to make you feel good, Glenna," he murmured. "I want to know I can do this for you."

Then his arms bowed as he bent his head and stroked his tongue across one nipple.

Glenna sucked in her breath. She'd known her breasts had grown sensitive, but she was undone with how incredible it felt to have him touch her there. She couldn't have held back her reaction if the hounds of hell were after her; she arched her spine almost painfully as her hands came up to dig her fingers into his hair and pull him against her. Reid obliged her, taking the whole of her nipple into his mouth as he lowered himself on top of her.

Through a sensual haze she felt him kiss her, caress her, touch her everywhere. Except the slight roundness of her abdomen.

That didn't stop her from exploring his body just as thoroughly, sliding her fingers across his wide shoulders, down his stomach and up again to bury in the mat of hair on his chest. Too restless to remain there, her hands roved bumpily over his ribs, then downward to flatten against his firm flanks, warm and slightly damp from exertion. She'd warned him once not to compare her to a high-spirited mare, yet she couldn't help thinking how he himself was so like the animals he trained, with the heart of a champion, the wildest and strongest of hearts, which required the most intuitive of talents to ensure that spirit wouldn't be damaged in one's quest to bring it to fruition.

She would not break this man's heart so, Glenna silently vowed. It would be the greatest travesty of all.

And yet she was more frantic than she'd been that evening over two months ago when she had practically thrown herself at him. How could she want to join with him more now than she had then, when she'd been driven by some subconscious need to hold on to her youth?

It wasn't just her, though. Both of them were as out of control as a couple of unseasoned adolescents carried on a wave of pure sexual instinct. Except there was a world of difference with Reid and Glenna. Unlike two callow youths, they knew what was in store for them, and it would be an affirmation of life of a different kind. For they had both the wisdom and experience lacking in youth, while still having a good portion of its energy and vigor, to make the most of this experience.

This was what middle age was all about, Glenna decided, filled with joy at the discovery.

"Please," she begged as she had before, straining beneath him, opening to him. With a deep groan he slid inside her, filling her as he had already filled her with this sweet hope of a child. And for the first time in a very, very long while, Glenna did not feel empty. Or alone.

Her throat tightened perilously, and she flung her arms about him, fingers digging into his shoulders as she tried to hide the tears that would not be stopped. They slipped down her temples and dampened her hair. And dampened Reid's cheek, pressed against hers.

He raised his head, his expression stricken. "God, Glenna, am I hurting you?" He began to pull out.

"No!" She held him with a leg wrapped around the back of his thigh. "No," she assured him, sniffing as she smoothed the back of her hand down his cheek, drying it. Wondering at how being with Reid, here and now, could feel so right. She simply wasn't the kind of woman to give herself time and again to a man with whom she was not of one accord. Of one heart. "I'm just... Oh, it just feels so good to be with you this way!"

"Believe me, I've wanted so badly to give you this kind of pleasure."

He kissed her with such tenderness it brought more tears to her eyes. "I—I'm sorry," she apologized between kisses and hiccups. "You must think I'm the cryingest woman in the world."

"No," he contradicted throatily. "No, I think you're the most passionate woman in the world."

He moved within her, deeply, bringing her home with each stroke, bringing them both home, until they were truly moving as one, in total partnership. Everything that was wrong in the world—in *their* world—seemed temporarily righted as together they rode out this stormy stretch of road, taking each other faster and harder and higher, until Glenna stiffened, rigid with exquisite anticipation, pounding with a powerful longing she dared not even wish to satisfy.

Reid held, too, his right hand lacing tightly with her left as he pressed it to the mattress beside her head in a wordless plea to make this moment the most and best it could be for both of them, even if neither of them could say it out loud.

Then he stroked into her one more time as they both came apart, shattering and scattering like a million, billion points of light flung up against the velvet backdrop of one perfect night, one endless moment.

One. Together. For now.

Reid didn't sleep, and he knew Glenna didn't, either. They simply lay silently, her head pressed to his shoulder, his arm cradling hers, his other hand spread possessively on her hip, holding her against him. It was as if they were afraid that any words, any separation would cool the intimacy they felt—craved—right now. Because, Reid thought, it would ebb as soon as they separated. It was just how life and loving were. Yet such was life, too, that that's when the doubts crept in.

As if to refute the fact, Reid said, his lips against Glenna's temple as he held her, "So it's decided. You're sleepin' in this bed from now on, even when I'm gone."

"Yes," she said, soft but definite. As always.

"And you're to consider this house yours. All of it. I want you to feel you can do what you want to change it to your liking, just as with the cottage."

He didn't mention moving her things over from the little house, and he wouldn't, not yet. He didn't want to press her, would take his time, having learned that was the best way to handle her, even if he still wasn't sure what she might want. Maybe she wasn't sure herself, and that's how they'd both failed so far. He knew in horse training a vital element to one's success was knowing from the first what one wanted from the animal placed in one's care.

But Glenna was no skittish filly. And he'd be a fool to treat her like one.

So how did a man handle a woman? A snippet of a song popped into his head from out of nowhere. It was from an old musical, he realized, that he'd watched on TV late one night with Miranda, who hadn't been able to sleep. It had been only a few weeks before she died. He'd been so worried about her, it surprised him anything had sunk in. Yet apparently some part of the plot or theme had remained with him, for he recalled the lines from a song: how to handle a woman was to love her. Simply love her.

Had he not tried that already? And it hadn't worked.

On reflex, Reid clasped the soft body in his arms closer to him, and Glenna responded by curling her fingers into the hair on his chest and sliding the inside of her thigh up the front of his. Oh, she was so responsive. So passionate. So needful. Him, too, as he grew instantly aroused, wanting to be inside her again almost desperately.

At least they could have this.

Would it be enough, though, for Glenna? Because Reid knew right now that it wasn't enough for him. Not by a mile. He wanted more—from her. From himself— for her. And he knew then that he'd subconsciously held such an aim from the first, despite his resolve that he would not make the mistake again of trying to meet this woman's every need.

What was the fatal flaw in him that made him feel he must act so? But she just naturally made him want to, this impassioned spirit who refused to be shut out, who demanded they meet together whatever trials lay ahead of them, who vowed she'd not let life just happen to her or to their child.

Yet even as he tugged Glenna's chin up so he could cover her mouth with his, slid his hand from her hip to caress her full breast and experience the satisfaction of her immediate response, even as he made sweet, passionate love to her, Reid wondered how he could be any different than he was. How could he not protect and take care of . . . and cherish . . . this woman, his wife?

It was impossible. Impossible as roping the moon.

Chapter Eleven

He felt like a kid again, green as a spring day. On the road in his brand-new dually, hauling two of his best cutting horses in the gooseneck trailer behind. Most of all with his wife at his side. And the whole experience felt damn good.

"Comfy?" Reid asked Glenna as he downshifted to make it up a hill. The pickup took the incline like a pro.

"Just fine," she answered.

"Now, you let me know if you need to make a pit stop or you start feelin' the least bit queasy."

"I will, but the mornin' sickness has calmed down quite a bit in the past few weeks. I think Jamey's method of eatin' two soda crackers before you even get out of bed in the morning and never lettin' your stomach get empty during the day does the trick."

Glenna had seen her doctor, as the two of them had discussed, and had ultimately decided against taking something for her nausea. Reid discovered she was quite stubbornly protective when it came to their child, the thought of which brought an unexpected fullness to his chest.

"Jamey's actually had a worse time of it than I have," Glenna went on. "She told me the other day she still won't let Kell or the hands so much as clear their throats in her hearing. And you know the way Charley and Purdy hawk and caw like two old crows—" She shuddered. "Odors always get me. Thank God I don't have to deal with a bunch of hands comin' in from doin' the chores smelling like a feedlot. I didn't tell Jamey that, because sometimes the mere suggestion is enough to set you off."

Reid gave a chuckle before sobering. "Sounds like you and Jamey have been gettin' closer to each other since you're not in each other's back pockets any longer."

"Yes, havin' a baby does have a tendency to bring women together, no matter the years between them," she acknowledged softly.

"I'm glad the distance between y'all hasn't affected your relationship."

"Mmm," Glenna said. Chin down, she tucked a lock of hair behind her ear, transporting Reid back to the afternoon when they'd talked of departed spouses and growing older, of adult daughters and sons... and babies.

Funny, to think that the relationship between him and Glenna had begun so much by chance, that neither of them would be here today had he not happened upon her on that lonesome stretch of road.

He shook his head, not relishing the prospect. "Well, if the move to Piney Rise had anything to do with strengthening relations with Jamey, then I'm glad."

"But what about the relationship between you and Clan?"

"God, I forgot. There's 7-Up in the cooler on the back seat. And plenty of soda crackers in the sack on the floor." He baldly changed the subject. He simply wasn't going to let anything spoil this day. "Don't hesitate to make use of 'em if the motion of the truck starts to get to you."

Glenna raised her eyebrows. "I wouldn't dream of gettin' crumbs on your seats. I'd rather brave a sick stomach."

"Lady, the last thing I'd do is kick you out of my pickup, or my bed, for eatin' crackers." He winked. "Especially when they've been one and the same."

She gave him a long look that took them both back to the night they'd made love on the back seat. Once, he would have balked at making any reference to that episode. That mistake. But now he was somehow glad to have certain moments with this woman that the two of them alone had shared, theirs alone to remember.

"Seems someone else besides Doc gets full of P and V before a show," she commented primly, speaking of the stallion who was recovering nicely from his ailment. Another reason Reid was feeling particularly fine today.

"Yeah, it's a good thing I got a workout last night or I'd be unlivable today."

Glenna blushed but didn't hide the shy, sexy smile that warmed him all over, yet another thing that made him feel like a kid of twenty again. He was finding it incredibly hard to keep his hands off her for even one minute. It wasn't just sex, he told himself. It might never have been just sex between them.

A week and a half had passed since he and Glenna had slept together the first time. They'd done so every night he'd been home, although it wasn't sleeping he fantasized about every minute of the day. Leaving her to attend last weekend's show had been an absolute hell. At least for Reid; he hadn't the nerve to ask Glenna if she felt the same way. They were both still too new with each other, too vulnerable. Too naked. Yet he could tell she liked being with him. An almost physical wall between them had toppled. Two people didn't share their bodies so intimately without them learning a little about how the other's mind worked. Without growing closer.

And in their totally unique way of doing everything bass-ackwards, he'd spent days screwing up his courage, like a bashful cowpoke at the county dance, to ask her if she wanted to accompany him to a cutting show in the hill country of central Texas. She'd have the pickup to come and go as she pleased. Drive to Austin and see the sights. Do a little shopping. Or she could stay around the arena with him, maybe meet some of their clients. Maybe have them meet his wife.

Damn, but he was in deep.

Pull back, warned a cautious voice. But it seemed more impossible each day.

"We should be getting to the equestrian center west of Brenham around four or five. I figured we'd get the horses settled and pick up our numbers before checking in to our hotel." He shot her a glance. "We do have a room reserved, don't we? I just assumed you made arrangements, but I should have asked."

"It's taken care of. In fact, Sonny Wescott recommended a place we could stay, even went ahead and booked the reservation."

"He did?" Reid was surprised. Sonny was a good friend as well as a client, but he was even less a detail man than Reid, sometimes bunking with Reid if places were booked up and he couldn't find last-minute accommodations. "Where're we staying?"

Ever organized, Glenna pulled a file folder from the canvas bag at her feet and flipped through it. "It's the Hearts o' Plenty Inn."

Now Reid wasn't surprised. Sonny Wescott was also a bit of a practical joker. "Oh, really?" he said inanely.

She glanced up. "Have you stayed there before?"

"No-oo, can't say as I have."

"Sonny said we'd like it. In fact, he told me he'd already taken care of the bill. A belated wedding present, he said." She replaced the folder in her bag. "I hope that's all right with you."

"I hope it's all right with *you*," Reid said without thinking.

Glenna looked at him with a tinge of apprehension in her eyes. "Is there something wrong with the place? I mean, I had a hotel booked when Sonny called me with the information on this inn just a few days ago. What if this Hearts o' Plenty Inn isn't very nice? You should have a clean, well-kept room to come back to after working hard all day." She sighed. "Somethin' told me I shouldn't have let our reservations go."

How could a woman being conscientious and scrupulous arouse him so? Reid wondered as he gave in to his need to have physical contact with her and reached over to give her hand a squeeze. Her slim fingers laced with his as if they were made to.

"I imagine the Hearts o' Plenty will have all the amenities we could desire," he said cryptically. *And then some.*

He couldn't wait to get there.

Reid unlocked the door to their hotel room and motioned for Glenna to go ahead of him, which she did.

She gasped. He grinned.

Pushing the door closed with his heel, he set down the bags and had a look around of his own. He had to admit it would be a shock to the unsuspecting party.

The room was a veritable lair of seduction, with a heart-shaped bed the approximate size of a football field eclipsing every other piece of furniture. Off in one corner sat a huge bathtub, big enough for two water buffalo to slip-slide around in, let alone two people.

Hearts seemed to be the dominant theme throughout the room, hence the name of the inn, Reid discerned. Setting the mood seemed to be another theme, with a soft, gauzy glow coming from the tassel-shaded lamps on either side of the bed and the low sound of romantic music issuing from a speaker in the wall. The room lacked any windows, and he guessed that the intent was much the same as with the casinos in Vegas: one was to forget about whether it was night or day outside, or any passage of time, allowing a couple to immerse themselves in the here and now of this place and moment.

Which would have been a real trick not to do, what with the sensory overload of red velvet and black satin everywhere, as well as more mirrors than in a sideshow magician's act. There was even a mirror on the ceiling. Or, more accurately, a mirror *was* the ceiling.

Glenna stood gazing pensively up at it.

"Reid Shelton," she said reproachfully. "Just what kind of a woman does Sonny Wescott think I am?"

"What I've told him, I'm sure."

"Which is?"

"That you're the prettiest and smartest wife a man could have. I didn't say sexy but I think he must've figured it out or we wouldn't be standin' here right now." He added softly, "Sonny knows without a doubt that I married a real lady."

"Oh." She blushed abashedly, and somehow Reid found the willpower—just barely—not to pull her down on the bed and take her swiftly and fiercely.

Instead, he leaned against the wall and watched her as she took a turn around, just as she had the evening he'd shown her the cottage for the first time.

"Do you like it?" he asked. "That is, as a den of in-iquity rather than a decorating scheme?"

"I don't know what to think." She still looked rather taken aback, almost as if she wondered just what kind of folks this cutting-horse set included.

He ambled over to her, sliding his arms around her from behind. "I did mention to Sonny that we hadn't had a honeymoon. Of course, he asked me point-blank, and I try not to lie to my clients." Nuzzling her neck, he murmured, "I didn't tell him we never had a wedding night. That's just between you and me."

He turned her in his embrace and kissed her with small, moist strokes of his tongue over her lower lip. "How about a real wedding night now?" he whispered against her mouth.

Quickening instantly to his touch, as he'd found she always did, Glenna made that ambiguous "mmm" sound, which Reid had no trouble interpreting at this moment. He crushed her against him with a hot, unbri-dled urgency that had been straining in him for hours, and sealed her mouth with his.

Yet as he lowered her tenderly to the bed he was deter-mined the seduction would be not swift and fierce but slow and sweet. The cool, slick satin shimmied around them. It would be heaven against bare skin, would grow quickly warm from the friction of their two bodies twin-ing upon it.

He reached for the buttons on the front of her dress, trailing kisses down the area exposed. He'd undone only a few when her hand covered his, halting his progress.

Reid looked up. "What is it, darlin'?"

Her gray eyes were filled with painful shyness. "It's this room. I mean...I'm really pretty conventional, Reid."

"Oh?" Affecting vast disappointment, he rolled across the bed to pick up the telephone, punching random buttons before saying, "Yes, Acme Circus Supplies? Tell the boys not to bring up that trapeze I ordered for Room 10. Thanks."

He replaced the receiver as Glenna stared at him, then broke out in laughter. She made to punch him in the arm but he caught her hand and dragged her on top of him.

"Don't worry 'bout being bashful. It's just us two," he said huskily.

"I know." She plucked at his collar, avoiding his eyes. "But I'm . . . pregnant. At forty-two. And like I said before, I'm no spring chicken—"

He was about to ask what in tarnation that had to do with the situation when he glanced up at the ceiling and caught a glimpse of the view Glenna had had a second ago: the reflection of them tangled together on the bed. Once they were naked, every inch of them both would be exposed to sight.

"Glenna." He took her face between his hands. "Does this mean when you look at me you see some washed-up old cowboy? Because I'm even older than you. Do you look at me in my reading glasses and think, Good Lord, how did I ever end up with this old coot?"

"No, of course not," she flared, then whispered achingly, "It's just that this room is made for two people who really know each other. Trust each other—"

Love each other. And then he knew what she wanted. Knew, as he had the evening of her birthday, what he could do for this woman.

"I have an idea," he said tenderly. "Let's leave the lights on, and I promise I won't look. But you can, all you want, or not at all. I won't know either way."

Without waiting for her assent, he swung his legs over the side of the bed to sit with his back to her. He tugged off his boots, then rose and began unbuttoning his shirt. True to his word, he refrained from looking at her as he shrugged out of it and tossed it on a nearby chair.

Reid paused, his hand on the snap of his jeans. He knew he was no beefcake, but he was in pretty good shape for a man his age. His work kept him fit, and he'd always tended toward lean rather than brawn, which could easily go to fat in one's later years. Still, he *was* no spring chicken, and he experienced a twinge of the vulnerability he'd seen in Glenna's eyes. Of being exposed, certainly, with every scar of his youth bared for examination, yet also of his need being exposed. Of wanting too much and dealing with the resulting disappointment. But still being so very, very needy.

Reid unzipped his fly and swept both jeans and briefs off in one movement. He turned to face her, knowing she would see beyond a doubt how much he wanted her, how that need was not something he could control or deny. He couldn't have looked into her eyes at that moment even if he'd had the right to, and he understood her more completely then than he ever had in the past. Understood himself, too, as it struck him how far he was willing to go for this woman.

He dropped to the bed, lying on his side, and pulled her across the slick surface so that she lay on her back against the length of him as he concentrated on taking off her clothes. Luckily, what she wore was easily removable—a crinkly floral print dress with pearly buttons all the way down the front. It was a modest dress, loose and free flowing, yet he found it as sexy as anything he'd ever seen her in. He almost told her she looked like a girl of twenty in it, untouched and irresistible as a rose in the bud—which he wanted to gather to him while he may—but he had a feeling now was not the time for such words. She mustn't think he couldn't desire her for exactly who she was: forty-two, a grandmother, pregnant. His wife.

He undid each button and parted the sides of the material. By touch he determined that beneath the dress she wore underwear frilled in soft lace. Aroused beyond measure, he stroked one hand over the flare of her hip, across her ribs and up to cup one lace-covered breast, knowing she would see everything he did. And he knew that Glenna was looking. He could just tell somehow, with some instinct. Reid wanted her to comprehend what he saw when *he* looked at her, a beautiful woman at the peak of her allure. He didn't have to open his eyes to know that was what he'd find.

Rising up on one elbow, he kissed the breast resting in his palm before taking her nipple between his lips. She surged against him, and he couldn't resist pulling her deeper into his mouth as he stroked his thumb over her other nipple. He loved the incoherent sounds she made, the way she clutched at his shoulders, buried her fingers in his hair to bring him closer to her. Quickly divesting her of every scrap of clothing, he wedged one leg between her knees as she drew them up toward her chest, which rocked them together and brought his thigh into contact with the softest part of her.

He could have gone on forever kindling her passion, but something told him Glenna had closed her eyes. He gave her breast one last kiss before settling back down beside her, affording them a minute to catch their breaths, although his hand continued to roam over her. Because he wanted her to watch a while longer. He wanted her to see how they could be partners in a way that had nothing to do with sex and everything to do with trust. And maybe, perhaps, with love.

Caught up in pleasuring her, Reid inadvertently passed his hand over her slightly rounded abdomen, and it caused him to pull back a bit in his actions and thoughts before he swept his palm around to the small of her back and turned her to him, not wanting, as before, anything to intrude upon this moment. Yet he couldn't help pondering: did she think because he never touched her there that he was somehow repulsed by her swollen belly?

It wasn't that, not at all. But Reid didn't tell her that, either, because then he would have to explain the reasons he hesitated to lay his palm, as he'd seen her do so often, upon that tangible evidence of a living being growing inside her. Up to now he had refrained from thinking too hard about the baby Glenna carried. He thought about her and the pregnancy, certainly, but he had yet to conceive of a baby in real terms. And he knew it was because he didn't want to dwell on the circumstances that had brought it into being. Brought them, him and Glenna, together, and yet, conversely, would always be there between them.

Because without this child, there would be no "them" at all.

It didn't matter! he told himself, crushing her breasts to his chest as he kissed her deeply, urgently. Not now, not here. This was the present, the one point of time he had some control over as he had no control over the past or the future. And he wanted to make it the best it could be. Make it last as long as it could. Because he knew, even if he was able to fulfill her here in bed, some other need in Glenna was still going unmet. Every time he looked at her, he could see it in the back of her soulful gray eyes.

Yet this *was* their moment.

With loving hands and lips Reid caressed his wife, knowing her in that physical yet most spiritual of senses as he covered her and slid into her. And touched her most intimately...almost touching the child that was a part of her.

He rose on one elbow so he could see Glenna's face. "Open your eyes," he commanded, his voice rough-edged.

Her lids drifted open to reveal eyes glazed over with passion, and they shut almost immediately as he moved within her.

"No," he pleaded raggedly. "Look at me! Please. Don't shut me out, Glenna. Not now."

Her lashes fluttered with the effort to do as he bid, even as he continued to drive them both higher. Then her eyes, clear and steady, met his. He held her gaze, seized upon it as he would a beacon in a storm, needing to in order to give her as good as he asked for.

Then the storm hit, its waves crashing around them with the force of a hurricane, tossing them about as if they had no more control over their actions...over their fate...than two matchstick figures.

And as Reid floated back down to earth, he knew that he and Glenna had just created something nearly as precious as a child. They had created a memory that would live within them both and, hopefully, bind them together for all time. He knew, too, that the more such experiences they shared, the better equipped he and Glenna would be to deal with whatever else life threw at them. No guarantees, of course.

But maybe, just maybe, this time it'd be enough.

"Sonny Wescott," Reid announced, "must be a mind reader."

He lay on his back, one hand behind his head, Glenna snuggled against his side, and stared unabashedly up at their reflection in the mirrored ceiling. He'd pulled the red satin coverlet over them as they lay in their heart-shaped bed, and he thought the picture they made looked like nothing so much as a living, breathing valentine.

"Are you going to tell Sonny that?" Glenna asked drowsily, apparently not half as worried about outside opinion as she'd been an hour ago.

"I would never say a word about such a private matter." He wondered, though, whether he'd be able to keep the telltale grin off his face.

"Mmm. We should do something to thank him for his thoughtfulness, I guess. I just can't think of what would be appropriate."

"Yeah, somehow a fruit basket just doesn't seem to strike the right chord."

Glenna actually giggled, then she pulled herself up on one elbow, revealing a tantalizing swatch of breast. "What time is it, anyway? We're supposed to meet the Wilkersons at the equestrian center and go from there to dinner."

"Oh, right. And I need to check on the horses. It always takes Solly some time to settle in. He gets a little nervous before shows."

Reid reached for his watch and squinted at it in the gauzy light. Finally he handed it to Glenna with a, "Shoot, you know my eyes. What's it say?"

"We've got plenty of time." She settled back down beside him, and his eyelids drifted closed as he savored the feel of her.

"Reid," she said a few minutes later, "do you ever get nervous about performing?"

His eyes popped open. "Beg pardon?"

"Do you ever get nervous about showin' your horses?"

"Oh. No. Well, maybe a little. I'm anxious for the horse to do its best, and not just so's to get me into the finals."

"What do you mean?"

Idly, he rubbed a thumb across his collarbone. "A horse can tell when it's doin' well, which helps build its confidence in itself—and in me. Because it can tell, too, when I'm doin' good by it, givin' it the direction and purpose it needs to bring it to its full potential. Y'see, I'm not failin' my client when I'm unable to do that. I'm failin' the horse, and that's darn near a crime. You do an animal that way, it eats into the trust you've fostered along. So every time I get on a horse, whether in competition or not, my aim is to make that experience one that brings me and that animal a little bit closer in spirit, because that's what's going to make champions of us both.''

Glenna again pushed up onto her elbow. Laying a supporting palm on his chest, she regarded him gravely. "Is that how you see us, Reid? Is that how you...handle me?''

Oh, she was smart, as he'd told her. She knew that, when at a loss for how to handle not her but the relationship between them, he fell back on his horse-training skills.

He met her gaze straightforwardly. "No," he answered, "I'd be a fool to do that, wouldn't I? But one of the first things I learned, years ago, was to be a partner, more than a taskmaster or a passenger, with an animal. You need to give yourself over to it, lose your ego, become one with it. Until you do that, you won't know the kind of peace a good relationship with a horse creates...a harmony that helps you sort of separate yourself from your frustration and disappointment with all the pain and stupidity in the world—''

He realized he was preaching, which, he knew from experience, didn't work with Glenna—or anyone else for that matter, he'd wager. But this particular outlook was not one he felt he had to sell to anyone, including himself. Rather, it had become a part of him, this means of achieving connection with more than another being, but a connection with himself, and with his place and purpose on this earth.

"Is it so wrong," he went on softly, drawing one finger along her jawline, "to apply some of the lessons I've learned over the years to other areas of my life? To the people in my life?''

Glenna continued to study him solemnly. Then she answered, "No, it's not wrong at all, especially if it does bring you understanding. And peace."

She *was* smart, and he was so damned in love with her.

Then she smiled bashfully as she confessed, "I think I already knew the answers to my questions. Many an afternoon I've found myself at the window watching you work different horses, from the greenest to the most experienced. You never let up, never stop asking each animal for its all, even in practice. But you never stop givin' your all right back."

Scooting higher on his chest, her breasts rubbing deliciously against his skin, she kissed him, almost in thanks, which led him to believe he had given her something, perhaps a confirmation of some kind. Which made him want to give her another by telling her he loved her, desperately so. But he held back, more than from out of habit. He had just failed so terribly before....

Such dampening thoughts had no place here.

Hauling her fully on top of him, he kissed her passionately, becoming instantly aroused by her own swift response as they both got caught up in the moment.

"Mmm," she positively purred, obviously completely at ease with him now. He experienced more than a surge of male satisfaction; Reid felt thankful that he had not failed her, in this at least. If only things could always be like this—her so happy with him—but no, he refused to think about what ifs and the foggy future.

"I'm so glad you asked me along," she murmured. "Glad this turned into a honeymoon, of sorts."

"We both deserve it," he told her ardently, gripping her behind the knees so she straddled him.

Her eyes turned silvery as the moon. "Yes. We do. Even if it's a workin' holiday. But I've wanted to see you at work, in real action."

Don't you know, darlin'? Reid thought, clutching her waist to hold her still as he buried himself within her softness, plunging them back into a whirlpool of desire. *Don't you know you already are?*

Chapter Twelve

Glenna slid the last batch of cookies from the oven rack and set them on an unlit burner on the stove before turning off the oven with relief. She pressed her palms to the small of her back and arched it, trying to ease the ache, which only lately had truly begun to worry her.

It was because she was older that she felt so tired, so achy; her body just wasn't as resilient as it used to be. Well, her three-month checkup was next week, and she'd talk to Dr. Kirby about it then. She had a feeling, though, he'd tell her to slow down and not try to do so much.

A well-known pang of remorse pricked her. Reid had told her the same. He was ever mindful of her, incredibly solicitous, but she was apt to put on an energetic front when he was around.

It was the least she could do for him.

Stretching over the sink, she opened the window for a bit of fresh air. Glenna braced her palms on the counter and filled her lungs with the breeze in an almost a mental catching of her breath, glad for the moment alone. The sounds of horses settling for the evening drifted to her. Kell and Reid had driven over a fresh bunch of cows for cutting practice, and every now and then one bawled, apprehensive in the foreign surroundings.

Despite the restlessness that still plagued her, the familiarity of the setting brought Glenna a certain peace: she in the kitchen, Reid in his office, hunting and pecking on the new personal computer they'd picked out together. Of course, Clan wasn't home, but that was actually as usual. She wondered why he had exhibited such indignation at potentially being relegated to the cottage. The young man was never here for it to have made much of a difference. Reid had mentioned Clan was riding in every rodeo possible to make the Finals. She also wondered how Clan was doing with that aim. But she didn't ask, and Reid continued to say nothing on the subject of his son. As usual.

Glenna sighed, mentally switching gears. At least one of Reid's aims for cutting costs while increasing the level of service had panned out—a loper now inhabited the cottage. The occupant was Delaney Briscoe, the young woman who had lived on Piney Rise earlier this year to train her mare under Reid's tutelage. Glenna had willingly consigned her retreat to the girl, who'd come back to Piney Rise for some intensive training to prepare her three-year-old for the World Championship Futurity in December.

Her arrival had been somewhat fortuitous. After the incident with Doc, Bobby Ray had come to Reid and said he thought it time to move on, and in the way of cowboys the two men had left it at that. So it was a weight off everyone's mind to have, even temporarily, a stable hand with real horse sense around to take up the slack and keep an eye on things, although Glenna still didn't see why part of that obligation couldn't have fallen on Clan's shoulders.

"Lord, that smells good."

Glenna turned as Reid entered the kitchen, empty coffee cup in hand. He filled it from the pot forever brewing on the counter. Sipping from his mug, he sauntered over to get a closer look at—and sniff of—the cookies.

"I was just going to bring a few in to you."

"I couldn't wait," he murmured as he bent over the stove, giving her the opportunity to treasure the look of him. As always, that shock of black hair hung over his forehead. With his thick lashes lowered, fanning his cheek, he suddenly appeared a much younger man. Much like Clan. She'd had that impression before, except Reid had lost the reserve, so like his son's, that she'd detected in him at first. Now he was anything but reserved, at least with her.

Besides, she had a feeling Reid Shelton would be forever young in her eyes.

He straightened, catching her looking at him. "Darlin', it ain't the cookies I can't wait for," he drawled as those hazel irises glinted like the morning sun off a river.

No, she decided, it was in *his* eyes that she would see him forever young.

A wave of heat swept over her, as if the oven still stood open. Glenna swayed, wondering that he could make her feel so weak inside with one look.

"Are you all right?" Reid asked, concerned. "It is perishing hot in here." He slid a supporting arm around her and she leaned against him, relishing the familiar feel of him. She knew his body almost as well as her own now. "You shouldn't work so hard, Glenna. Much as I appreciate your cookin', I won't die of starvation if I don't get a square meal with all the fixin's every night."

"But it's my responsibility to feed you. To take care of you. I'm your wife."

He nuzzled her neck. "Yes, you are, and I'd like to keep you around for a while."

Glenna was glad he couldn't see her face as she experienced another pang of remorse. She knew she was trying so hard to meet Reid's physical needs because of the secret she still hid in her heart. She simply couldn't get over the belief that she had somehow caused herself to get pregnant to avoid dealing with the prospect of middle age. Of course, she knew she wasn't the only woman to reach forty and find herself suddenly yearning to have a child for no better reason than it might be her last chance at motherhood. It was as if a woman didn't really comprehend how much her ability to bear children meant to her until she was threatened with that gift being taken away.

But even if that deep-seated need had been what motivated her to have sex with Reid that first time, logic told her such longing couldn't *make* her pregnant. And yet the human spirit was a mighty force to be reckoned with.

Regardless of how she had become pregnant, it still wasn't fair to Reid. The fact was she had taken advantage of him.

With an inchoate urgency Glenna clutched him to her, and he responded by wrapping his strong arms about her and holding her as if she were the most precious thing in the world to him.

"What is it, darlin'?" he asked, but she only shook her head and held him tighter, remembering that she must be strong for him, knowing it would hurt him terribly to unburden herself, yet greatly fearing that her guilt would always be between them.

Did it matter for nothing that she loved him now? Perhaps she had from the first, without even knowing it. Perhaps this was the nature of the force that had driven her to throw herself at him so frantically that night. How else could she have acted so out of character by giving herself to a man with whom she was not of one accord, one heart? Still, even if she did love him, would it ever be possible for them to set aside the circumstances that brought them together and live this marriage to its fullest?

It already lay between them, however, tangibly so. Glenna knew Reid had yet to reconcile himself to the fact that he was to be a father again. He never voluntarily talked of the child. Never touched the place where the baby grew, when he made a point of touching her everywhere else, knowing her intimately.

She ached for him. Ached for the little life inside her, too, for Reid had been right to wonder if this child would pay for their folly.

"Hey," Reid murmured, raising his head at the sound of her choked-back cry of denial. "What's goin' on here?"

"N-nothing," Glenna fibbed, avoiding his gaze, hating herself for being so weak. "Part of bein' pregnant is mood swings. Perfectly normal."

"I've got an idea that'll cheer you up," he said, giving her a squeeze before releasing her. "Why don't we go through the house together and talk about where we'll put the things we took out of the cottage that are sittin' in the barn. And maybe we can talk about what you'd like to do to the rooms while we're at it. I've noticed you haven't done anything to change them—"

"Oh, but I don't need to," Glenna protested. She'd noticed that, outside of Reid's office, everything in the house appeared barely broken in, affirming her assumption that he had always spent most of his evenings in his retreat—and Clan somewhere other than home. As for Miranda . . . where had her refuge been? "And I haven't got so much furniture I couldn't find places here and there for it. For instance, the rocker can go in our bedroom, and my sewing machine in one corner of the office, now that the cot's gone." She didn't mention that it would be a tight fit all around, especially once the baby came.

He gave her a significant look. "I'd buy that, except I know you're particular about your surroundings."

"Isn't it enough I've already commandeered the kitchen and thoroughly invaded your office?" she joked feebly.

He frowned. "This is your home now, Glenna. All of it."

"But it's really not necessary—"

"I think it is," he said with uncommon persistence. She remembered how not so long ago he'd have let the matter go rather than get drawn into an argument. Become involved. Or was he actually looking to her to make the changes he hadn't felt up to making himself? "I'd like you to consider every room yours as equally as it's mine. I don't want you to feel shut out of any one."

"Clan's, too?"

Even as she witnessed the chill that entered his gaze, she made herself go on. "Reid, I know you told me he was your son and you'd handle him, but if this is his house, too, wouldn't it be only fair to ask him for his input?"

And, the question occurred to her, have Clan be the one to bring the matter out in the open by asking her how on earth she thought she could take his mother's place?

"All I'm saying," she continued doggedly, "is ask him what he thinks. Don't you wonder what *he'd* like...what he's feeling?"

At her questions, Reid's mouth tightened. "Sure I wonder. What kind of a father do you think I am?"

"I don't know," she said, surprised at the apprehensiveness of her tone, which she consciously suppressed to add, "but I'm counting on you bein' a good one to our child."

Chin dropping, Reid slid his weight onto one hip and strung his index finger through his belt loop in that now-familiar stance in which he did his thinking. Then he shook his head with a shrug of his shoulders. Glenna's heart clenched, for she recognized that gesture as the one he used to pull himself back, disinvolve himself.

But no, she was mistaken, for he said in a low voice, "I don't know how to deal with him, Glenna. You know, I used to think Clan was like me in a lot of ways, and I'd try to handle him accordingly. I don't think I was short-sighted to have taken that direction with him. He looks like I did at that age. He's a man, like me. A...a rodeo cowboy, like I was."

He continued to stare at the floor, musingly. "But in the past few years I've finally seen how he's more like his mother, in the way he shuts out—"

He broke off with a dissatisfied huff. "Hell, Glenna. It's just a...a stage he's in, like you and me dealin' with coming up on middle age, and there's not much I feel I can do to ease his way through it. That's just...life."

Glenna chewed on the inside of her mouth. She supposed there was some truth in that statement. Then she thought of Reid's remark of having been a rodeo cowboy, like Clan. Had it been a hard choice to make, giving up that life to pursue a more stable career for a married man? And equally hard to deal with Clan's success—much as Glenna herself had found it hard to stand by and watch Jamey fulfill all of her dreams, even though, contradictorily, as parents they wanted their children to have what they themselves hadn't.

Did Reid ever dwell on the prospect that by the time their child, boy or girl, had reached maturity, every unfulfilled dream he might still dream, even now, would have faded completely into his life's background?

Suddenly needing at least some inkling of how he truly felt about their child—whether he *did* think about it at all—she asked, "As long as we're rearranging the house, have you considered where we're going to put the baby?"

His thoughtful gaze settled on her for some seconds before he said, surprising her, "Yes, I have."

He led her to a door tucked at the end of a hallway and opened it. She'd never looked inside, had always thought it held only a closet. Yet as Glenna drew close she could see the interior of a room. A small one, but a room nonetheless.

She stepped inside and caught her breath as realization struck her.

This had been Miranda's retreat.

The walls were a pale blue with dainty lace curtains at the small window. The floor was covered with a faded Oriental rug. Against one wall was an old console piano in dark walnut, a basket beside it filled with sheet music. A painting of a peaceful rustic scene hung above it. Opposite sat a Victorian period chair upholstered in a flowered print. Next to it stood a small table, a brass lamp and a sewing stool. On it lay an embroidery hoop with cloth stretched over it.

The stitching upon it had only been half completed, and would remain so forever.

Feeling incredibly intrusive, Glenna glanced away, her vision blurred by tears. Reid, the man who never looked backward, always forward, had obviously preserved this room, this memory.

It was a revealing moment for Glenna, because not only did she see she'd been mistaken in her judgment that Reid had put his past behind him, but also that she had caused him to dwell on it even more as she had effectively made his future too daunting to face. A future barren of the belonging evident in this room.

"Oh, Reid, no," she choked.

"No, what?"

"You don't want to change Miranda's room. Not just for... for the baby."

She watched as his gaze roved over every inch of it, as if committing it to a memory that would then be put away. Forever.

"It's time," he said definitely. "Time to move on." Reid turned to her. "There's no other place we can put it." He hesitated. "The baby, I mean."

Shaking her head, she started backing out of the room. "No, it's not fair—"

He caught her by her upper arms. "Maybe not, but it's how it's supposed to be, Glenna. How it should be. I never changed this room because there was never a reason to before. Now there is." His fingers tightened in emphasis of his words. "There's not much I can give you, Glenna, but what I have is yours, this house included. I can do this for you, Glenna. I want to. You're my wife."

"No!" She saw immediately how her automatic denial hurt him, and she tried to mitigate it by smoothing that shock of hair off his forehead. "What I meant is, I don't deserve this... this much from you."

"Why do you keep saying that?" he asked with unchecked frustration. "Is it me? What am I not doing?"

"It's not you!" God, she wanted to tell him the whole story, straight from her aching heart, get it out in the open. But all a confession would do was hurt rather than heal, she was sure of it. It would wound Reid, and she would do anything rather than hurt this man.

Or were her intentions really that noble? For Glenna knew she'd actually do anything rather than lose him.

She stared up at him, saw the pain in his eyes she'd already caused him.

"Hold me," she pleaded suddenly.

His gaze softened as he drew her into his embrace, and for a few minutes Glenna found a measure of peace as she always did in his arms. They did have this between them. For now.

"Oh, Reid, I'm so afraid," she whispered against the side of his neck.

"Of what, darlin'?" He stroked a calming hand down her hair as he might have stroked an agitated horse.

She had to tell him; she couldn't live with herself if she didn't. Glenna swallowed, fighting nausea that had nothing to do with her pregnancy. Finally she said, "I— I can't take Miranda's place, Reid. It's just not possible."

His hand stilled. "I see. And I think at last I understand what's held you back from me."

Her heart cracked in two. She wanted to run, but she didn't think there was any place on earth where she could escape this terrible reality, because she couldn't escape herself.

But then he was gathering her even closer to him. "Do you remember, Glenna, saying somethin' to me once about how you intended to learn from your mistakes?"

Her fingers clenching a handful of his shirtfront, she nodded, simply unable to speak in this moment of revelation for them both.

"I know I'll never forget it myself. God, you were so determined, so intense, so passionate...." He pulled back a bit to lift her chin so she was forced to look at him. "Yes, I've been wonderin' for some time now how you could ever take Miranda's place—"

"Reid, no." She'd found her voice only because she couldn't listen to him admit he finally realized how little they did have in common, and how it would never be enough to make their marriage truly a happy one. "I'm sorry. Please—"

"Look at me, Glenna," he commanded, and she was helpless not to obey. And, unbelievably, she saw in his hazel eyes such light, such warmth, such...love, she found herself daring, for one solitary moment, to dream the impossible.

He seemed to read her mind, for he said, "It is impossible, isn't it? Impossible as ropin' the moon." His voice grew rough as it fell to a near whisper. "That I might..."

Almost shutting the words off before they came out— or perhaps because words simply weren't enough?— Reid crushed his lips against hers. Glenna nearly sobbed for the bittersweet relief brought her by this reprieve, no matter that certain issues lay unresolved between them. At least they could have this. As if to deny the spiritual breach that held her apart from him, she twined her fingers in his hair to pull him closer as their open mouths melded together. With a low groan Reid bent her back across the arm around her waist with which he supported her, bowed his long, hard body over hers, and still it was not close enough. It wouldn't be until she opened her heart to him completely and told him the absolute truth: that she loved him, would always love him forever for bringing back to her life that which she'd feared she would never have again—renewal, hope, a bright future—and she didn't mean only in terms of this unborn child. It didn't matter, truly, how they had come together, or why. All that mattered was she loved him now.

She tore her mouth from his, desperate to say it, but then she saw that something over her shoulder had caught his attention. His face went abruptly grim.

Puzzled, Glenna pivoted in his arms. Five feet away, at the end of the hallway, stood Clan. His expression was hidden by the dim light.

"Evenin', son," Reid said calmly, still holding her. "We didn't hear you come in."

"Obviously." His tone was barely polite. He took a step forward, and Glenna noticed that he looked not at them but past them, into the room beyond.

"Reid was just showing me your mother's—this room," she explained hastily, hoping her blush wasn't evident to the young man. How much had he seen—and heard? "To redecorate it. But I was thinkin' it might be best left exactly as it is."

"I thought..." His gaze shifted suspiciously between her and Reid. "I thought you had the cottage."

"Delaney's come back and lives there now," Reid put in. "She's taken over Bobby Ray's duties. And Glenna's moved into the house. She is my wife, after all."

Glenna wondered at his tone of defiance, so like that one he used when speaking to her of Clan.

"I see," the young man said, as if his father's statement surprised him not in the least. "Seems like you've got all the bases covered, doesn't it, Dad? The question is, why even fool with changing Mom's room?"

"It's time, Clan," Reid said definitely, just as he had to her.

"Time for what? For me to get a clue and move out of my own accord?"

"Look," Glenna broke in, "nothing need be decided now. We can put the nursery anywhere—"

"The *nursery?*" Clan interrupted.

Oh, Lord, she'd forgotten Reid hadn't told him. Glenna saw realization strike Clan like a blow, saw him make the calculation of them being married barely two months. And saw him come up with an accurate conclusion.

She was suddenly angry—at Reid. When was he planning to tell him, or was he at all? Didn't he care how it would affect Clan?

She was diverted from such thoughts by Clan himself. Yet he hadn't moved a muscle, just stood staring at his father. And the contempt in his green eyes was something to behold.

"Funny, ain't it," he drawled, his inflection deceptively careless, "how the more things change, the more they stay the same."

"Clan," Reid said warningly. A warning the young man didn't heed.

"What I mean is, you may call yourself a horse trainer, Dad, but you're still a rodeo cowboy underneath the polish, rising to every challenge put in front of you, never thinkin' past the next rodeo. The next *ride*."

The word held an insulting implication.

Reid's hazel eyes glittered as his arms dropped from around her and he squared off in front of his son. Clan shifted on his feet, twitching the hand hanging at his right side like a gunslinger loosening up before a shoot-out.

Glenna glanced from one to the other as the two men, so physically similar, stared each other down. She felt utterly helpless. She wanted to step between them, but she'd already come between them enough as it was.

Tension radiated from Reid, the muscle in his jaw twitching as if he barely contained himself. She wondered what he held back with such superhuman effort. And why.

"Get out of my house," he finally said, impassive as stone.

The young man's eyes widened in reaction. Then Clan nodded curtly. "Fine. Just give me twenty-four hours to pack my gear and make arrangements elsewhere and you won't see me again."

He turned and left. Seconds later a door slammed down the hall just as definitely as Glenna sensed one had shut between father and son.

"Reid, do something," she pleaded suddenly.

He looked at her, his manner still detached. "Do something?"

"Yes. Say something. How can you let him go?"

"I won't have him disrespect either of us. Besides, what would I say that he'd listen to?"

"Tell him...tell him...I don't know. Reassure him that he's still part of the family, that this is his home to come back to, that you want to work things out between you two eventually. Please, Reid. He's your son!"

"Leave it, Glenna." That warning again.

But she persisted. "You saw how he reacted to your saying it's time to change this room, Reid—oh, how it must've hurt him! Maybe he feels this is the one place where his mother still lives in some way. Or maybe he believes it would be going against his mother's wishes to change—"

"No!" Reid nearly shouted. His jaw bulged with the emotion he held back. Then he said, deadly quiet, "There're a thousand sins I own in this world, Glenna. But disregarding Miranda's wishes isn't one of them."

She stared at him, completely baffled by his remark. Completely shocked by its bitter tone. Yet before she could ask him what he meant, he brushed past her, turned the corner at the end of the hallway. And she heard another door slam shut.

She remained rooted to the spot where she stood, just outside the threshold of that small, perfectly preserved room, as ice water trickled forebodingly through her insides. Because for the first time it seemed to her that Reid might have a secret of his own he kept from her.

And with secrets on both sides, which neither of them trusted the other enough to confess, how would their marriage ever have a chance?

Chapter Thirteen

"She's the finest broodmare I've ever owned."

"Mmm," Glenna murmured noncommittally into the telephone receiver, leaning forward in the desk chair to massage her lower back. It was all the comment needed to keep up her end of the conversation as she listened to Sonny Wescott go on about the eight-year-old sorrel mare for which he was trying to find a suitable stud, and how he wanted Reid's input.

"Reid's out workin' the horses right now," she explained quickly when Sonny paused for breath, "but could have him call you this evening if you like." Usually she didn't mind chatting with clients, but today she was feeling particularly achy. And tired. She'd been too upset to sleep much last night after the vehement exchange between Reid and Clan—and her and Reid.

In contrast, the rest of the evening had passed in conspicuous silence, even after the two of them had gone to bed. He had lain beside her stiffly, as she herself was while the clock in the hall ticked, a constant reminder that with each minute they experienced the passing of a time forever lost, not only to them but to every solitary human being in the world.

It had been in the deepest part of that endless night that Reid had turned to her, taken her in his arms and made love to her urgently, powerfully, as if for the last time. She'd been helpless, as always, not to respond to him. Yet for once, the act hadn't salved her restless heart, even briefly.

Glenna shook her head of such thoughts and tried to concentrate on Sonny as he replied, "No, Reid doesn't have to call me. Seein' as how you're keeping his schedule these days, you can just make an appointment for a time in the next month or so for us to go on down to a ranch in Louisiana to look at a couple of likely stallions standing there."

"Sure." She flipped through the calendar she'd taken over for Reid. "Let's see . . . October's better than November. How about the tenth? No, wait—" Reid had already written in something on that date. "Declan 27." What did that mean?

She frowned in puzzlement before turning the page. "The next week is pretty clear. Shall we say the seventeenth?"

"Sounds good to me," Sonny replied. He hesitated. "You know, you've done a fine job of gettin' Reid organized, Glenna. He's needed someone like you. And I don't mean just to help him with his business." Another pause. "You're good for him. The best thing that's happened to him, if I might say so."

"Th-thank you, Sonny," Glenna replied, nonplussed and a bit disbelieving. Sonny had been a client of Reid's for years; he would have known Miranda even before she became ill.

Saying goodbye, she replaced the receiver and sat back with closed eyes. Now that she had a moment to rest, she realized how poorly she really was feeling. Not only did her back throb but she noticed a twinginess in her abdomen.

She rested her hand protectively over it, reassured by the warmth that seeped through the thin layer of her elastic-waisted broomstick skirt. She'd taken to wearing them instead of her jeans, which by the end of the work day became as binding as a straitjacket.

Yet it wasn't nearly the end of the day yet. A stack of filing lay at her elbow, and her call list was a page long.

Opening her eyes, she glanced at her watch. What if she lay down for a while? The answering machine would catch any calls. Maybe Reid was right; she was working too hard.

Maybe he was right about a lot of things, and she should just put the unchangeable past behind her and move on. There were events and happenings in every person's life that one would like the opportunity to go back to and at the very least tie up a few of the loose ends. It wasn't often possible, though. That was just how life was. *Get over it and go on.*

Thus resolved, Glenna grabbed the filing papers and stood in one move, then swayed with light-headedness. She clutched the edge of the desk to steady herself, head dropped between her shoulders as she breathed deeply. Maybe she would lie down, just for five minutes, right here in the office.

As she slid out of her shoes and padded barefoot across the floor to the sofa, Glenna couldn't help wondering if she'd ever felt this worn-out with Jamey. Of course, when she'd carried Jamey she'd been nineteen, younger than her daughter was now. And more resilient, both physically and psychologically.

Glenna sank onto the sofa, tucking her feet under her as she adjusted one of the sofa pillows under her cheek. Lord, it felt good to close her eyes, even if her thoughts continued to turn around in her head like autumn leaves whipped into a spiral by the wind. The Wilkersons needed an update on their stallion. She should put in an order at the feed store that Delaney could pick up tomorrow. And then there was something. . . something having to do with the calendar.

But she was just too tired to make sense of it right now. Maybe later, when she felt better....

"Glenna?"

She didn't stir, and Reid experienced a moment of alarm as he sat on the edge of the sofa next to her. He'd come in to use the bathroom and had found her here.

The rhythm of his heart quieted as he saw that she was asleep. Poor thing, she was probably exhausted from a fitful night. His gut wrenched as he thought of his part in causing the turmoil in her life. She didn't need it, especially now.

Tenderly he brushed Glenna's auburn hair back from her face as he'd done the day she'd nearly fainted by the Breaks. How young she'd looked then, as she did now in sleep. The highlights she'd put in her hair had faded, and he noticed the odd silver strand here and there amongst the red-brown. Somehow they only made her more precious to him, made him realize how lucky he was. Those strands of gray told him she was no youngster; she was a woman in her prime, seasoned by four decades of living and loving, who understood, without placing blame, the defeats and disappointments that were part and parcel of that living. He had a feeling, though, that he would look at her with the same view ten, twenty, thirty years from now, long after they had truly grown old—together.

If he was given that chance. No, he'd already been given the opportunity. The question now was whether he would be able to live up to it.

At his touch, she sighed, and he wondered if she still dreamed, what she dreamed.

He hadn't done much to add to her dreams last night, had he? He'd wanted to, though, as he held her on the threshold of that room, to give this woman what she so wanted, what he believed with all his heart she needed from him. But somehow he'd sensed it still was not enough. That something lay between them. Was it Miranda—still?

Perhaps. He knew for certain, however, that his late wife had come between him and Clan.

Clan. His son. What was he to do with him? And why was it when it came to dealing with Clan that he found himself reverting to his old way of drawing back, telling himself he couldn't change the past and so should put it behind him as if it didn't matter. It *did* matter, though, Reid realized. Obviously it did, or he wouldn't have reacted as he had last night, not with stoicism but with anger, nearly rage. Nearly saying things he shouldn't. But was that the better way to proceed rather than holding back, keeping his emotions inside him while he feigned indifference?

Because he wasn't indifferent, not anymore, if he ever truly had been. And he couldn't let himself become that way again, not with Glenna. He'd die inside.

Then a memory pricked him. What about how Clan had reacted last night, completely out of character? It had stunned Reid, for it wasn't like the boy to pick an argument. To care enough to do so. Not his son.

Yes, Clan was his, too.

He must have tightened his fingers involuntarily in her hair, for Glenna's lashes fluttered open, her eyes hazy with sleep as she tried to focus on him. "Reid? What...what time is it?"

"Four or so." He relaxed his fingers, tried to stroke away the pain he might have caused her, but his hand fell away as, groaning, she pushed herself into a sitting position. "Heavens, I must've passed out." She started to rise.

"Well, there's no need for you to get up now, if you're still tired."

Glenna made a face and sank back down. "Hoo. Maybe I am. But I—I'll be all right. You can go back to work." She glanced up at him. "Unless there was somethin' you wanted from me."

Everything. I want everything you can give me— whatever it is. Just don't hold back on me. But it worked both ways.

He concentrated on a plaque on the wall behind the sofa. "Actually, I...do want something. To apologize to you for last night, for what happened with Clan. You see, there's something I need to tell you. Tell you both—"

"Clan," she broke in, drawing his gaze back to her. "Is that...Declan?"

"Yes, it's an old family name." He frowned. "I didn't think I'd ever told you that."

"You didn't." She closed her eyes. "I saw it on your calendar. Some date in October."

"The tenth. It's his birthday."

"Mmm." Eyes still shut, she bracketed her face with her hands, massaged her temples. "And how old will he be?"

"Twenty-seven," Reid answered readily as he removed her hands from their occupation and took them in his. They were ice-cold. "Glenna, are you all right? Why don't you lie down again?"

She didn't answer him. "But weren't you and Miranda married two years before James and I were?"

"Yes." He wondered what these questions were all about, when obviously she wasn't feeling well.

"But you said Clan'll be twenty-seven," she persisted, opening her eyes and looking at him. They were that muted gray he'd seen before, when she seemed to stifle emotions that were too intense, too vivid.

It struck him what she was getting at. "Yes," he answered calmly, relieved it was out at last.

"Then unless Clan was months premature..."

"Yes, Glenna. Miranda was pregnant when we got married."

Her lips made a round O of realization.

"I know it's kind of a shock," he said, "but it doesn't affect us."

A shutter slipped down over her gaze, distancing her from him. "Then why didn't you tell me before?"

He set her hand on her thigh, patted it, then drew his own away. Getting a little distance himself? "First of all, what would I have said? That I'd covered the whole shotgun wedding scene before? Secondly, why would I have told you? What happened with Miranda...it's over and done with, Glenna, just like it's not an issue for me anymore that you and I had to get married."

"Anymore?" she asked quietly.

"I didn't mean it that way!" He put a hand on her arm, and she actually shrank from him.

Wounded, Reid stood and paced away from her, so tempted to retreat more than physically, to draw into himself again.

His back to her, head angled to the side, he pointed one finger at the floor in emphasis. "Don't tell me things aren't different now in your mind, too, than they were before."

"But how were they...before? Your feelings, that is. About the baby? About...me?"

He should have known Glenna wouldn't let the subject drop. How could he have been such a fool to believe he might have had a chance to atone—not to avoid making the same mistake twice, but to correct the mistake he had made, if only in his own mind.

Sighing roughly, he said, "All right, I'll admit at first I was near to kickin' my sorry ass into the next county at the thought that I'd been careless enough to let this happen again." Difficult as it was, he made himself face her. "I wanted to tell you, Glenna. I almost did, the moment you told me you were pregnant. But then, I... I'm not sayin' this was right, but I took some exception to your attitude."

He studied the pattern on the rug just beyond his boot toes. "I'm talkin'," he said softly, "about your shame over what happened. Because even though you blamed yourself most, I knew the lion's share of it rested on my shoulders. I of all people should have known better than to try to..."

He gestured vaguely, unable to admit out loud he had been trying, foolishly, to meet her needs. And had apparently failed.

"Yes," Glenna said as softly. His head shot up. "Yes, we both should have known—should know now—what's in our minds and in our hearts."

He remembered her saying something very like that the day by the Breaks. And he caught her implication. "I do know now, though. I have learned something in the past twenty-odd years. And what I know is that with you and me—" He gestured between them even as he registered the mounting desperation that drove the action. "It's not the same as what happened between me and Miranda."

"Not what," she said.

"Come again?"

She stared not at him but past him, as if she had to in order to concentrate on what she had to say. "It's not a what—the conceiving of this child—that's the issue here. It's the matter of how it was conceived, in the heat of passion when the last thing we were thinkin' of was how this act, this gift from God allowing two people the physical expression of the...the love between them, is also meant to bring children into the circle of that love."

She focused on him, eyes so very regretful. "And that wasn't on our minds. Not at all."

"So what?" he argued. "We can't put that behind us and be happy together now? For crying out loud, Glenna, an unplanned pregnancy is not the end of the world! Anymore, people don't even make a pretense of keepin' it from a kid that he was an accident, like we did—"

He broke off, spun away from her, his fingers shooting through his hair, digging into his scalp as if to wrench from his brain whatever ingrained thought pattern continued to work against him. He did not want to get into this. It was over! And nothing could be gained from rehashing the past.

"Clan doesn't know, does he, Reid?" Her voice was very, very soft.

"No." *Leave it at that, Glenna,* he wanted to warn, would have if he'd thought she take heed.

"And I'm supposed to believe it doesn't matter?"

"It wasn't my choosing, not to tell Clan," he said from between clenched teeth. He felt the hurt, decades old, rising up in him again, and he tried to push it down, hold it back. But it would not be tamed this time. "It was...it was Miranda. She took one look at Clan's face after he was born and made me promise never to tell him."

"Why?"

"Yeah, that's a good question, isn't it? Why?" He snorted cynically. "I didn't ask that at the time, not wanting to press the issue when it seemed so important to her. And I didn't ask later, either, because it didn't take me long to figure out the situation for myself, what she'd known from the first."

He hesitated, could not go on. He'd never said the words, never told another soul of how he had failed his wife, had failed within himself. But it didn't matter anymore! Glenna's and his marriage was different, for even in a few months of being married he was closer to her than he'd ever been to Miranda. He knew that closeness was because this time he was not only wiser but more motivated; neither of them had the leisure of an entire lifetime to work into their relationship. He couldn't wait, wish and hope that true intimacy with this woman might eventually develop. He had to push as Glenna pushed, demand as she demanded, and never hold back, never look back....

"Tell me, Glenna," he said, staring out the window at the white pipe fences and tidy buildings that contained the only beings with whom he had ever felt he'd achieved real accord. "Do you intend to keep the fact we had to get married from the . . . from it?"

The question apparently startled her, for she paused a moment before answering, "I—I don't know. I hadn't thought about the subject, to tell the truth. I'm still trying to deal with . . . with us."

He pivoted to look at her. "Well, I'm insistin' right now you turn your eyes straight ahead, look down the road as far as you can, and by God start thinkin' about it. Because I won't go through the rest of my life bein' made to feel I have to hide something because it can never be corrected or forgiven. I refuse to make *that* mistake again."

"So you *do* consider our being married a mistake."

"Damn it, no! Won't you, for once, try to see things my way? You asked once why someone can't benefit from our experience, and I'm wondering who deserves it more than you and me. Why not look at what's happened between us from a whole different direction, as an opportunity? A chance to do things different?''

''Because it won't work! This marriage will never work as long as you're unable to set aside for good the part of your past that still plagues you!''

''It's over and done with, I tell you! The past is past, it can't be changed, much as you might want to, Glenna. Unless—''

He stared at her, hardening his gaze, hardening his heart against the hurt. ''Are you suggesting, now that the kid's been legitimized, that we just give up? Go our own ways and forget this marriage?''

''No! But can you honestly look forward to years and years of living in the same house with each other, sleeping in the same bed, with our difference of opinion on this matter between us? Because you obviously resent being put in this predicament again, and you'll always resent our child because of it.''

Visibly trembling, Glenna rose to her feet, her stance resolute but tense, as if she braced herself for the shots from a firing squad. ''You tell me, Reid. What did you figure out? What did Miranda know from the first?''

''I told you it doesn't matter. It doesn't matter with us, either, how it happened—''

''*It's not an it!* It's a her—or him. You can't even give our child a gender, much less call him a baby. And you never touch me here, Reid!'' She pressed both palms over her abdomen as he'd seen her do so many times, even before she was pregnant. ''The place where he's growing inside me. So don't tell me how this child was conceived doesn't matter! I'd have to be blind not to see how the past still separates you from Clan. And I won't have it. Not for my baby.''

Her fists clenched at her sides, she held her chin high, gray eyes snapping, her pale skin suffused with color as her hair bobbed around it in an auburn billow. And damn him, he wanted her then. Right now. Wanted her forever, and he was going to lose her for sure if he didn't tell her the truth.

A truth she already apparently knew, for she went on, "If you're in earnest about not repeating your mistakes, then you better resolve the situation with your first child before your second arrives. If you'll do that, then...we'll stay married, make the best of it we can, even if you don't...even if I can't—"

Her mouth trembled as she blinked slowly once, twice. Then she dropped her chin, wrapped her arms around herself and bent forward as if in physical pain. "Oh...God, what've I done?" she said, her voice strangled.

Reid went ice stone cold at the sound of her despair. Did committing to a future with him disturb her that much?

She choked on a sob before clapping her hand over her mouth and bolting for the door. But he knew it wasn't because she was going to be sick. She was running. Again. This time from him, because somehow, some way, he and his love still weren't enough.

Of course, he had never told her that he loved her.

Aw, hell, let her go anyway, the voice in his head urged him. *The past can't be fixed. Why you even tried in the first place...*

But then another voice, deeper, more profound, spoke up. *Never, never, never again will you have this chance.* Obviously, much mattered between them or they wouldn't be fighting like this. Fighting for their lives.

"Don't you dare!" Reid shouted after her, crossing the room and charging down the hall to find Glenna already halfway out the screen door. He reached her, grabbed her arm and spun her around. "Don't you dare go tear-assin' across the countryside!"

She fought his grip. "Let go!"

"The only way we're gonna be able to work things out between us is if we both stay and not run from whatever it is in us that we can't face about *ourselves*."

At that, Glenna abruptly stopped struggling. She looked up at him, her eyes filled with that desolation of spirit, that forlornness of having been forsaken, and he knew he'd hit the problem right smack on the head. But he also knew, in a flash of insight, that he would break Glenna's spirit, as surely as he might break the spirit of a horse, should he try like some roughstock rodeo rider to dominate such a passionate soul, make it submit to his will.

He *wasn't* that kind of cowboy.

"All right, then," he said. "Go on. Go lookin' for whatever you're not finding here, but I'll tell you this, Glenna—I'm not chasing after you again, trying to find out what's wrong or how I can make it better, and comin' up short. Because this is it, as far as I go. If you come back, it's got to be by your own choosing, under your own power, with your eyes wide open."

He dropped his hand as she stood motionless, head down, for one long moment in which Reid's heart nearly pounded out of his chest. Then, barefoot, she ran down the steps and across the yard. Her flight was arrested, however, when she spotted Clan, who was tying down the load in the bed of his pickup. They exchanged glances, though what message might have been communicated between them was lost to Reid. Then she caught up her skirt and ran to the red dually parked next to Clan's. Within seconds she'd pulled it around, gravel spitting under the tires, and headed for the road in a plume of red-brown dust as he stood looking after her.

And Reid knew that just because he stayed while Glenna chose to run did not mean he was any better at facing his problems than she was.

Chapter Fourteen

Reid stewed for a good minute after Glenna left. Then he crossed the porch in three steps and stalked across the yard to Clan.

"C'mon," Reid ordered peremptorily as he passed by on his way to the stable. "We're goin' for a ride, you and me. I'll take Rogue and you can have Nasty."

He didn't wait to see if Clan followed, just proceeded to the tack room, grabbed a saddle, blanket and bridle, then went on to the paddock where the gelding and the mare were grazing. He whistled them both over, and they came willingly, their gaits loose jointed, heads bobbing and tails flicking off flies. Setting the equipment on the top railing, Reid swung over the fence and snagged hold of Rogue so he could saddle up the gelding.

Pretty soon he heard the opening and closing of a door, the jingle of a bit as it banged against the pipe fence. With the same ease and efficiency of his father,

Clan brought Nasty around to stand docilely next to Rogue.

The two men were silent as they readied their mounts, although after a minute Clan commented sardonically, "Never did understand why the hell you name your animals what you do." He grunted as he tightened the cinch on one of the mildest horses Reid had ever trained. "Or why you named this place Piney Rise, for that matter."

"Well, now, you wouldn't know 'cause I never told you." Reid automatically ran his hand across the gelding's flank and down to the hock of one back leg, ever vigilant for the beginnings of any problems. "All it is, is my little way of rebelling, not fadin' all the way into the scenery."

He fitted the toe of his boot into the stirrup and hoisted himself effortlessly into the saddle. "I like to think it says, maybe more to myself than anyone else, that I'm still alive and kickin', even if I've stuck myself out here in the middle of nowhere. And might even have a bit of P and V left in me yet."

Leaving Clan to make what he would from that comment, Reid rode Rogue out the gate and headed him north at a slow walk. Clan and Nasty followed.

Again the two men said nothing, even when they reached the Breaks and dismounted. Forefinger hooked in his belt loop, Reid just stood for a moment taking in the panorama of that wide, long, deep canyon, carved an age ago by a river that was now a mere trickle of water. It occurred to him, for the first time, how the Breaks were the perfect companion for the flat, endless plains they rent in half. Any less dramatic an indentation, any less of an impression, would have been completely lost in the encompassing expanse.

His gaze lit on the lonely pine tree across the Breaks, poised on the brink as if ready to jump into the chasm. As if on the edge of goodbye.

Reid stooped and scooped up a hefty chunk of lime-stone, weighed it consideringly in one hand. Then in an abrupt movement he hurled it with all his might out into the canyon. It arced briefly before plunging to earth.

"Damn," he murmured, massaging his shoulder. "Glenna had the right idea. Does a world of good."

He squinted into the setting sun. "That was quite a little performance she and I treated you to just now, wasn't it? Like two hotheaded, hot-blooded newly-weds..." Of course, he and Glenna *were* newlyweds; should they be expected not to act like ones, just because they were older? "Surprised the crockery didn't fly. I don't know what's got into me lately."

He glanced over at Clan, who stood watching him im-passively. He recognized the expression; he'd felt his own face fall into the same lines all too often. Reid knew what emotions Clan hid behind that mask of detachment, and it wasn't just because the young man was his flesh and blood.

"I've somethin' to tell you, son, and I guess the best way to say it is just to have out with it." He looked Clan square in the eye. "Your mother was pregnant with you when we got married."

He waited. But there wasn't the flicker of a reaction in Clan's eyes, and Reid thought he might get let off the hook, not have to deal with questions he would have an-swered as best he could, as truthfully as he could. But even if there would be no recriminations, neither would anything be resolved.

Then Clan shifted on his feet and dropped a bomb-shell of his own. "I know, Dad. Mom told me."

Reid gaped. "She did?"

"About two weeks before she died."

"How...?" *And why, Miranda, when you swore me to secrecy?*

The young man removed his Stetson to swipe a forearm across his forehead, then held the hat in both hands while he scrutinized it, as if unwilling to meet Reid's desperately searching gaze. "She said she didn't want me to find out after she was gone and think she'd resented me. She said she *had* wanted me, entirely so, but she knew what it felt like not to be...loved that way, and she'd been thinkin' only to spare me the same."

Clan lifted his eyes, but he still didn't look at Reid, merely switched his scrutiny from his hat to the reddening horizon. "She made a promise to herself that I'd never feel like that." His fingers clenched on the brim of his Stetson. "That because how I came into being was a mistake, I wasn't loved as much as every person deserves to be."

Reid shook his head in utter confusion. "She told you all this?"

Finally Clan looked at him. "Yes."

"Well." His hand actually trembled as he thrust his fingers through his hair. Nearby, a large boulder readymade for sitting came into Reid's tunneled view. He made it over to the rock and sat down gingerly, as if shellshocked.

Setting his elbows on his knees, Reid clamped his head between his hands and stared at the ground, trying to work the situation out in his mind. Afraid it was already all too clear to him.

"Is that why you've been so...so distant since she died? Because you believed *I* held something against you?"

The young man shrugged unconcernedly. "I don't know."

"Well, think about it! Do you think I wasn't able to put aside the circumstances of your birth and be a good father to you, Clan?"

"I guess the real question is, do *you* think you did?"

Reid rose to his feet. "That's not what I asked."

"Well, it's what I want to know, what's important, isn't it?" Reid registered, with some surprise, the rising apprehension in his son's voice. Clan was far from unconcerned, it seemed. "Otherwise, why did you never tell me yourself!"

His anguished tone startled them both. Clan spun away, took a few rambling steps toward the lip of the canyon. "I've been waitin' two years, Dad," he muttered.

But oh, the desolation in those words!

"She...she made me promise never to tell you," Reid admitted, hating what he was doing, dishonoring Miranda's memory to her only son, breaking a promise a quarter of a century old. But perhaps it was time, for hadn't he his future relationship with his son to think about? "Surely she told you that, too. And I kept that promise, Clan. Never let it be said I didn't live up to that faith—"

"Even after she'd died, and you and I were the ones left to go on without her?" Clan peered skeptically over his shoulder at Reid. "Mom never said so, but the fact that she told me all this before she died made me think she was either going to have a like conversation with you—make sure you did talk to me about it—or that she expected after she died you'd tell me anyway, and she wanted to make sure I knew her...side."

The emotion in Clan's voice had ebbed, but now it erupted again. "Dad, it was going to be just you and me after she died! I'd have thought you would *have* to tell me, sort of get it off your chest so everything'd be open and square between us. Or didn't you *care?*"

With a sound of self-disgust Clan crammed his fingers into his front jeans pockets and stared at the immutable view. And Reid gazed at the stiff, proud back of his son. His only son, so very much like himself.

So. Now he understood. And Reid knew the real sin he had committed: he had let his self-doubt and vulnerability about his abilities keep him from seeing to the particular need in his son of knowing he had his father's unconditional love and acceptance.

"Clan." Reid cleared his suddenly tight throat and took a step toward him. "Son. I cared. I care now, very much, for you and what you feel. You've got to believe me. Just like you've got to believe that your mother never told me she had let you know. I can see how you'd have thought she would've but she didn't, not even at the last—"

The pain, the hurt cut into him afresh. Deeper than it ever had before, because now it was clear to him how grievously he *had* failed, through twenty-five years of marriage, to make it up to Miranda for getting her pregnant. For never being able to meet her emotional needs, no matter how hard he tried. Otherwise, Reid wondered, why couldn't she have told *him*, given him the confirmation he so needed, even on her deathbed?

Bleakly he searched the shadowed depths of the canyon, as he had when Glenna had given him the news she was pregnant. Searched the enormous sky above, as he had the evening they had turned to each other in wordless need. What answer had they expected to find? What did he expect now?

He himself had said that they would both have to find the answers in themselves. But what if he looked, looked hard, and didn't find them?

"Why?" he asked wrenchingly. So despairing was he at that moment, Reid simply had to seek the answer outside of himself. "Why didn't she tell *me*?"

And, miraculously, it seemed an answer might actually be there.

"There's...somethin' I didn't tell you Mom said," Clan admitted, his voice muted. "And that was she fell clean in love with you the first time she met you, and never stopped.''

Reid whipped his head around to find Clan studying him. ''She did?'' he asked with clear disbelief.

Again his son gave him that look of skepticism before going on. ''The problem was she knew it wasn't that way for you. Best I could tell from what she said, Mom saw from the first that you were pretty carefree, the kind of cowboy that sort of took one day at a time, livin' for the here and now, and nowhere near ready to settle down. Then she got pregnant, and even though you never made a fuss about marrying her, she said she was afraid that even if you might learn to love her, it'd never be the same as how she did you. Like . . . like a powerful longing she had no way of controllin', is what she said.''

Clan scowled to himself, whether embarrassed or feeling he was telling secrets that weren't his to reveal, Reid didn't know. ''And bringin' the subject up when she was sick so she might tell you, all the while fearin' you might not say the same in return, that you loved her as much . . . I don't think she wanted to die knowin' for sure.''

It was another bombshell, a life blow. For Miranda to have gone to her grave feeling she couldn't be honest with him . . . It nearly brought him to tears to think that even though he had been at her side, she had essentially died alone.

He observed the hard edge to Clan's expression, and wondered if he was doomed to see always that scorn in his son's eyes every time Clan looked at him that told him how much he had failed.

Yet there was no going back to the way he had been, believing the past was best left alone. Because it had become the here and now, and he must deal with it, however inadequately.

He cleared his throat. ''All I can say is, I did love her, son, as much as I could. I won't disrespect her memory, but in my defense I've got to say I tried to give her more, but she shut me out. Whether it was because she couldn't believe I could love her after having to marry her, I couldn't tell you. But I do know, now, that I shouldn't have let her hold me at arm's length. Then—shoot, what did I know? I was a twenty-year-old rodeo bum, and part of me was certain no amount of love could make up for ruinin' her own prospects by gettin' her pregnant.''

''Yeah? So what about what you said, you know, of having your little way of rebellin'? You weren't content, Dad. Even I could see you were restless.''

Reid noticed they were both standing the same way: hipshot, wrists cocked as their fingers crooked through a side belt loop. A relaxed stance that hid the emotions churning underneath the impassive facade.

''Well...'' Reid dropped to a squat, picked up a twig and discarded it. He must be scrupulously truthful; there could be no more secrets that would only continue to fester. ''If anything made me restless, it was livin' in a house with a wife I couldn't seem to make happy. Because there was you.''

''Me?'' Clan echoed. ''How could I have come into that situation?''

''See, your mother, she hurt me pretty bad with her distancing me. I mean, any fool could see that she did have it in her heart to love that way, because she loved you, without restraint. Even knowing that's how it always is with a mother and her babies, it kept me believin' all the love in me I had to give still wasn't enough.''

He shook his head. ''It's strange now, to have you tell me that she really did love me and thought I couldn't love her. Basically that was the same self-doubt I was feelin'.''

And now, had he only made the situation worse by telling Clan the truth? Had he set for good the tenor of his future relationship with his son by revealing just how backward he'd led his life up to now?

Reid focused on the object of those questions, knew he could only say one thing more that might help. "I'm sorry, Clan, for not bein' wiser when it came to handlin' the tender feelings of your mother, my own wife. At least I have learned from the experience, which I guess is what life's all about. Learning and growing and moving on."

"Yeah, well." Clan dropped to his haunches beside his father, elbows propped on his knees. "I just wish we'd both known the whole truth sooner." He sounded both apologetic and forgiving.

"Me, too," Reid said with feeling. "Me, too." But he had always believed nothing could be gained from dwelling on the unchangeable past, and so the situation had never been resolved.

"Even understanding why you didn't talk to me before," Clan said, "you still might have."

"Might I?" He scraped the edge of an index finger across his chin. "You're kind of a hard case, son, if you know what I mean."

"Yeah, I guess I can be. Like when I found out last night that you'd married Glenna because she was expectin', when I knew Mom had been, too.... I'm sorry, too, Dad, for sayin' what I did. I deserved being thrown out."

"I imagine it was pretty hard to stand there and feel like you might not have a place in your own home. You do, though."

Forearms braced on his thighs, Reid linked his hands between his knees and said exactly what he was feeling, even at risk of rejection. "I'd like you to stay, Clan, and help out with the business."

"Dad—"

"Now, hear me out. You won't be able to ride the bulls forever, son. I know you've got your heart set on taking the World Championship before you're through, and I'm behind you in that effort. When it comes to rodeoing, you're not like me," he said wryly. "You're better. You've got more natural talent in your little finger than I ever had, not to mention the drive to succeed at a mighty tough profession. It *is* a profession, for the serious, and I don't want you to think that I'm not proud of what you've achieved in just a few short years. But it won't be long before you'll be lookin' past that aim and wonderin' what you'll do with the rest of your life. You're coming up on your twenty-seventh birthday, which is a peculiar age for a man who does what you do. You're still young enough to have more than half your life ahead of you, but gettin' past your prime as a professional athlete."

"I know. That's why I've been goin' all out this season. I've got to win in the next few years or it's not likely to ever happen."

"And I agree that's the kind of effort it takes to win the World. I know how difficult it was for you to set aside that ambition and help me care for your mother. I've never forgotten that, never will, and that's why I haven't pressed you to contribute more to the operation since she died. Not because I haven't needed you, or wanted you there."

He squinted across the Breaks toward that lone pine tree before cutting a covert glance at Clan, who again unconsciously mirrored his father's pose, like a kid of six who still thinks his daddy hung the moon. It choked Reid up, for it gave him hope that he hadn't lost his son's love and respect throughout all this exhuming of past hurts and misunderstandings.

"I'm just sayin'," he went on gruffly, "that you'll always have a place to live on Piney Rise. And when the time comes, you have a job here, too. I haven't talked to Glenna yet, as either my partner or my wife, but I have a feelin' she'll agree to cuttin' you a share of the business if it'll mean you'll stay. Even with Delaney around to help out, I could use someone like you. I know horse training isn't your first love, but you're not half bad at it. Although I'd have to say any talent you got in that department came from me."

Clan snorted dryly even as one side of his mouth lifted in a smile. "I'll tell you who's getting too old to be whippin' the bull around."

Reid reached out and cuffed the younger man affectionately, leaving his hand on Clan's nape in a squeeze. "I mean it, kid. You don't have to go. I'll even help you unload your pickup."

"Thanks, Dad." He hesitated. "But it's really for the best if I do stay on the road, at least till after the Finals. And after seein' what I accidentally did last night, I'm thinking you and Glenna could use the time alone."

"Fine, then," Reid agreed. "Just remember, I'm always here if you need someone to talk to. In fact, I'd kind of enjoy the opportunity to lend you a bit of my experience, such as it is, if it'll help you even a little."

Yes, Reid committed himself then and there to using his experience and wisdom—for he *had* learned something of life in the past twenty-five years—to helping Clan work through the young man's regrets of missed opportunities.

So what of the opportunity now presented to himself? Reid wondered. Was it too late for Glenna and him to achieve real happiness? Hadn't he already done all he knew to get her to trust him and open up to him completely, had opened himself up to her, let her know the depth of his need for her?

No, Reid realized, he had only done what he'd had confidence in doing. If he was to get past his insecurity, he would have to humble himself completely, stop distancing himself. Until he did that, he would never know the kind of peace and harmony that comes from true partnership with a woman.

And he would find out, without a doubt, whether he was able to satisfy her needs.

The prospect scared the life out of him. He must remember, Glenna was not like Miranda. She'd hold inside what she was feeling for just so long, and then it came pouring out, good or bad, bringing along that youthful passion of hers. He could handle that, he told himself. He *would* handle it, somehow.

That decision made, Reid rose. "I need to get home." He scanned the horizon, this time in the opposite direction of the Breaks, as if he could actually see all the way to Piney Rise. He couldn't, but he knew it was there. "If Glenna's not back, would you lend me your truck to go find her?"

Also rising, Clan assented even as he lifted his eyebrows at his father.

"Yeah, I know I said I wouldn't go after her." Reid drew Rogue around into position and hoisted himself into the saddle. "I lied."

Clan took the statement without comment as he looped Nasty's reins over her head and climbed aboard the mare.

Their pace was not so sedate on the way back to Piney Rise. Clan looked askance at Reid as they jogged along. "Think she'll be there?"

"It's a toss-up. That was a pretty big row we had, though not our first." His stomach pitched around inside him in a way that had nothing to do with the ride. "Hopefully not our last."

"She's a real Texas tornado, ain't she?"

"Stormy as a two-year-old filly," Reid answered candidly. "She's told me more than once she's not normally this way, that it's a variety of things—turnin' forty-two, becomin' a grandmother, us gettin' married and this pregnancy comin' along—but you couldn't prove it by me.''

He thought of her in all her moods, as varied as the west Texas sky, as constant as the west Texas landscape. You could hang your hat on the reliability of knowing that whatever was going on inside her, it would be apparent to anyone who cared to take a look.

''All I know is,'' Reid said with conviction, ''I wouldn't change a hair on her head. Not for anything in the world.''

''Think things'll be different once y'all settle down and get used to each other?''

''Mmm,'' he murmured, which was Glenna's expression, he realized. It certainly had its uses, conveying either a yes, no, maybe, or all three. But not indifference. Never indifference.

''God, I hope not,'' Reid said. With feeling.

Chapter Fifteen

Glenna drove, having no idea where she might be going. Of course, why do anything different? she thought ruefully. However, the prospect of fetching up on the side of the road and going for the most hair-tearing, breast-beating crying jag she'd ever indulged in held little appeal.

So what *was* she going to do? Wander the back roads of west Texas into infinity?

Reid was right. Again. She shouldn't have run, but at that moment she just couldn't have stayed and told him the truth, take the chance that the love light would leave his eyes as he drew emotionally away from her. Or had the damage already been done by her pushing him to take an action that went counter to how he'd always lived his life?

And so on she drove. She would have to go back, though, sometime. It wasn't fair to ask him to take a page from her book if she wasn't willing to do the same for him.

Yet she didn't turn back to Piney Rise, for when the next crossroads came, it seemed perfectly natural to follow the road to Plum Creek.

The sun was still hot on the back of her shoulders as she pulled in the familiar driveway. Her old pickup, the one she and Jamey had driven to Texas from Nevada, was parked next to the house, which told her at least one person was home. She checked the digital clock on the dash of the dually. Coming up on six. Hopefully, Kell and the hands wouldn't have yet returned for the day.

Glenna climbed the steps to the mud porch and entered it, but she hesitated at the back door, uncomfortable with just walking into the house. This wasn't her home any longer. Had never been, really, in the few months she had lived here.

She knocked. It was only brief seconds before Jamey's concerned face, along with Hettie's curious one, appeared through the window.

"Momma!" She flung open the door and stared at Glenna. Hettie, on Jamey's hip, bounced with delight.

"Mama!" she parroted, lips smacking with each syllable. "Mamamamama!"

"No, sugar, I'm Grandma," Glenna corrected, reaching out to take a pudgy hand between her thumb and forefinger and giving it a fond shake. She looked up at her daughter. "May I come in?"

"Sure!" Her puzzlement evident, Jamey stood back as Glenna entered the kitchen. "You like to scared the life out of me. I couldn't imagine who would be knocking at my door. Or why."

"Mmm," Glenna answered—or didn't answer—as she avoided her daughter's searching gaze, which had dropped to take in her unshod feet. "I was just out for a drive and thought I'd check in on you."

The kitchen was warm and filled with the smell of baking. A pot of beans bubbled away on the stove. In this room, at least, there apparently was none of the usual staking out of territory that goes on in a family, for on the table was a jumble of half-completed projects that could have been either Kell's or Jamey's. Glenna recognized several leather-working tools—a stitch spacer, stitch awl and, of all things, the needle-nose pliers she'd nearly chucked into the scrub the afternoon of her birthday— that were being used to repair a headstall. An inventory listing lay side by side with a pile of invoices. A laundry basket stacked with clothes took up the most space. Another basket, this one filled with clean but unfolded diapers, sat next to it.

Glenna automatically started folding them.

"So how've you been feeling lately?" she asked briskly, finding a measure of comfort in taking on the one role right now in which she felt competent, that of being a mother to her grown daughter. "Any more morning sickness?"

Hesitating at her mother's questions, Jamey gave Glenna a strange look, then crossed the kitchen to strap Hettie into her high chair. "No. I'm through with that part, thank goodness. Now it's the itchiness. My skin feels stretched tauter than a banjo string." Absently she gave her stomach a scratch as she poured some dry cereal onto Hettie's tray.

Though four and a half months along, Jamey hadn't yet switched to maternity clothes, Glenna noted, although the younger woman had gone back to the loose-fitting jeans and shirts she'd taken to wearing after giving birth to Hettie.

"And then there's the cheerful thought that things are only going to get worse before they get better," Jamey added glumly.

Glenna gave her daughter a mildly concerned glance. "That doesn't sound like you," she said without reproach.

"Well, it is me." One hand grasping her other elbow, she pensively watched Hettie cram a fistful of cereal into her mouth.

"What's wrong, sugar?" Glenna asked gently.

"Shoot, Momma, you didn't come here to solve my problems." She studied Glenna. "Did you?"

Glenna laid her hand on the stack of folded diapers in pause. "Seein' as we're both pregnant and likely goin' through a lot of the same things right now...maybe I did."

Apparently finding the sense in that, Jamey nodded. "I've just been wonderin' lately how I'm gonna be able to handle two babies." She echoed the reservation Glenna herself had had upon learning of her daughter's pregnancy so soon after getting married. "I mean, I wouldn't give up having this little one with Kell for anything, but Lord, we're barely used to livin' with each other. And here I go, not only foisting one baby on him, but two! It's not like he isn't bein' the sweetest man you can imagine, because he really is. Patient and kind. Even with me so grumpy all the time."

"It's normal to have such fears and doubts when you're pregnant, Jamey." Glenna snapped the wrinkles out of the quilted cloth in her hands. "I know you had similar ones when you were pregnant with Hettie."

"Sure, but then there was a lot of other stuff goin' on in my life. But now...why now when I'm happily married and doin' what I love? Now should be the best time of my life. Besides, you'd think once you recognized your fears for what they were, you could put them aside. Stop yourself from feelin' so anxious. But it seems impossible.''

Paying undue interest to her task, Glenna murmured, ''Yes, I know what you mean.''

Jamey sighed and wrinkled her nose, giving her mother an apologetic look. ''Oh, well, there's no takin' it back now that the deed is done, even if I wanted to, right? And I don't want to *not* be pregnant—even when I want to. You know?''

''Y-yes,'' Glenna repeated, almost inaudibly. So there was no avoiding her problems even here. For she knew, very well, what it was to want too much. To want it all.

And now she was going to lose it all, for that same reason.

She sank into a chair at the table, a diaper crumpled in her fingers. ''Oh, Jamey, what've I done?'' she whispered.

''You *did* come here for another purpose, didn't you, Momma?'' Her daughter was beside her in a trice, taking the chair next to her. ''What is it?''

Closing her eyes, Glenna swallowed. To have to admit such things, as she was about to, to one's daughter. But she just had to talk to someone, even if Jamey wasn't the someone to whom Glenna really should be baring her soul. ''It all began on my birthday, and feelin' so alone. And old. And useless.''

Jamey reached out and took one of Glenna's hands in hers, squeezing tightly. ''I knew you were feelin' that way, Momma, and I ached for you. I just didn't know how to help you other than to try and make you feel, as much as I could, that you belonged. That we, all of us—Kell, Hettie, me and this baby to come—wanted you to be a part of our family.''

"I know you did, and I loved you all for your efforts. But..." But they just hadn't been enough. Nothing had.

Rising, Glenna crossed the floor to where Hettie sat munching her snack. One palm propped on her thigh, she bent to eye level with this child, who would always be so dear to her, because Hettie in particular had been a boon to her, at a time when Glenna had needed to care for another's welfare and future in order to keep from dwelling too greatly on her own.

She helped Hettie gather the scattered cereal into one bunch, smiling absently when long-lashed eyes lit on a rogue *O* near the baby's elbow before Hettie pounced on it. "You know, I never thought I'd be one of those women who'd be dissatisfied with growing older. Never. But I was. I... I've even been envious of my own daughter."

"I know, Momma."

"Mmm. I figured you did."

"I never blamed you. I couldn't."

"Well, I blamed myself. It surely wasn't like me. And then when I started goin' through the change—"

From behind her Jamey interrupted, "But, Momma, how could you be going through menopause if you're...?"

"I'm not, obviously, but right around my birthday I believed I was." She straightened, one hand pressed protectively to her abdomen, the other on her achy back. "I hadn't had a period for some months, I was getting hot flashes and having mood swings and feeling restless, not myself at all. I didn't see how it *couldn't* be menopause. And then to realize, too, that the last sign of my youth, that of my ability to bear children, was passing from my life... I'm afraid I went a little crazy. I guess it was one of those situations you just mentioned, of knowing what you're goin' through is normal, the emotions of loss and grieving, but you can't stop yourself from feelin' what you're feelin'. That's why I ran away the morning of my birthday, to stop myself from doing something I'd regret. Which I failed to do.''

''What're you talkin' about, Momma?''

This part was the most difficult of all to admit, but Glenna forced herself to go on. She stared, hard, at the spice rack hanging on the wall above Hettie's head, willing it not to blur before her eyes.

''That evening ... I th-threw myself at Reid. I barely knew him, even if we had a lot in common, both of us widowed, with grown children who were moving on with their lives. Both of us alone. But all that wasn't enough in common to excuse what I did.''

''You mean ... you made love with him, Momma?''

Glenna blushed, though not from embarrassment. From shame. ''It wasn't makin' love. It wasn't even sleepin' together, which signifies some type of ongoing relationship. No, it was once, which makes it sex, pure and simple. Or maybe not so simple, for I obviously had some deep-seated urge to hold on to the past, or to thumb my nose at my empty future, so that I used Reid Shelton.''

Her voice dropped to a whisper. ''And out of that night came this baby. When I found out I was pregnant, that's when I realized how much I'd really used Reid. I must have wanted, secret even to myself, to defy nature itself and conceive this child, no matter who was affected in the process.''

Glenna waited, her arms wrapped around her middle, for her daughter's reaction. Would Jamey be shocked? Disappointed by her mother's irresponsible actions? Or mightily disillusioned as she gazed at her mother and wondered if this was what she had to look forward to in twenty years: becoming a faded, foolish woman who persisted in grabbing for her lost youth.

It was a dismaying prospect that, still, chilled Glenna's blood.

Then Jamey spoke up, pronouncing judgment in her typical way. "Mother. That's about as farfetched a story as I've ever heard."

Glenna spun around. "What?"

"You did it once! How could you have 'meant' to get pregnant? Especially when you didn't for twenty-three years after me? I mean, you never said anything to me about it, but I know you and Daddy tried for more children." Her gray-green eyes turned misty. "I think that's the main reason, after Daddy died, that I really felt I'd let you both down. I was the only child you'd had."

"Oh, sugar, that's not true at all." She held out her hand to her daughter, suddenly needing vital contact.

Squeezing Glenna's fingers between her own, Jamey nodded. "I know that now. So it's not so difficult for me to see that you had no way of knowing you'd get pregnant by Reid."

"But that's what I must have wanted, deep down. Why else would I virtually throw myself at Reid? That's just not *like* me!"

She noted the rise in her voice and made an effort to calm herself, even though she felt like jumping out of her skin with the restlessness that had nothing to do with hormones or pregnancy or anything else physical. "Oh, Jamey. You see, that's not the half of it," Glenna admitted. "It's not right between Reid and me, it'll never be right, because how this child was conceived will always come between us."

Jamey's brow furrowed. "Why's that?"

Glenna hesitated. "Reid told me that he and Clan's mother had to get married. You need live in that house but one day to see how the fact continues to affect his relationship with Clan. And Clan doesn't even know! Reid told me that Miranda made him promise not to tell Clan, which seems to me means she was trying to preserve her son's future happiness, if no one else's. Somehow she knew from the very beginning that because of how she and Reid got married they would never be truly happy. And when Reid admitted as much himself—''

Fighting tears, she pressed the back of her hand to her lips then closed it in a fist. ''It hit me today during our argument that he *does* see me as taking Miranda's place, quite handily. Once again he's stuck in the middle of an unfulfilling relationship with a woman. No wonder he hasn't wanted to look back. Or forward.''

She swiped angrily at her eyes, disgusted with herself for what amounted to crying over spilled milk, which in essence was what she'd been doing for months now. ''I was wishing on the moon in the first place to even think we could overcome not only our mutual past but the experiences we had separately. We both have too much history, too much of living and being disappointed in life— in ourselves—to give completely of ourselves, which is what it takes to make a successful marriage. I should have tried to do as he did and just put the past behind me and move on, make the best of it. But I don't want to make the best of it! I want more.''

Closing her eyes against the onslaught of longing, she felt one rebel tear escape the confines of her eyelids and slip down her cheek. No, she couldn't run any longer; she had to face what she'd done, what she was, once and for all. Because she knew then it hadn't been just a baby she'd wanted. If it had been, why hadn't she released Reid of all responsibility for it, gone off and raised her child and never, ever seen him again?

The pain of that possibility, suddenly very real, hit her right where she lived. Because what she wanted, more than a child, was to be in love. Deeply, abidingly, in that once-in-a-lifetime way, and hadn't she already had that with one man? Hadn't she had all that heaven allowed one person? How could she be so selfish?

Forearms strapped across her middle, Glenna shook her head. She simply couldn't tell her daughter *that* secret. Yes, part of it had to do with her not wanting to taint Jamey's vision of romantic love, or perhaps of herself, the mother who should have been wiser. But Glenna couldn't tell Jamey the rest because her daughter wasn't the one she should be baring her soul to, nor the one she really wanted to. She wanted the one person on earth who would understand, as he had always understood, because he was her peer, friend, lover, husband, father of her child. He did understand—didn't he?—what it was to need that soul-deep connection with another being that brought a person true and lasting peace, that made the worst that either of you faced bearable because you did it together.

If she didn't find that sort of connection with Reid, then Glenna knew there'd be no one else, ever. And she would be truly, finally alone.

And if that was what she ran from, then why was she here?

Silence filled the kitchen. Outside, the sun had stolen tiredly away, but it left a few glowing torches of red and yellow to see the night safely in. And tomorrow the sun would rise just as surely as it had for centuries. Life would go on.

It was Jamey who spoke first. "Maybe what you did, Momma, whether accidental or on purpose, *is* just like you," she said. "You're a different person than you were a year ago. You've been through a lot, to say the least, and it's changed you. You've lost so much, and you're not going to sit by and let life happen to you again."

She tugged Glenna around so that the two women sat knee-to-knee. "Look at it this way—you've never had to fight for your happiness before. Now you've got to pursue what you want, instead of waiting for it to come to you."

She knew what Jamey was implying. She was forty-two—God wasn't going to send a man the likes of Reid Shelton to her again. Did it really matter how this whole situation had come about? Or was what they did with this chance the real issue here? Maybe they'd made a mistake, but it was actually only a mistake if they continued to look at it as such.

Wasn't that what Reid had said? That what they'd done together could be turned into something else. An opportunity. A chance to do things differently.

Oh, did they still have a chance?

Glenna covered Jamey's hand, as it lay upon her cheek, with her own, knowing she had been fruitfully blessed. Because Jamey understood perhaps not all of her mother's anguish, but enough of it—*because* she was in love. And love was ever hopeful, trustful, enduring. Such truths came not with age but were universal.

She must hope; she must look forward.

"How," Glenna whispered with a catch in her voice, "did you ever get so wise?"

"Everything I know I learned from you, Momma. You raised me up right as rain. And you can do it again." Jamey pressed her palm to her abdomen in that age-old gesture of maternal love and protectiveness. "We both'll raise our children with faith and hope and love."

Leaning forward in her chair, Glenna embraced her firstborn, who hugged her back, fiercely. Yes, soon she would be able to say for the first time in her life, that Jamey was her firstborn.

"Oh, sugar," Glenna said against Jamey's ear, "I'm so lookin' forward to this baby, but I've a feelin' you're the one who's going to be the real comfort to me in my old age."

As she straightened, her back spasmed. She sucked in a breath.

Jamey drew away, looking at Glenna in concern. "What is it?"

"Just a slight backache. Although it seems worse than it was earlier."

"Are you all right? Why don't you lie down here till you feel better?"

"No. I want to get home. Home to Reid."

Yes, Piney Rise was her home, where she belonged. Fortified by that thought, Glenna felt much better, both mentally and physically, on the ride back to Piney Rise. Yet when she experienced a sudden wetness between her legs as she climbed out of the truck upon reaching the ranch, some of her apprehension came back. Scolding herself not to jump to conclusions, she walked into the house and straight to the bathroom. There she found a bright red stain on her underwear.

Glenna closed her eyes, fighting panic.

"Reid?" she called faintly, not wanting to strain in any way. But perhaps the damage had already been done. "Reid?" she called out more loudly. "Please... answer me if you're here."

Where was he? Where had he gone?

Slowly, cautiously, she made her way down the hall to their bedroom, then to his office. The house was indeed empty. She was alone. She glanced out the window and saw Clan's pickup still parked in the driveway; she hadn't noticed it on the way in. There was no sign of Clan, though. Where were both men?

Glenna's gaze fell to the phone on the desk. Easing down into the chair, she did what she should have done immediately and called Dr. Kirby at home. In his calm, efficient way he asked her a few questions, gave her some quick instructions on what to do or not do. She should stay as quiet as she could, preferably in a supine position; she shouldn't drive, if at all possible.

But she should meet him at the hospital in Borger as soon as she could get there.

Glenna hung up, now gulping back sheer hysteria. Where was Reid? She couldn't do this alone. She needed him, more than to get her from Piney Rise to the hospital. If she was going to make it through this, she needed his support, his strength, his love. She must believe that he did love her, if perhaps that love was not all that it might be. Yet. Because she would show him how much she loved him, that with that love they could overcome any differences they had, and not just for the sake of this child.

This child they'd made—that now might not be.

Again with great care, Glenna made her way to the back door and out onto the porch. Maybe Reid was in the stable. She'd left him pretty agitated himself—perhaps he'd ridden out to the Breaks in his own brand of escape from his troubles. If he had, there was no way she could fetch him, either by horse or by pickup.

How could she have made him feel he couldn't stay in his own home, that he had to go somewhere else to find solace? She had no one to blame but herself for pushing Reid away, for being so shortsighted and foolish.

But please, don't make this child pay for my folly! she prayed.

Then she saw him as he emerged from the stall barn and began walking toward the house, his son at his side.

"Reid," she whispered, grabbing the porch post and leaning against it in relief.

As if he'd heard her, his head came up and he caught sight of her standing there. He turned and said something to Clan, then started at a brisker pace toward her as she came down the steps to meet him, arms extended to bring him to her just that much faster.

She knew the instant he saw the stark fear in her eyes.

"What is it, Glenna?" He took her hands in his. "What's wrong?"

"It's the baby. Reid—" She was shaking like a leaf. "I'm b-bleeding! It happens sometimes, Dr. Kirby said, in the f-first trimester, and it doesn't always mean for certain that the baby's mis . . . miscarry . . . But Dr. Kirby wants me to come to the hospital right away. I'm supposed to stay c-calm, but how—"

Without waiting for her to finish, Reid lifted her into his arms, crossed the yard toward the dually in ground-eating strides. He called to Clan over his shoulder, "We've got an emergency here, son. I need your help."

The young man was immediately at his father's side, opening the back door of the passenger side of the pickup and helping Reid settle Glenna on the seat before sprinting around the front to the driver's door.

"Lie down, Glenna, and put your knees up," Reid commanded calmly. He climbed in, half-perching on the seat beside her. A pillow appeared seemingly out of nowhere, and he put it behind her head. "Clan'll drive, and I'm going to be right here with you and help you stay relaxed."

He tucked her flowing skirt around her, then looped an arm around her bent knees, clasping them against his side. The other arm he hooked over the back of the front seat and steadied them both as Clan turned the corner out of the driveway. "We'll be there before you know it, darlin'."

Glenna focused on him with anxious eyes, trying to do as he said, taking deep breaths that seemed to stop midway in her chest no matter what she did. Even given Reid's concern and sure actions, his gaze remained remote, his demeanor distant.

Oh, had the damage already been done?

"Reid, I'm sorry!" she burst out, her chest swelling with her struggle to hold her sobs in check. "I shouldn't have left! It was wrong! But I know now—"

"Hush, hush," he interrupted gently, smoothing back her hair.

"No! I know I asked too much from you! I had no right, but I wanted...I wanted..." All her worries came bubbling to the surface; she couldn't stop them, no matter how irrational. "I'm too old to have a baby! That's why Dr. Kirby wants me to get to the hospital. There're certain risks with women my age, he said. And I'd been having a backache for some weeks now, but I thought it was nothing! How could I have been so neglectful—"

"You have to stay calm, Glenna," Reid broke in forcefully, then said with more composure, "We can talk later. There's nothing that can't be worked out."

"Yes," she agreed, grasping hold of that idea like a lifeline. "We're in this together, right?"

He hesitated for a split second, then nodded. Was he merely pacifying her?

Desperate to find in his touch some sign of what he actually felt—the one way she knew he couldn't hold back from her—she groped for his hand, and he laced her fingers in his. "Oh, Reid, I'm just so afraid!"

Then she saw in his hazel eyes, bright and tender, what made him so remote. What he'd tried to hide. "I am, too, darlin'," he whispered. "I am, too."

He pressed their twined hands against his chest. "Relax, now. Everything's going to be fine."

It had to be. And though that belief remained a beam of light she must continue to focus on lest she lose sight of it, she simply had to pour out the fear in her heart. It came up from the deepest, most womanly part of her, straight to this man, her husband, the father of her child, the only person on earth who shared this vital link with her. The only person in whom she could both find and give solace as they contemplated the most terrible possibility of all.

"W-what if we lose this baby, Reid," Glenna whispered. "What if we do?"

Chapter Sixteen

Reid squeezed Glenna's hand but didn't respond. Couldn't respond. Hadn't he asked for this, that she be completely open with him, and hold back nothing of her wants, desires—or fears? What if he failed to live up to that trust, failed to meet her needs in this most desperate of moments?

He could feel himself blanch, and he sought to hide it from her by leaning forward to say to Clan, "How're we doin', son? I don't need you breakin' any laws, but I imagine the sheriff would understand if you took this truck up to eighty or so. The shocks're the best, so don't worry about jostling Glenna."

"Got it, Dad."

He gave Clan's shoulder a squeeze, then stared out the windshield, clamping and unclamping his jaw in herculean restraint from what he really wanted to do. Which was bellow his frustration, howl out his own fear. Throw a boulder the size of Amarillo into next year. He understood completely what had caused Glenna fits, what she'd been railing against when he'd found her parked on the side of the road: the realization of how easily and senselessly one's expectations for the future could be torn apart and scattered to the four winds.

Sure, at first he wasn't keen on having another child, but that had more to do with how it had come about, not the child itself. Now, though, Reid wanted it—for many reasons. Despite the circumstances behind this child's conception, he knew Glenna thought of it as a gift. A gift, as he knew *he* thought of it, that he had been able to give to her. A gift that was now threatened with being taken away from them.

What if they lost this baby? Would they try again? Would she even be able to conceive again? Searching his store of horse knowledge, Reid knew that the chances of conception lessened with a female's age. And even if he and Glenna had been lucky once, they might not be so again. It might not even be wise to try, considering her age.

Yet without a child to bind them to each other, there might not be enough reason for them to stay married and try to work things out between them.

Without her, he'd die inside.

His gaze fell to her face, and he found she studied him with troubled eyes. He hadn't responded to her question. It was because he hadn't known what to say, still didn't. So he came up with the only assurance that was in his power to give, inadequate as it might be.

"Just hold on to me, Glenna," he said roughly, "and together we'll make it through this somehow."

Solemnly she continued to contemplate him for an endless minute, in which he was sure she found him as lacking as any cowboy who'd ever pledged to tame what was so obviously beyond his control.

Then, closing her eyes, she nodded and seemed, at least for the time being, appeased.

Finally they arrived at the Golden Plains Community Hospital. Once Reid had helped her out of the pickup, her feet didn't touch the ground as again he carried Glenna. He knew Clan would take care of parking the truck.

Dr. Kirby was waiting at the emergency entrance and even had a wheelchair ready for Glenna. With raised eyebrows he took in the picture of his patient in the arms of one rather worse-for-wear-looking cowboy.

"And you are ... ?" the doctor inquired delicately.

"I'm Reid Shelton. Glenna's husband."

"I see." Dr. Kirby smiled. "I'm very glad to meet you."

"Likewise," Reid acknowledged with a curt nod. He settled his precious cargo into the wheelchair, wondering if he would be allowed to go with her, ready to ask, but she was holding fast to his hand. There was no question he was staying with her all the way.

The room they took Glenna into wasn't a regular hospital room but had a bunch of equipment in it, including one machine they wheeled over to the bed onto which Glenna was transferred.

A nurse secured a blood pressure cuff around Glenna's arm, then took her pulse and temperature. Once those stats had been duly noted, the nurse laid a drape over Glenna's lower body before helping the patient out of her skirt and underwear. Dr. Kirby came in and gently palpated Glenna's stomach, asking question after question about the nature and location of any pain or other symptoms. His murmured *I sees* and *uh-huhs* gave away nothing.

Yet Reid knew very well the complications that could arise in an equine pregnancy and, while he would never equate Glenna's condition with a horse's, those complications crowded into his mind, ectopic pregnancy foremost among them. It was often the reason for pain and bleeding at this point in a pregnancy. And could be fatal to a mother.

Immediately he was plunged into the memory of a similar situation, as he sat at Miranda's side, both of them contemplating the inevitability of her passing. Even knowing that it was a fact of dying—or in Glenna's case, please God, of giving life—that such an experience was by its nature deeply personal, unable to be shared, Reid still felt left behind, distanced.

He gave Glenna's hand a hard squeeze to counter the sensation. He simply would not fail her now.

The staff was incredibly efficient, and Reid's worry eased as he saw that his wife was in good hands even if people were poking her here and prodding her there, as if they were picking out a frying hen at the butcher shop. His mild indignation fueled his nerve as he watched a white-coated fellow draw blood, and kept him from thinking about the imminent situation.

"Well, now, Glenna," Dr. Kirby said, drawing up a low stool, "I'm just going to check to see how the bleeding is."

Glenna's hold on Reid's hand was like a vise grip. Neither of them said anything. What could they say? He felt absolutely helpless, at fate's mercy. The question kept coming back to him: What *would* they do if they lost this baby? Now, though, was not the time to worry about whether their marriage was strong enough to sustain such a blow. It was too late to shore up the foundation if the house was already falling down around their ears.

Please, give all of us one more chance. Please.

"Not too bad," Dr. Kirby pronounced. "No tissue, and the color's turned dark, an indication that the bleeding is slowing. Let's see what the ultrasound picks up."

The lights were lowered as a technician coated Glenna's exposed abdomen with a pale blue gel and proceeded to move some sort of sensor in a circular motion on it. Reid watched as the woman slowly shifted the oblong device on that white expanse of skin. It didn't seem possible to him that there was actually a baby in there; Glenna's stomach seemed flat as ever.

He glanced at her. She had her eyes glued to the computer monitor, filled with indiscernible images in a radar-screen-shaped space, at the technician's elbow. Reid wondered if Glenna could see anything in the shades of gray that he couldn't.

"What've we got, Terry?" Dr. Kirby asked the technician.

"I'm having a hard time picking up..." She typed on the keyboard below the monitor, marking certain darker areas with crosses and magnifying them, before continuing to manipulate the position of the sensor.

Then, like an optical illusion, Reid spied a familiar shape, a tadpole—no, more than a tadpole—that moved out of focus as quickly as it had come.

"Darn." The technician made another half circle with the disk, as if sneaking up on the site from a different angle. "I had something for a second there—ma'am, could I ask you to hold your breath just one minute?"

Everyone held their breaths. Reid's heart thudded to a stop, almost as if he was able to impart his strength—and love—to the one who needed it most at this moment.

Then he and Glenna gasped as one as they saw it, a tiny person-shaped swelling. A pulse throbbed in it. A heartbeat.

Reid's own heart started up again. His throat grew tight as Glenna squeezed the hell out of his hand and they stared at the movement. *A heartbeat!*

"Looks like we've got a baby," Dr. Kirby said. "Right where he's supposed to be and doing fine."

"He?" Reid jumped on the inference, not taking his eyes from the screen. "It's a he?"

"No, I'm afraid it's too early to tell the baby's sex yet. I was simply speaking as the father of two boys. Expectant parents tend to do that, I think, rather than continually refer to an unborn child as an it. Makes the child more real to them."

Reid avoided Glenna's gaze as the technician cleaned the gel off Glenna's stomach and helped her to sit up.

"So," he asked after a few minutes, "are we out of the woods completely, or what, Doctor?"

Slapping his thighs, Dr. Kirby stood. "I'm going to go look at the blood work, check for anemia and how the pregnancy hormone levels are, but from all the indications, there shouldn't be any problems on that score. I'd like to admit you to the hospital overnight, Glenna, just to keep an eye on things. We'll give you a very mild sedative to relax you, and keep your uterus relaxed, too. But the fact that the bleeding was never profuse and has stopped, and that we've obviously got a viable fetus that's going strong, I don't see why you can't have a perfectly normal pregnancy."

"Even after this scare?" Glenna asked skeptically. No, Reid noted, hopefully. "Even . . . at my age?"

"Of course. You may be a bit past what doctors would call prime childbearing age, but you're healthy. Certainly there are more risks, but since more and more women are having babies into their late thirties and mid-forties, a lot more information is available and more medical technology is being developed to deal with those pregnancies. Besides, what these women are proving more than anything is that you're as young as you feel.''

Reid's and Glenna's gazes met, and they shared a private look that conveyed their concurrence—and relief.

''Are there any precautions we should take to ensure there're no more problems like this?'' Reid asked.

The doctor patted Glenna's arm. ''Just follow all the prenatal care instructions I've given you already. Oh, and avoid any undue stress.'' His gaze switched from one to the other of them. ''Am I correct in assuming the worst of that is over?''

Before Glenna could even open her mouth, Reid had answered for them both. ''I guaran-damn-tee it, Doc.''

Dr. Kirby laughed. ''I'll take you as a man of your word, Mr. Shelton. Let's get you settled into a room, Glenna.''

''One more thing, Doctor,'' Reid interrupted the other man's departure.

''Yes?''

''I'll be stayin' with Glenna through the night.'' It wasn't a question or a request.

Dr. Kirby nodded. ''Then we'll try to make you as comfortable as possible, too.''

Twenty minutes later Glenna found herself situated in a semiprivate room in which the other bed was unoccupied. A cot had already been brought in for Reid, although he hadn't arrived yet, having taken this opportunity to inform Clan of the goings-on and tell the young man he could go home for the night and return for them both in the morning.

She was glad for the moment alone.

Resting her head back against the pillows that propped her into a sitting position, Glenna closed her eyes. The sedative must be kicking in. At least, she thought it was the sedative that made her feel calm. At peace.

Her baby was safe, its future held in trust. Now she must live up to that trust by seeing to her own future—the one she must share with Reid.

Glenna heard the door open and close, and turned her head. Reid stood with his back against the door, holding his hat at his side.

Would it ever cease to thrill her to see him without it? He'd admitted he felt awkward without the security of a hat protecting his head, shading his face, shielding his expression. It seemed to her a measure of trust for him to reveal himself now, to be somewhat vulnerable.

But he'd always been such, even when he'd looked at her with that impassive expression that couldn't negate the emotion in his changeable eyes. Even when he told her not to want too much from life, while still trying to give her all that he could.

How lucky she was, how blessed, to have him enter her world at a time when she'd believed part of her life was over. Not the childbearing part. The falling-head-over-heels-in-love part usually reserved for the young.

"Clan still here?" she asked inanely, suddenly nervous and shy with her husband.

"No." Reid pushed off from the door and walked over to the bed. "I sent him home."

"Then I'll have to thank him tomorrow for his help tonight."

He set his hat, brim up, on the tray table at the foot of the bed. "He knows." His voice was subdued. "I told him."

She nodded, dropping her gaze to the quilted fabric of the blanket spread across her lap. Obviously, father and son had managed to come to some sort of an under standing. She wouldn't press him for information though; it was none of her business.

She wondered how to bring up what did concern both of them, namely the argument they'd had this after noon. How to tell him that she wanted to make the most of this chance that had been given them. But first, she must put the past behind her, be scrupulously honest with him, if she was truly to be able to go on.

Reid shifted on his feet, boot soles scuffing on the li noleum floor. "I owe you an apology, Glenna."

Her chin shot up. "You? Why?"

"For actin' like a stubborn old coot too set in his opinions and views to consider another's," he answered ruefully.

It was the opening she'd been looking for.

"No, *I'm* sorry, Reid, for runnin' off this afternoon. promise you, it'll never happen again. Although the pri vacy did give me a chance to do a little thinking. Fac some things about myself I'd been avoiding."

She drew in a deep breath, realized only then she' been holding it for hours, trying not to do anything tha might put pressure on the baby. "Y-you were right, yo know," she made herself continue. "And I was righ too. What's happened in either of our pasts, it is all wa ter under the bridge, in one sense. But in another, thos experiences linger in us, become a part of us, make u who we are today. For better or for worse."

His gaze turned abruptly inscrutable. "For worse?"

She nodded jerkily. "You see, all my life I was.. content just bein' a wife and mother. A wife to James, mother to Jamey. I probably even took it for grante some. And I thought I'd learned very well how to dea with whatever disappointments and hardships life ha brought me. But when James died, suddenly I was force to redefine myself and how I looked at things. I wasn't a wife anymore, wasn't really a mother, either—so who would I be? Suddenly I wasn't thinkin' about what I'd had to deal with already, but what I was going to have to deal with—a future where all the possibilities and expectations I had for my life, even the certainties I'd come to depend on, were no longer there. And I wanted to just keep lookin' back at that past, not because I thought it would solve my problems, but mainly because the future seemed more than I was feelin' up to."

Her throat grew tight and her nose began clogging up. Glenna sniffed, forcefully; she simply must get through this without crying. "Anyway, I tried to deny I was completely daunted by life for many, many months. I think you understand, when you work at securing your future—makin' a life, a living, a marriage that's supposed to sustain you in the years to come—and then have that future wiped away so that you're faced with going on without even a clue of which direction to take now that all direction has been taken from you.... I wondered where I'd find the strength to face another day, wondered if I even wanted to try, when all I had to look forward to was years and years and years of bein' alone. So alone that little mattered to me any longer, and what did matter was slowly losing its ability to sustain me."

Her gold wedding band glinted in the soft light of the bedside lamp, reminding her of Reid's eyes. She latched on to that omen, choosing to see it as encouraging. Certainly it helped her to go on. "Everything just seemed too much to bear right around my birthday, with the realization that my life with James was over for good, that Jamey had made peace with his passing and was movin' on with her own life. And so I needed to, too. I needed to come to terms with my new role of mother to a grown daughter, as a mother-in-law, a grandmother—all the

capacities I'd hoped and planned to take on as I go
older. Just not *yet*. And so I latched on to the one tangible way in all this that I could defy fate. I thought I
wanted a baby. Or what a baby meant—a beginning instead of an ending to an era in my life. I know now
though, that I wanted much more. I wanted...*you*."

With a quick glance at Reid, Glenna gave an embarrassed laugh. "I bet that's somethin' a lot of men would
like to hear more often from a woman, that she wanted
him with a need that wouldn't be denied. But it wasn't
just a physical wanting, not just sex that I wanted with
you, a moment of passion that would ease both our
troubles. Or give me a child. I wanted love."

That jarred the detachment from his eyes. "Glenna,
do—"

"Let me finish, please." She stayed his comment.
"While I can." She traced the pattern in the blanket,
fingers shaking, heart pounding. "Yes, I wanted love,
but that doesn't absolve my actions, what I did to pursue love. Even so, I'm bold enough—selfish enough—to
ask that I not have to pay for those actions for the rest of
my life."

"What do you mean, Glenna?"

Swallowing painfully, she answered, "What I'm sayin'
is, I don't want to take Miranda's place, Reid. I want to
make my own place in your heart. Somehow. I'll do
anything, in fact, to try to do that."

Did she sound as desperate to his ears as she did to her
own? She was, though, as desperate as she had ever been
in his presence.

"This has simply got to work, Reid," Glenna choked
out past the lump in her throat. "This marriage, and not
just because of the baby. Even though you've given me
that baby and so much more I don't deserve, I'm askin'
you to please open your heart and give me a chance. A

I have to give you in return is my heart, because I love you with every bit of it, and I can't... I can't live without you.''

Her ears rang with the ensuing silence. Oh, she shouldn't have sounded so needy! She shouldn't have put that burden of her happiness on him! It was another mistake, she realized. When would she learn?

"Say somethin', Reid," she whispered.

She heard boot steps walk away from her, though he didn't leave the room. No, he was too honorable and upstanding a man; he wouldn't shirk his responsibilities—or the truth. But, God, she wanted more than his obligation to her!

Out of the corner of her eye she saw Reid had stopped in front of the window, his back to her.

Finally he said into the quiet, ''Why not?''

Glenna raised her head. ''Why not what?''

''Why is it wrong to want what every other person in the world wants? To have a place to belong, to have a purpose. To love someone special to you, be loved the same way. What you want for yourself, Glenna—they're simple things. God-given rights, not extras. And I don't know of anyone else more deserving of havin' them than you. What's wrong with wanting something for yourself for a change?''

He had asked her the same question before. ''Was it fair, though, for me to take so much, not even considering what I might have to give in return?''

''But you have given me something, Glenna—my son. You know, there were a lot of things Clan and I said to each other today that should've been said years ago. And while I was talking to him, in the back of my mind I was wondering, why did I decide to tell Clan today the secret his mother wanted kept from him? I figured out it was partly because he's my son, too, and I'd every right to tell

him. But most of all because of you. If it weren't for you
we'd probably have gone God knows how many mor
years before Clan and I cleared the air between us. I
ever."

"I told you, Reid, I had no call to demand that o
you."

"No, you were right, and not just because I learnee
some things that would have made a difference in how I'
have lived the past two years of my life—hell, the pas
twenty-five years of it. Things havin' to do with Clan an
me...and Miranda." He hesitated. "You see, all m
married life I felt like no matter what I did, I was neve
able to make it up to her that I'd gotten her pregnant."

Shock rolled through her. That was a much differen
view of the situation than Glenna had perceived. Bu
suddenly, taking that view, things began to make sense
Still, she knew that, like her, Reid had a need to unbur
den himself. For himself to understand. "Why did yo
feel that way?" she asked gently.

"Because...she shut me out. Oh, not out of our be
or the house or whatever. Our marriage wasn't som
sentence to Siberia for either of us. We shared a lot c
good times—and bad times—that naturally brought u
closer. And then there was Clan, raisin' him. But I wa
inexperienced in life, in dealin' with people, and not wha
you'd call naturally perceptive. I was a typical rode
cowboy, livin' and lovin' for today. Anyway, when
married Miranda, I quit messin' around at rodeoin
somethin' I was never going to amount to much in, an
buckled down learnin' about horse training, which su
enough instilled in me a little of the insight I never had
a kid. I learned over the years that I'm not some car
less, carefree cowboy.

"Even then, Miranda never let me into here—" in th
reflection of the window, she saw that he touched h

chest "—into the innermost part of her, something you'd think would happen as the years went by. But it didn't, though I never stopped trying. I finally came to the conclusion that there must've been something lacking in me that made it impossible for me to reach the part of her that couldn't let her forget—or forgive."

He bent his head and ran his hand through his hair. "Even...even at the last, when she lay dying, when she was so scared, so damned scared she shook with it, she'd let me get just so close, and that was it."

Glenna's own concerns receded into the background as she ached for the raw hurt in his voice. "Oh, Reid..."

He shifted his shoulders as if adjusting them against a weight. "When she died, I guess that's when I did give up, in a way. Gave up expectin' a lot from life or people. Or me."

He finally turned from the window to face her. His features were drawn but peaceful. "Then I was drivin' along the road one day, and I saw this woman crying and hollering and letting it all hang out, not holdin' a thing back. And...and, well, she took my breath away." One corner of his mouth turned up wryly. "I'll admit part of me thought, if this is how they grow 'em in Nevada, then I surely wanted to get me some. But part of me was scared to death. Because you made me want to try to meet the need I saw in you. I won't deny that I'd have done just about anything for you—because you asked for that. Demanded it, and still do. Everything I can do, everything I can give. And more."

Deliberately he walked to her side and sat in the chair next to the bed. He leaned forward, elbows on the mattress, hands clasped with his forehead resting on his crossed thumbs as he stared at the blanket, as if in prayer. "There's one more secret I've not kept but hidden inside me, one I didn't tell Clan today and will never tell him

and have him build up his own doubts of never being
enough. For years I'd hoped and believed that if Miranda and I had other children, things might resolve
themselves between us. In my mind, another son or
daughter would have seemed to confirm the rightness of
our marriage, redeemed me in her eyes. We didn't conceive again, though, and it was another nail in the coffin
of my self-doubt.

"But now...I *have* been able to give a child to you, and
it hopefully returns some of what you've given me,
Glenna, and that's your full and unconditional love. And
so it's fitting that what I give you of myself that just
might be worth all the trouble you've gone through, what
I wanted to tell you last night, is this—you can't take
Miranda's place. It'd be impossible as ropin' the
moon—" he drew a shuddering breath "—because I
know right now I never loved her the way I love you. God
forgive me for sayin' it, but it's the stone truth."

Hands still clasped, he laid one forearm across her ribs,
the other across her hips, creating a cradle of her pelvis.
And slowly Reid lowered his head until his cheek rested,
oh, so tenderly upon the very place where their child
dwelt.

"Oh...oh, my precious love," Glenna choked as she
leaned over him, her own cheek pressed to the crown of
his head, an arm hugging his shoulders as she smoothed
back that shock of black hair, over and over.

"God, Glenna," Reid said raggedly, his voice muffled
against her. "I was so damned scared that without this
baby to hold us together we'd have no reason to try at this
marriage."

"Never!" she cried. "Never!"

They lay so, for several minutes, as tears spilled from
her eyes onto Reid's neck. She wiped them away as best

she could. "You—you must think I'm the cryingest woman you've ever known," she whispered jokingly.

"No," he denied vehemently, raising his head and taking her face between his hands. "I think you're the most passionate, loving, deserving woman I've ever known."

His hazel eyes were brighter than she'd ever seen them, and she realized it was because of the unshed tears in them.

It shocked her, made her cry even harder. "Hey. Th-that's my job."

"And this is mine," Reid murmured as he hitched one hip onto the edge of the mattress, took her in his arms and kissed her. She clung to him, and pretty soon he'd climbed completely onto the bed next to her, boots and all.

"Do you really, actually comprehend," Glenna said between kisses, "the gift you've given me in your love? I feel like there's nothing we can't overcome or do together."

Reid rested his forehead against hers. "Like raise this kid? I've been thinkin', we'd probably do best to hope for a girl."

At his words, her heart soared within her. He was talking about the baby to her! "But I've raised a girl," she said lightly. "I'd like to try a different challenge this time."

"Challenge is the word, believe me. Take it from me, boys are hell on wheels."

"And girls aren't?"

Reid snorted.

"All right, then." Glenna gave in to him willingly. "Have it your way. Just wait'll she's eighteen or nineteen and decides she's old enough to know what life and love are all about, when just a few years ago she was in pigtails. And now she's got her heart set on some cow-boy..."

Reid gulped audibly. "Damn. What've we let our-selves in for?"

They chuckled softly at their foolishness. But it felt so good. She was thrilled to her toes that they were sharing this most intimate of subjects with each other, as she had so dreamed of doing.

Yes, she was lucky to be so blessed, to have everything that heaven allowed.

It was as if she'd been given the gift of this child all over again.

Reid bent his head and kissed Glenna softly, but it quickly escalated, as they both couldn't keep from want-ing more from each other.

He was nuzzling her neck when she found her voice several moments later. "I'm afraid Dr. Kirby gave me some bad news."

He froze. "What?"

"No sexual relations. For a few weeks, at least. We shouldn't even be doin' this much," she added miser-ably. "Nothin' to get me...excited."

He relaxed against her, nose buried in the crook be-tween her ear and collarbone. "Oh. Well, it won't be easy keepin' my hands off you, believe me, but I have learned to have a little restraint in my old age."

"But, Reid, I don't know if I can restrain myself."

He lifted his head, eyebrows raised. "I always knew that conventional-lady act was a ruse."

"I'm not joking! I need to be close to you," she told him fervently. "I need to make love with you."

His gaze turned tender. "I know, darlin'. I do, too."

Settling back against the pillow, a hand behind his head, he snuggled her against him and whispered, "I do like the sound of you saying that—making love. Makes me feel like a kid again.''

His lips brushed her temple, and Glenna sighed, truly, completely, marvelously at peace. And right where she would always belong. ''It is something at our age, isn't it,'' she said, ''to feel so young and alive—''

''And in love,'' they finished together.

Always . . . together.

Epilogue

Six months later.

Glenna was having the strangest dream. First, she heard Patsy Cline singing "I Fall to Pieces." Only Patsy's voice had dropped to a baritone. Then the pace picked up as Glenna heard George Strait singing "Amarillo by Morning"—except George had a little bit more trouble reaching those high notes than Glenna remembered him ever having.

Finally, as she drifted to wakefulness on the strains of "Mack the Knife," she realized where she was and who was doing the singing. And to whom.

She opened her eyes to find Reid standing next to the window of her hospital room. He was completely engrossed in the swaddled bundle of pink he held awkwardly in his two large hands. The light pouring in from outside cast shadows upon his face that, despite the youthful shock of hair springing out over his forehead, made him look haggard. She knew how he felt, though. It had been a long night for everyone, and he had stayed with her every minute.

Heavens, how she loved this man!

"Hey, there," she said shyly, sitting up.

She must have surprised him, for he jumped slightly before looking up. "Hey," he said gruffly. "I was just tryin' to quiet Mandy here. She was frettin' a bit, and I thought you could use the sleep. I wasn't quite sure yet what her taste in music is, so I went with a little of everything."

He looked somewhat embarrassed, likely at being caught practically cooing over his infant daughter, but it only made him more endearing to Glenna. He would make a good father to their child.

The bundle started squirming as snorty, fussing sounds issued from it. "She's probably hungry, the poor little mite," Glenna said, holding out her arms. "Bring her on over."

Reid did so, gingerly relinquishing the baby to Glenna's capable hands before sitting on the edge of the bed next to her. She unbuttoned her gown and settled the little one against her, thrilling to the feeling of holding such a precious armful again. And this one was all hers—hers and Reid's.

She'd done so earlier, but Glenna couldn't prevent herself from taking another inventory: ten small fingers and toes, two pink ears, two eyes buttoned up tight, a pug nose, and a rosebud mouth currently working like crazy.

"Isn't she beautiful?" Glenna breathed, gently stroking the down atop the small head. "She'll have black hair, I think, just like yours. I was so hoping she would, even though I know you were holding out for a redhead." She glanced up at Reid, who had braced an arm next to her hip on the other side of her as he did his own thorough perusal of his wife and child. "But you got what you wanted—a girl. I'm glad."

"Shoot, Glenna, I'd have been thrilled to death with a boy, too. You know that." He reached out to touch one impossibly tiny fist. "Funny, though, how we're still managin' to get the best of both worlds, with Jamey and Kell havin' a redheaded boy. Oh, that reminds me."

He reached for something on the floor beside the bed and came up with a new video camera. "Jamey and Kell called earlier to say they wanted to drop by to visit, and I asked them to bring little Luke along." Turning the camera back and forth, he admired his new toy. "Thought we should start both tykes out right, recordin' their lives for posterity."

"You did, did you?" Glenna asked absently, her gaze focused on her little girl.

"Yep. I figured we'd put a baby in each of your arms and show everyone the world's proudest momma and grandma."

Her head snapped up as Reid now had her undivided attention. "You're not serious!"

He actually looked surprised. "I'm not?"

"Honestly, Reid." She pushed a hank of limp hair off her forehead. "I've just been through twelve hours of labor, for pity's sake."

"Yes, and I've already missed gettin' on film our child's first moments in the world." Reid laid the camera aside. "I won't take your picture right now if you don't want me to, Glenna, but I'll tell you this—I'm done with regrets. I feel I have got to make the most of this chance I've been given, not just to see to Mandy's future, but to her past. Our past, the one we're building the memories of as we speak."

"Mmm," Glenna murmured as she dropped her chin again to drink in the view of her daughter's face—and to think about what Reid had said.

They'd finally decided on names last week, after much discussion—Amanda for a girl, Jason for a boy. And it was only after they had come to that decision did Glenna realize how close those two names were to Reid's and her deceased spouses, Miranda and James. She thought it fitting that they might wish, even subconsciously, to acknowledge the two with whom they had raised Jamey and Clan. But although that past would forever be a part of them both, the present was hers and Reid's. He was right. Now was their time in the sun—theirs and their child's. Still...

"So what did that particular *mmm* mean?" Reid asked.

She wrinkled her nose. "Oh, it's just hard to believe I'm here right now, when not even a year ago I was feeling so desperately old and useless, what with coming up on middle age and being a grandmother twice over. And it's not like those facts have changed at all."

"*Glenna,*" Reid said.

She looked up and was captured anew by those hazel eyes filled with warmth and fire. "I said it once, and I meant it—you don't look like no middle-aged lady to me. And you *sure* don't look like anybody's grandma. But I know how you feel."

He shook his head as he gazed at his daughter. "When I was holdin' her just now, all I could think was, I'll be an old man when she's just comin' into the first bloom of her life. Because middle age isn't around the corner for me, I'm up to my knees in it right now. I probably look more like a grandpa to this little one than a daddy."

Glenna reached up and brushed his hair back, bringing her hand around to lay tenderly against his cheek.

"You know what *I* thought when I saw you with Mandy?" she whispered. "I thought you looked darlin'. And you'll always be young in my eyes."

His fingers came up to grasp hers as he turned his head and kissed her palm in thanks. Yes, they could do this for each other, provide for one another that connection of being in accord, of one heart. Of finding in each other perfect understanding and peace.

"God, I love you, Glenna, more than my life." He laid his hand over hers as he cradled their child's head to her breast. "And this little girl. She's just a bitty thing," he said, voice rough. "Right now, I can't even imagine how I'll be able to let her go out in the world and spread her wings. Where will I find the wisdom and strength to do it?"

"I don't know, love," Glenna murmured. "But we'll find the way—together."

*   *   *   *   *

Who can resist a Texan...or a Calloway?

This September, award-winning author
ANNETTE BROADRICK
returns to Texas, with a brand-new
story about the Calloways...

SONS →OF← TEXAS

Rogues and Ranchers

CLINT: The brave leader. Used to keeping secrets.

CADE: The Lone Star Stud. Used to having women
fall at his feet...

MATT: The family guardian. Used to handling
trouble...

They must discover the identity of the mystery
woman with Calloway eyes—and uncover a
conspiracy that threatens their family....

Look for **SONS OF TEXAS:** Rogues and Ranchers
in September 1996!

Only from Silhouette...where passion lives.

The exciting new cross-line continuity series about love marriage—and Daddy's unexpected need for a baby carriage!

It all began with *THE BABY NOTION*
by Dixie Browning (Desire #1011 7/96)

And the romance in New Hope, Texas, continues with:

BABY IN A BASKET
by Helen R. Myers (Romance #1169 8/96)

Confirmed bachelor Mitch McCord finds a baby on his doorstep and turns to lovely gal-next-door Jenny Stevens for some lessons in fatherhood—and love!

Don't miss the upcoming books in this wonderful series:

MARRIED...WITH TWINS!
by Jennifer Mikels (Special Edition#1054, 9/96)
HOW TO HOOK A HUSBAND (AND A BABY)
by Carolyn Zane (Yours Truly #29, 10/96)
DISCOVERED: DADDY
by Marilyn Pappano (Intimate Moments #746, 11/96)

DADDY KNOWS LAST continues
each month...only from

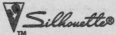

Bestselling Author
LISA JACKSON

Continues the twelve-book series—FORTUNE'S CHILDREN
in August 1996 with Book Two

THE MILLIONAIRE AND THE COWGIRL

When playboy millionaire Kyle Fortune inherited a Wyoming
ranch from his grandmother, he never expected to come
face-to-face with Samantha Rawlings, the willful woman
he'd never forgotten...and the daughter he'd never known.
Although Kyle enjoyed his jet-setting life-style, Samantha and
Caitlyn made him yearn for hearth and home.

MEET THE FORTUNES—a family whose legacy is greater than
riches. Because where there's a will...there's a *wedding!*

You can run, but you cannot hide...from love.

This August, experience danger, excitement and love on the run with three couples thrown together by life-threatening circumstances.

Enjoy three complete stories by some of your favorite authors—all in one special collection!

THE PRINCESS AND THE PEA
by Kathleen Korbel

IN SAFEKEEPING
by Naomi Horton

FUGITIVE
by Emilie Richards

Available this August wherever books are sold

 *Silhouette*®